Sugar & Spice

Sugar & Spice

Sensational Desserts with Vivid Flavor

Carole Bloom

HPBooks

HPBooks
Published by The Berkley Publishing Group
200 Madison Avenue
New York, NY 10016

Book design by Richard Oriolo
Cover design by James R. Harris
Cover photograph copyright © 1995 by FoodPix®

Text illustrations by Jeane H. Stetson

First edition: November 1996

Published simultaneously in Canada.

The Putnam Berkley World Wide Web site address is
http://www.berkley.com/berkley

Library of Congress Cataloging-in-Publication Data

Bloom, Carole.
    Sugar & spice : sensational desserts with vivid flavors / Carole
Bloom.—1st ed.
        p.   cm.
    ISBN 1-55788-254-1
    1. Desserts.   2. Spices.   I. Title.
TX773.B617   1996
641.8'6—dc20   96-13199
                                                            CIP

Printed in the United States of America

10 9 8 7 6 5 4 3 2 1

Dedicated with love to my husband, Jerry,
who puts the spice in my life
and who knows where to find
the better bits.

Acknowledgments

• • •

Many thanks to my husband, Jerry Olivas, superb taste tester, world's best computer expert, excellent editor, great motivator, great dishwasher, and genuinely funny person. His constant enthusiastic support keeps me going.

Thanks to my agent, Jane Dystel, for helping me to fulfill my goals, for always being there when I need her, and for having the right answers to my questions. Thanks also to my editor, Jeanette Egan, who was a pleasure to work with.

Charles Perry, staff writer for the *Los Angeles Times* and culinary historian, generously gave me some great research tips, which led me to find much fascinating background information about spices.

A serendipitous meeting at the home of our mutual friends, Kitty and Owen Morse, led to Jeane Stetson's drawings. I appreciate her thoroughness and attention to detail.

Warm thanks to my many friends and neighbors who gleefully volunteered to be taste testers: Kitty and Owen Morse, Lily Loh, Kira Kane and Simon Lynn, Marguerite and Bill Butler, Sam and Semra Gurol, Denise and Jim Quigley, Hugo and Edith Hahn, Grace and Bill Stone, and my ice-skating buddies Susie Hostetter, April Stinis, Mindy Tremblay, and Mindy's daughter, Kara, who thinks I'm "the best cooker in the world." Thanks also to good friend and adviser Betz Collins for her words of wisdom and for eagerly cheering me on.

. . . Sugar and spice, and everything nice . . .
—Anonymous

She that hath Spice enough may season as she likes.
—Thomas Fuller, *Gnomologia*

Contents

◆　◆　◆

Preface

◆ ◆ ◆

My inspiration to write this book comes out of my love of spices. Every chance I get I include a spice, or two, or three in whatever I make. When I go out to eat I almost always order a dish that has spices in it. Spices not only enhance existing flavors, but they add a new dimension of their own. The best way to describe this is to simply say it is exciting. It causes your taste buds to stand up and cheer. Although I like spices in just about all foods, dessert made with spices is double happiness. You get all the pleasure of the flavors of the dessert with the extra added spirit and liveliness of spices.

Most of us use spices like cinnamon, ginger, and nutmeg in baking without even thinking about it. We keep these spices in our kitchen cupboards as a matter of course. But what about other less well known spices like cardamom, caraway seeds, coriander, saffron, and sesame seeds? Many of us have never used them or even tasted them. You would be amazed at how they can enhance and expand the flavor of your desserts.

I've been fortunate enough to have experienced the wonderful qualities of spices for many years. I studied pastry making and confectionery arts in France and England and have worked in both Europe and the United States in hotels and restaurants. I can remember many spice cabinets in front of which I would often stand for a few moments before choosing a spice to take in all the great fragrances. I've also traveled a fair amount and during each of my forays I made it a point to eat as many different desserts, pastries, candies, and confections that were made with spices that I could find. All this exposure has given me an opportunity to taste many different spices and to create some sensational desserts with them.

In the beginning of the book I have included a good deal of background information regarding spices. Here you will find information that defines just what spices are, a brief history of spices, as well as information about equipment for working with spices. Each chapter covers a separate spice with information about its history, lore and myths, and characteristics. Here you will find information on where the spice is grown, how it is cultivated, how it tastes and smells, and the forms in which it is used. Tips for choosing, buying, storing, and preparing the spice for use in desserts is also included. The recipes are written in an easy to understand step-by-step fashion with the ingredients clearly listed in the order in which they are used. If there is something special regarding a particular recipe, it is covered in a brief headnote.

The end matter of the book includes mail-order sources for spices, a table of weight and measurement equivalents, a table of temperature equivalents, a table of conversions to and from metric, a table of sugar temperatures and stages, a table of comparative baking pan sizes, and a bibliography listing some great resources for spices.

Many of the more common desserts that are made with spices are named by their predominant spice. For example, Vanilla Bean Ice Cream, of course, is made with vanilla. Gingerbread and gingersnaps are made with ginger. However, many dessert recipes, including several recipes that I created for this book, do not have the name of the spice in the name of the dessert. In this book each chapter is organized by a particular spice so it is easy to see which desserts use which spice. If you would like to make a dessert with saffron, like Saffron Ice Cream, just turn to the chapter on saffron.

Although the title of this book, *Sugar & Spice*, is almost a cliché, coming as it does from an anonymous poem that most of us heard as children, it fits perfectly. Sugar and spices have a natural affinity for each other. Spices have been used for thousands of years to add aroma, vivid flavor, and excitement to desserts. I have a great appreciation for spices; although they are only used in small amounts, their impact on flavor is great. I invite you to share this appreciation and to enjoy the excitement of *Sugar & Spice*.

Sugar & Spice

Introduction: All About Spices

What Are Spices?

Spices are fruits, seeds, berries, buds, barks, and the dried roots of various plants. These plants are usually grown in tropical regions, like nutmeg, which is grown in Indonesia. One of the primary uses of spices is to flavor food. In most cases this gives food a robust flavor and an aromatic scent. Each spice has particular distinguishing flavor and aroma characteristics, its essence, which sets it apart from other spices. Spices are used either in their whole state or ground. The form in which they are used is determined in large part by what they are used for.

Spice History

◆   ◆   ◆

Since ancient times many cultures have used spices not only as food enhancers but also as medicine; anointing oils; cosmetics ingredients; perfume for the body, home, and places of worship; and embalming preparations for the dead. There have been numerous times in history when spices themselves have been the preferred form of currency. Also, the desire to find spices has been the primary incentive behind many of the great explorations in history.

Although the specific origin of many spices is cloudy, most of them can be traced back to the tropical regions of the Far East. Ancient overland caravan routes, known as the Silk Road, that came from China, Asia, and India through the Middle East, brought spices to the eastern Mediterranean basin and Europe thousands of years ago. Arab traders became wealthy by acting as middlemen in the spice trade. They made sure to keep the sources of their products shrouded in myth and mystery so they could maintain their monopoly on the trade.

When Europe was in the Dark Ages, the use of spices came to a halt. Trade between the Arabs and Europe ceased and spices disappeared. However, during the Middle Ages and the Renaissance there was a greatly renewed interest in the use of spices, and they became much more widespread. During these periods spices enhanced the lives of Europeans by adding spectacular flavors to their cuisine. Spices themselves became symbols of status and power, and were highly prized as luxury goods.

In the thirteenth century, Marco Polo traveled to China, where he spent many years in the service of the Emperor Kublai Khan. He traveled widely throughout China and the Far East recording his observations about the people, the culture, the cuisine, the weather, the crops, and society in general. When his stories were published many people thought they were too fantastic to be true (an opinion still shared by many). He conveyed much information about crops and their cultivation, especially about spices.

During the Middle Ages, Venice controlled the monopoly on the spice trade in the Mediterranean. The Venetians were able to control the types of spices and the amounts that filtered into Europe. As a result, they grew rich while the other countries of Europe strained to be able to afford these much sought after commodities. Spices were so highly valued that often they were used as payment for debts. They were also taxed at every opportunity. In fourteenth-century England, the taxes levied on spices helped pay for repairs to London Bridge.

In the fourteenth and fifteenth centuries, it was the search for a short ocean route to India to buy spices directly from the source that sent Prince Henry of Portugal, also known as Prince Henry the Navigator, and his contemporaries, including Christopher Columbus, on journeys of exploration. Columbus, of course, didn't get to India. However, his discoveries in the "new world" changed eating habits forever. Fortunately for us, he and others brought to the attention of the rest of the world such fabulous items as allspice and vanilla.

Spain and Portugal built great empires and vied with each other for many years for control of the Moluccas, the Spice Islands in Indonesia. In the sixteenth century, Ferdinand Magellan led an expedition that sailed westward across and through the Atlantic Ocean to the Pacific Ocean, and finally did reach the Moluccas in the Far East. However, by the time they arrived, most of the crew had perished from the rigors of the journey. The ship eventually returned with its hold loaded with precious spices.

In the seventeenth century the Dutch, English, and French began to exert their influence on spices as they expanded their empires. Large companies that controlled and managed the spice trade were created. The Dutch were the most ruthless, eventually cornering the world market on many spices.

In the eighteenth century, the demand for spices began to subside. The monopoly on the spice market was broken when plants were smuggled out of the Moluccas by Pierre Poivre (French for "pepper"), who established plantations on other islands. This made spices much more readily available and, as a result, cheaper.

Today spices can be found on every supermarket shelf. They are virtually taken for granted. The use of spices has become so interwoven in our lives that they have enriched not only our cuisine but our language as well. "The spice of life," "to spice it up," and "spicy," are phrases and words that connote excitement and gusto. They imply that spices give pleasure, are provocative, and offer a touch of the exotic. Spices are used so extensively that if they were eliminated many dishes would completely lose their appeal.

Equipment for Working with Spices
◆ ◆ ◆

Although many spices are used in their whole state in desserts, often they need to be ground or grated. Freshly ground or grated spices are much more flavorful than those that have sat on a shelf for a long time. Once ground or grated spices are exposed to the air, they quickly lose their flavor and aroma. The following tools can be used for preparing spices.

Mortar and Pestle

The mortar and pestle, a very ancient implement, is still one of the most effective tools for grinding spices. A shallow slope-sided bowl, the mortar, measuring between 2½ and 4 inches in diameter and 2 to 5 inches deep, is used to hold the spices, while a pestle is used to grind the spice against the bowl. The pestle is a round, solid, tapered tube about 6 inches long with a bulb-shaped end. A mortar and pestle are made from the same material, which is usually marble, ceramic, porcelain, clay, or wood. Olive wood is the most popular of the types made of wood because it is the most durable, but mortars and pestles are also made from alderwood and poplar.

Coffee Grinder

A coffee grinder is a mechanical device that has a cylindrical shape with a cavity on top that holds rotating metal blades in its base. The grinder has a removable clear plastic cover that allows you to see how finely a spice is being ground. Coffee grinders do a superb job of evenly grinding spices to a fine powder. Keep a small brush handy to clean out the inside of the grinding cavity. Keep a separate grinder to use only with spices. Be sure to thoroughly clean the grinder of coffee grounds before giving it over to your spices.

Spice Grinder

A spice grinder resembles a pepper mill with top and bottom sections that can be twisted in opposite directions to grind the spice. The top of a spice grinder is made of clear acrylic so it's easy to see how fine the spice is being ground. Some spice grinders can be set to measure out a specific amount of ground spice.

Nutmeg Grater

A nutmeg grater is specifically designed for grating a whole nutmeg. It is about 4 inches long and 2 inches wide. The back side is flat and the top is a tapered half-moon shape with fine mesh for grating the nutmeg. A nutmeg grater often has a compartment with a cap on top that clamps shut where the whole nutmeg can be stored. A nutmeg grater can be used to grate other hard spices, such as cinnamon sticks.

Nutmeg Grinder

A nutmeg grinder, sometimes called a nutmeg mill, is a 3-inch round, stocky-shaped mill a few inches high with a hand crank on top. A whole nutmeg is held in place inside the mill in a small shaft. A small plate with tiny prongs on one side holds the nutmeg in place while it is being ground. This plate is at the end of a centrally mounted, spring-loaded shaft that forces the nutmeg against sharp cutting blades at the base of the grinder. A clear cover for storing whole nutmeg surrounds the top portion of the grinder. A nutmeg grinder is easier and more efficient to use than a grater. However, it should be noted that a nutmeg grinder produces more of a fine shaving of the nutmeg as opposed to a fine powder that you get with a nutmeg grater.

Pepper Mill

A pepper mill is usually cylindrical in shape, about 1½ inches in diameter, ranging in size from a few inches to almost 2 feet tall. A pepper mill has either a small hand crank on top or two sections that twist in opposite directions with a stainless steel shaft that runs down the hollow center of the cylinder. The peppercorns are kept in this hollow center. As the crank is turned or the two sections are twisted, the peppercorns are pushed against a metal grinding mechanism in the base. Some pepper mills have grinding mechanisms that can be adjusted to different settings of coarseness. Pepper mills are made of many materials, including wood, acrylic, brass, porcelain, and stainless steel.

Measuring Ingredients for the Recipes
◆ ◆ ◆

Recipes for desserts, pastries, and confections are precise formulas that have been carefully worked out through trial and error. If the proportions of ingredients are changed, the formula becomes unbalanced and as a consequence the recipe may not work successfully.

When measuring dry ingredients such as flour, sugar, powdered sugar, cornstarch, and nuts, it is important to use dry measures. These come in a graduated set of sizes that nest together. They are flat on top, with long handles. They are made to be filled and leveled off. To be accurate in your measurements use the "scoop and sweep method." Scoop the measuring cup into the ingredient and sweep it off cleanly at the top. Measuring by this method will ensure that the proportions of your ingredients correspond to those called for in each recipe.

Spice Blends

◆　◆　◆

Spices have been blended together for hundreds of years to create unique, exciting, and lively flavors. By combining spices they enhance each other, bringing out each other's best qualities and creating a totally unique flavor.

In Europe during the Middle Ages the possession of spices was a symbol of wealth and prestige. Many spices were used together to indicate one's prosperity. Although this is no longer the case today, there are still many classic spice blends that have special uses, such as *quatre épice* in France.

Many countries have mixtures of spices that are characteristic of their cuisines, such as Japan, China, India, Thailand, Indonesia, Ethiopia, Saudi Arabia, North Africa (Morocco, Algeria, and Tunisia), France, Italy, the British Isles, and the United States. Curry, *garam masala, harissa, ras-el-hanout,* five-spice powder, creole seasoning, and cajun seasoning are some of the world's classic spice blends.

For desserts one of the most classic spice blends contains cinnamon, nutmeg, ginger, and cloves. Other classic blends include allspice and/or mace. There are particular blends that are labeled "pumpkin pie spice," which usually consists of cinnamon, nutmeg, ginger, and cloves, or "apple pie spice," generally made up of cinnamon, ginger, and nutmeg.

Cinnamon and sugar are combined together to create cinnamon-sugar, which is usually sprinkled on top of freshly baked items while they are still warm. It not only adds extra sweetness and flavor, but texture as well.

These spice mixtures can be made up in advance of use or blended as needed. They should be stored in tightly sealed glass containers in a cool, dark, dry place where they will last up to a year.

Making your own spice mixtures can be a great way to create your own uniquely flavored desserts.

Allspice

Allspice has the distinction of being the only spice to come from the New World. It is native to the West Indies, where sixteenth-century Spanish explorers found it on the island of Jamaica. They mistook it for pepper, calling it *pimienta*, the Spanish word for pepper. Later, the English translated *pimienta* to "pepper" and the spice took on its alternative name, Jamaican pepper.

The Spanish introduced allspice to Europe in the late sixteenth century. When the English colonized Jamaica in the late seventeenth century, allspice had already been established as a cultivated crop. The English then took over the thriving allspice trade, expanding it greatly.

During the seventeenth century, pirates who roamed the seas throughout the West Indies used allspice to flavor the smoked and barbecued meat they ate before their raids. The meat was called *boucan*, taken from the French verb *boucaner*, meaning "cured." The pirates became known as *boucaners*, which later became "buccaneers."

Allspice is used extensively in Scandinavian, Russian, and Polish cuisines, in both sweet and savory dishes, and in Middle Eastern, Central American, and West Indian cuisines, primarily in savory cooking. In the United States, allspice is mostly used in baked good such as cookies, cakes, and pies like pumpkin pie.

Lore and Myths

◆　◆　◆

Allspice has been reputed to be a digestive aid.

Characteristics

◆　◆　◆

The botanical name for allspice is *Pimenta officinalis*. Allspice is the berry of the *Pimenta dioica* evergreen tree, a member of the myrtle family. The tree has shiny dark green leaves and tiny white flowers during the summer. It reaches heights of up to 30 feet when fully grown. The round, small berries are the size of a small pea or a large peppercorn. They are hard, dark reddish-brown, with a roughly textured outer surface.

Where and How It's Grown

◆　◆　◆

Native to the West Indies, allspice is grown primarily in Jamaica, where the highest quality is produced. Allspice is also cultivated in Mexico and in Central and South America.

The trees are grown in orchards called pimiento or allspice walks and emit a powerful fragrance when their flowers are in bloom. The berries are harvested when mature but unripe, so that they retain the most flavor. They are dried in the sun for about a week, which turns them a dark reddish-brown color.

How It Tastes and Smells

◆　◆　◆

Allspice has a strong, sweetly aromatic scent with a pungent slightly sweet flavor that resembles a combination of cinnamon, nutmeg, and cloves, with a hint of pepper.

Use and Preparation

♦ ♦ ♦

In desserts, allspice is used primarily ground. It is best to grind it just before use to prevent flavor loss. Allspice should be ground using a spice grinder or pepper mill.

Tips for Choosing and Storing

♦ ♦ ♦

Buy either whole or ground allspice from a source with high turnover to be sure of freshness. Whole and ground allspice should be stored in tightly sealed glass jars in a cool, dry place. Use whole berries within two years, ground allspice within 6 months.

Allspice Torte

Classic elements with a new twist are combined in this delectable *genoise* torte. *Genoise* is a light, buttery sponge cake that is extremely versatile and is the basis for several layered cakes and desserts throughout Europe and the United States. Here it's embellished with a medley of spices. The torte is assembled with a classic buttercream flavored with allspice and ginger and decorated with toasted hazelnuts. I think you'll find this worthy of center stage at your most cherished celebrations.

Makes 1 (9-inch) cake, 12 to 14 servings.

◆ ◆ ◆

Genoise

1 tablespoon unsalted butter for pan and parchment round

2 teaspoons all-purpose flour for pan

3 large eggs at room temperature

3 large egg yolks at room temperature

½ cup plus 1 tablespoon sugar

4 tablespoons all-purpose flour

4 tablespoons cornstarch

1 teaspoon ground cinnamon

1 teaspoon ground coriander

1 teaspoon ground ginger

¼ teaspoon ground cardamom

¼ teaspoon ground cloves

Pinch of freshly ground black pepper

2 tablespoons unsalted butter, melted and cooled

Buttercream

1 cup plus 2 tablespoons sugar

¼ teaspoon (heaping) cream of tartar

½ cup water

2 large eggs at room temperature

2 large egg yolks at room temperature

3½ sticks unsalted butter, softened

16 allspice berries or 1¼ teaspoons ground allspice

¼ teaspoon ground ginger

¼ teaspoon freshly grated nutmeg

¼ teaspoon ground cloves

Sugar Syrup

¼ cup sugar

½ cup water

Assembly

¼ cup apricot preserves

½ cup toasted and finely ground
hazelnuts

14 whole hazelnuts, toasted and skinned
(see page 71)

Genoise

Position a rack in the center of the oven. Preheat oven to 300F (150C). Using the 1 tablespoon butter, butter the inside of a 9 × 2-inch round cake pan and a 9-inch parchment paper round. Dust pan with the 1 tablespoon flour and shake out the excess, then place the parchment round in the bottom of the cake pan, buttered side up. Set pan aside while preparing cake batter.

Place the eggs and egg yolks in the bowl of a stand mixer or a medium bowl. Using the wire-whip attachment or a hand-held mixer, beat at low speed while slowly adding the sugar. Turn the speed up to medium and beat until the mixture becomes very pale yellow and holds a slowly dissolving ribbon when the beater is lifted, 5 to 8 minutes.

Sift together the flour, cornstarch, and spices. Fold flour mixture into the beaten eggs in 3 stages. Then fold in the melted butter in 2 stages.

Pour the mixture into the prepared cake pan and bake until golden colored and the top of the cake springs back when lightly touched, 45 to 50 minutes. Cool cake in the pan on a rack 10 minutes. Place a 9-inch-round cardboard cake circle over the top of the cake pan and invert the cake onto the cardboard. Gently remove the cake pan. Carefully peel the parchment paper round off of the back of the cake and re-invert the cake onto the cardboard cake circle. Leave the cake to cool completely on a rack.

The *genoise* will keep for 4 days, well wrapped in the refrigerator, or it can be frozen for several months. If frozen, defrost the *genoise* in the refrigerator 24 hours before using. The *genoise* is easier to cut if made the day before it is to be used.

Sugar Syrup

Combine the sugar and water in a heavy-duty 1-quart saucepan and bring to a boil over medium heat to dissolve the sugar. Cool.

Buttercream

Combine the sugar, cream of tartar and water in a saucepan and cook to 242F (116C) over high heat, stirring until sugar dissolves. Brush down the sides of the pan 2 or 3 times with a pastry brush dipped in warm water to prevent crystals from forming. As the sugar is cooking, beat the eggs and egg yolks in the bowl of a stand mixer or in a mixing bowl using the wire-whip attachment or a hand-held mixer, on medium-high speed, until they are very thick and pale yellow, 5 to 8 minutes. When the sugar is at 242F (116C), slowly pour it into the eggs in the mixer, then beat the mixture at medium-high speed until the bowl is cool to the touch, about 5 to 8 minutes.

When the mixture is cool, add the butter, a few tablespoons at a time. Then beat 2 minutes, until the mixture is smooth and fluffy.

If using the allspice berries, grind them to a powder in a spice mill or coffee grinder. Combine with the other spices and add to the batter in 2 stages, stopping to scrape down the sides of the bowl with a rubber spatula after each addition. Reserve ⅓ cup of the buttercream for the final decoration.

The buttercream can be prepared in advance of use and refrigerated, covered, 3 days, or frozen up to 4 months. If frozen, defrost in the refrigerator 24 hours before using. To rebeat the buttercream, place chunks of it in the bowl of a mixer and place the bowl in a saucepan of warm water. When the buttercream begins to melt around the bottom and sides of the bowl, remove the bowl from the water, wipe it dry, and beat the butter-cream with the flat beater of the stand mixer or with a hand-held mixer on medium speed until it is fluffy, 2 to 3 minutes.

To assemble

Slice the *genoise* horizontally into 3 equal layers. Place the bottom layer on a 9-inch cardboard cake circle. Brush the layer with the sugar syrup, then spread evenly with the apricot preserves. Cover the preserves with a thin layer of the buttercream using a metal flexible-blade spatula. Position the middle *genoise* layer over the buttercream and brush with the sugar syrup. Spread with a layer of buttercream, about the same thickness as the *genoise* layer. Position the top *genoise* layer over the buttercream and brush with the sugar syrup. Spread the top and fill in the sides of the cake with the buttercream. Smooth buttercream over top and sides of cake.

Sprinkle the ground hazelnuts onto a piece of waxed paper. Use a flexible-blade spatula to wedge underneath the cardboard cake circle to gently lift up the cake. Hold it up carefully from underneath with one hand. With your other hand, press the hazelnuts into the side of the cake up to the top edge. Carefully set the cake down on a serving plate, using the flexible-blade spatula under the cake circle to help guide it. Use a small knife to mark the serving pieces around the top outside edge of the cake.

Fit a pastry bag with a large open star tip (number 3 or 4) and fill with the remaining buttercream. On the outside edge of each marked piece, pipe a rosette or a small mound in the center. In the center of the rosette place a whole hazelnut, pointed end up.

Keep the cake in the refrigerator until 30 minutes before serving. Cut the cake with a serrated-edge knife or with a sharp knife dipped in hot water and dried. The cake will keep, well covered, in the refrigerator up to 3 days.

Allspice-Ginger Wafers

These crisp wafers take their flavor from the combination of allspice and ground ginger blended with rich, robust brown sugar. They are a scrumptious addition to an assortment of cookies or an ideal accompaniment to ice cream.

Makes 60 wafers.
◆ ◆ ◆

1¼ cups all-purpose flour
¾ teaspoon ground allspice
½ teaspoon ground ginger
Scant pinch of ground cinnamon

½ cup firmly packed golden brown
   sugar
½ teaspoon baking powder
1 stick (8 tablespoons) unsalted butter,
   chilled, cut into small pieces

Sift the flour with the allspice, ginger, and cinnamon into the work bowl of a food processor fitted with a steel blade. Add the brown sugar and baking powder and pulse the mixture for 15 seconds to blend. Add the butter and pulse the mixture to cut the butter into very tiny pieces, resembling meal, about 1 minute. Continue to pulse the mixture until it is smooth, about 1 minute.

Using waxed paper, form the dough into a 1-inch-square block. Wrap the block in waxed paper and chill in the refrigerator until firm enough to cut, about 30 minutes.

Position racks in the upper and lower third of the oven. Preheat oven to 400F (205C). Line 2 baking sheets with foil, shiny side down.

Remove the block of wafer dough from the refrigerator and peel off the waxed paper. Cut the block into 1-inch-wide strips. Cut each strip into ½-inch-thick pieces. Place the pieces on the lined baking sheets with 1 inch of space between them. Chill the baking sheets 30 minutes.

Bake the wafers 6 minutes. Switch the baking sheets and bake another 3 to 4 minutes, until golden brown. Cool wafers on the baking sheets on racks.

Store the wafers up to 6 days in an airtight container at room temperature.

Tropical Coconut Cake

Two flavors of the Caribbean, allspice and coconut, were the inspiration for this cake. Cream of coconut provides the coconut flavor in the buttercream. It is sold in cans and is available in the baking or specialty foods sections of most supermarkets, or in large liquor stores. Be sure to stir it thoroughly before use.

Makes 1 (8-inch) cake, 10 to 12 servings.

◆ ◆ ◆

Cake

1 tablespoon unsalted butter, melted and
    cooled, for pans
1 tablespoon all-purpose flour for pans
6 large eggs at room temperature
1 cup sugar
¾ cup all-purpose flour
2½ teaspoons ground allspice
½ teaspoon freshly grated nutmeg
Pinch of salt
¼ cup grated or shredded coconut,
    preferably unsweetened
1 teaspoon pure vanilla extract
3 tablespoons unsalted butter, melted
    and cooled

Buttercream

1 cup plus 2 tablespoons sugar
½ teaspoon cream of tartar
½ cup water
2 large eggs at room temperature
2 large egg yolks at room temperature
3¼ sticks unsalted butter, softened
1 teaspoon pure vanilla extract
½ cup cream of coconut
1 teaspoon ground allspice
½ teaspoon freshly grated nutmeg

Assembly

½ cup papaya, passion fruit, or apricot
    preserves
½ cup coconut, lightly toasted

Cake

Position a rack in the center of the oven. Preheat oven to 350F (175C). Brush the insides of 2 (8 × 2-inch) round cake pans with some of the 1 tablespoon butter, then lightly dust with the 1 tablespoon flour, and shake out the excess. Place an 8-inch round of parchment paper in the bottom of each pan and brush with butter.

In the bowl of a stand mixer or in a medium bowl, using the wire-whip attachment or a hand-held mixer, beat the eggs and sugar together at medium-high speed until they hold a slowly dissolving ribbon when the beater is lifted, about 5 minutes.

Sift the flour with the allspice, then toss with the nutmeg, salt, and coconut. Fold the dry ingredients into the egg mixture in 3 stages, being sure to blend thoroughly. Fold in the vanilla and melted butter in 2 stages.

Divide the batter evenly between the 2 prepared pans and bake 25 minutes, until the cakes are golden and spring back when touched on top. Cool cakes in pans on racks 15 minutes. Then invert the cakes onto 8-inch cardboard cake circles, remove and discard the parchment paper rounds, and re-invert so the top is up. Continue to cool completely. (The cakes can be prepared up to 2 days in advance of assembly. They should be wrapped in plastic and refrigerated until ready to use.)

Buttercream

Combine the sugar, cream of tartar, and water in a saucepan and cook to 242F (116C) over high heat, stirring until sugar dissolves. Brush down the sides of the pan 2 or 3 times with a pastry brush dipped in warm water to prevent crystals from forming. As the sugar is cooking, beat the eggs and egg yolks in the bowl of a stand mixer or in a mixing bowl, using the wire-whip attachment or a hand-held mixer, on medium-high speed, until they are very thick and pale yellow, about 5 to 8 minutes. When the sugar reaches 242F (116C), slowly pour it into the eggs in the mixer, then beat the mixture at medium-high speed until the bowl is cool to the touch, 5 to 8 minutes.

When the mixture is cool, add the butter a few tablespoons at a time. Then beat 2 minutes, until the mixture is smooth and fluffy. Add the vanilla extract and then the cream of coconut. Add the allspice and nutmeg and beat again until the buttercream is smooth and fluffy.

To assemble

Slice each cake in half horizontally. Place 1 layer on a cardboard cake circle and spread with a thin layer of preserves. Top the preserves with an even layer of buttercream, about ¼ inch thick, using a flexible-blade spatula. Repeat this procedure with the remaining layers. Do not spread preserves on the top layer. Spread the top and fill in the sides of the cake with the buttercream. Smooth buttercream over top and sides of cake. Reserve about ½ cup of buttercream for decorating. Carefully set the cake on a serving plate, using the flexible-blade spatula under the cake circle to help guide it.

Place the toasted coconut on a sheet of waxed or parchment paper. Use a flexible-blade spatula to lift up the cake, and carefully hold it up from underneath with one hand. With your other hand, press the coconut into the side of the cake just up to the top edge. Fit a 10- or 12-inch pastry bag with a large closed-star tip (number 3 or 4) and fill with the remaining buttercream. Pipe a border of alternating shells around the outside top edge of the cake, then pipe a large rosette in the center. Sprinkle the rosette with toasted coconut.

Serve the cake immediately or refrigerate until 45 minutes before serving. The cake will keep up to 4 days in the refrigerator, tightly covered.

Molasses Wafers

Rich and spicy, these yummy wafers are some of my favorites for fall. They are the perfect cookies to eat with a steaming mug of apple cider, tea, or coffee by a warm fire. But don't feel you have to wait for cool weather to make a batch. They are truly delicious anytime.

Makes 24 cookies.

◆   ◆   ◆

½ stick (4 tablespoons) unsalted butter,
    cut into small pieces, softened
¼ cup dark molasses
¼ cup firmly packed dark brown sugar
½ teaspoon ground allspice (preferably
    freshly ground)

¼ teaspoon ground cinnamon
¼ teaspoon ground ginger
1 cup all-purpose flour
2 tablespoons granulated sugar
1 to 2 tablespoons all-purpose flour

Add the butter and molasses to a 1-quart saucepan over medium heat and bring to a boil. Remove saucepan from the heat and transfer mixture to the bowl of a stand mixer or a medium bowl. Using the flat-beater attachment or a hand-held mixer, stir 1 to 2 minutes to cool the mixture. Add the brown sugar and the spices and blend thoroughly. Add the flour in 2 stages, blending thoroughly after each addition.

Transfer the mixture to a smaller bowl, cover tightly with plastic wrap, and chill in the refrigerator 1 hour or in the freezer 15 minutes, until the dough is firm enough to handle.

Position racks in the upper and lower third of the oven. Preheat oven to 350F (175C). Line 2 baking sheets with parchment paper. Place the granulated sugar in a small bowl.

Remove the bowl of cookie dough from the refrigerator or freezer. Dust your hands with flour. Pinch off pieces of the dough the size of a walnut and roll these into balls. Place each ball in the bowl of sugar and roll it around to coat it, then transfer to a prepared baking sheet. Leave 2 inches of space between each ball.

Use the bottom of a drinking glass that has been dipped in cold water and dried to flatten each ball. Bake the cookies 5 minutes. Switch the baking sheets and bake another 3 to 4 minutes. Cool cookies on baking sheets on cooling racks 10 minutes, then transfer the cookies to the racks to cool completely.

The cookies will keep up to 1 week at room temperature in an airtight container.

Spiced Sugar

Spiced sugar is an intriguing way to add spice flavor to any dessert recipe. Use it instead of the granulated, superfine, or powdered sugar called for. It's best to use whole seeds, berries, or sticks to flavor the sugar because they can be easily removed, but grated or ground spices can also be used. Some good choices for spiced sugar are allspice, anise, cardamom, cinnamon, and cloves.

Makes 4 cups.

◆　◆　◆

4 cups granulated, superfine, or powdered sugar

1 tablespoon spice

Alternately layer the sugar and spice in a glass jar or plastic container, starting and ending with the sugar. Tightly cover the container and let the sugar stand for at least 24 hours so the spice can permeate the sugar.

Lemon-Allspice Chiffon Cake

This classic, light chiffon cake is updated and enhanced with a blend of spices highlighted by allspice. The cake is great on its own, but for an extra treat try it with Honey Mace Ice Cream (page 133) or Vanilla Bean Ice Cream (page 208).

Makes 1 (10-inch) tube cake, 14 to 16 servings.

♦   ♦   ♦

½ cup water

½ cup unflavored vegetable oil, such as canola or safflower

¼ cup freshly squeezed lemon juice

1 teaspoon lemon extract

1 teaspoon vanilla extract

28 to 30 allspice berries or 1¾ teaspoons ground allspice

1 teaspoon ground ginger

¾ teaspoon ground cinnamon

½ teaspoon freshly grated nutmeg

2½ cups sifted cake flour

1 tablespoon baking powder

¼ teaspoon salt

1½ cups superfine sugar (see Note, below)

Zest of 1 large lemon, finely diced

6 large eggs at room temperature, separated

½ teaspoon cream of tartar

Powdered sugar for garnish

Position a rack in the center of the oven. Preheat oven to 325F (165C). Cut a round of parchment paper to fit the bottom of a 10 × 4-inch tube pan with removable bottom. Cut a center hole out of the parchment paper round to fit over the tube of the pan and place the round in the bottom of the pan.

In a small bowl or a 2-cup measure, mix together the water, oil, lemon juice, and extracts. If using the allspice berries, grind them to a powder in a coffee grinder or with a mortar and pestle. Combine the ground allspice in a small bowl with the ginger, cinnamon, and nutmeg.

In the bowl of a stand mixer or a large bowl, sift together the flour and baking powder, then blend in the spices, salt, and 1 cup of the superfine sugar. Make a well in the center of the mixture and add the lemon zest, the egg yolks, and the liquid ingredients. Using the flat-beater attachment, a hand-held mixer, or a wooden spoon, blend the ingredients together on low speed until smooth and well combined, 30 to 60 seconds.

In a greasefree bowl, whip the egg whites with the cream of tartar until frothy. Slowly sprinkle the remaining ½ cup superfine sugar over the whites and continue to whip them until they are glossy and hold firm, but not stiff, peaks. Fold a large scoop of the egg whites into the batter. Then gently fold in the remaining egg whites in 4 to 5 stages until thoroughly blended.

Pour the batter into the prepared pan, using a rubber spatula to smooth and even the top. Bake the cake until it is golden brown, springs back when lightly touched, and a cake tester inserted near the center comes out clean, 55 to 60 minutes. Remove the pan from the oven and immediately invert it onto its feet over a cooling rack, or hang it by the center tube over a funnel or the neck of a bottle. Leave the cake to hang for several hours, until it is completely cool.

To remove the cake from the pan, run a thin-bladed knife around the inside of the pan and around the tube. Gently loosen the cake from the edges and push the bottom of the pan up, away from the sides. Run the knife between the bottom of the cake and the bottom of the pan and invert the cake onto a plate, peel off the parchment paper round, then re-invert, so it is right side up. Dust the top of the cake heavily with powdered sugar. Slice the cake into serving pieces with a serrated knife.

Store the cake up to 3 days at room temperature, well wrapped in plastic wrap, or it may be frozen up to 2 months.

Note

Superfine sugar has much smaller crystals than regular granulated sugar. It dissolves very quickly and leaves no gritty traces, making it the ideal choice for fine-textured cakes, candies, meringues, cold desserts, and caramelization. In Britain, superfine sugar is called castor sugar. In the United States, superfine sugar is produced by C & H. It is available in many supermarkets. However, if you have trouble locating superfine sugar, you can make your own by pulsing regular granulated sugar in a food processor or blender 1 minute. Regular granulated sugar can also be substituted for superfine sugar.

Anise

*Woe unto you, Scribes and Pharisees,
hypocrites! for ye pay tithe of mint
and anise and cumin.*

—*New Testament*, Matthew 23:23

Also called anise seed, anise is one of the most ancient spices. It is native to the Middle East, where it can be traced as far back as ancient Egypt.

It was the Romans who first used anise seeds to flavor their food during the Middle Ages. By the fourteenth century anise was so highly valued in England that it was heavily taxed.

The colonists brought anise seeds to the New World, where the Shakers grew it primarily for medicinal uses. Anise was so highly valued that the laws enacted in the colony of Virginia required every new arrival to plant six anise seeds.

Anise is widely used in the Mediterranean countries, Russia, Poland, and Scandinavia to flavor cabbage, fish, shellfish, meats, and sausages. It is especially popular as a flavoring in pastries, cakes, and cookies in Europe and the United States. Anise is the prime ingredient in many licorice-flavored liqueurs that are popular throughout the Mediterranean.

These include Absinthe, Pernod, Ouzo, Sambuca, Anisette, and Pastis. Anise is also used to flavor cough drops and other medicines.

Lore and Myths
◆ ◆ ◆

There is much lore and myth surrounding anise. It has been considered to be an aphrodisiac and to have magical powers. It was also thought that if it was tucked under your pillow you would have a restful night without nightmares.

For medical purposes anise oil has been used to get rid of body lice and to aid in healing scorpion bites. During the Middle Ages, anise comfits, anise seeds that were coated with sugar, were chewed to aid digestion. Throughout the ages, anise has been chewed to sweeten breath. This is still in practice in India today.

Anise has also been valued as a perfume. In the fifteenth century, King Edward IV of England had his bed linen and clothing perfumed with sachet bags of anise seeds.

Characteristics
◆ ◆ ◆

Anise is the seed of an annual plant that is a member of the parsley family and is related to caraway, cumin, dill, and fennel. Its botanical name is *Pimpinella anisum*. The plant has feathery bright green leaves with clusters of small white flowers. It grows to a height of about 2 feet. The small oval seeds range in color from gray-green to light brown, with a fuzzy, ribbed outer coating. If the seeds are dark brown, this indicates they are stale and have lost their flavor. Occasionally, the fresh leaves are used as a flavoring in salads, cooked vegetables, fish, and fruit dishes.

Where and How It's Grown
◆ ◆ ◆

Anise is native to the Middle Eastern countries of Egypt, Turkey, Lebanon, and Greece. Today it is cultivated in hot, sunny climates throughout the world, including India, Pakistan, Russia, Spain, France, China, and the United States. China, Turkey, and Spain are the biggest producers of quality anise seeds.

Anise is easily grown from seed in well-aerated soil. It is a slow-growing plant that needs a frost-free growing season. Harvested shortly before the seeds ripen, the plants are pulled up by the roots and placed in piles to dry. The seeds are removed from the plants and spread on trays to dry further, either in a warm indoor area or in dappled sunlight. A pound of anise yields about 10,000 seeds.

The essential oil, *anethole*, also found in caraway and fennel, is extracted from the seeds and is used to impart a licorice flavor to liqueurs, cough drops, and other medicines.

How It Tastes and Smells

◆ ◆ ◆

Anise has a sweet licorice flavor that is very aromatic. It is a warm flavor that imparts a soothing sense. The smell of anise is distinct but not overpowering.

Use and Preparation

◆ ◆ ◆

In desserts anise is used both as whole seed and ground. To obtain the maximum flavor from ground anise, it is best to use it right after it has been ground. Anise should be ground using a spice grinder, pepper mill, or a mortar and pestle.

Tips for Choosing and Storing

◆ ◆ ◆

Buy either whole or ground anise seeds from a source with high turnover to be sure of freshness. Store whole and ground anise seeds in tightly sealed glass jars in a cool, dry place. Use whole anise seeds within 6 months and ground anise within 2 weeks.

Fig & Anise Cake

There is a local European-style bakery that makes a fig-and-anise bread that is so good it's like eating cake. I think the combination of flavors is sensational and created this cake to showcase them. It's so good, you'll find yourself nibbling at it all day.

Makes 1 (9-inch) tube cake, 12 to 14 servings.

◆ ◆ ◆

2 teaspoons unsalted butter, melted and cooled, for pan

2 teaspoons all-purpose flour for pan

2 cups plus 3 tablespoons sifted cake flour

1 teaspoon baking powder

1 cup coarsely chopped dried Calmyrna figs (about 12)

3 tablespoons anise seeds

¼ teaspoon salt

2 sticks (16 tablespoons) unsalted butter, softened

1⅔ cups sugar

5 large eggs at room temperature

1½ teaspoons anise extract

2 tablespoons powdered sugar

Position a rack in the center of the oven. Preheat oven to 325F (165C). Brush the insides of a 9-inch-round tube or kugelhopf pan with the melted butter, then lightly dust with the flour, and shake out the excess.

Sift together cake flour and baking powder into a small bowl. In a small bowl, toss the chopped figs with 2 tablespoons of the flour mixture. Toss the remaining flour mixture with the anise seeds and salt.

In the bowl of a stand mixer or in a medium bowl, using the flat-beater attachment or a hand-held mixer, beat the butter until light and fluffy, about 2 minutes. Gradually add the sugar and beat the mixture until creamy. Add the eggs, one at a time, beating well after each addition. Stop and frequently scrape down the sides and bottom of the bowl with a rubber spatula. Add the anise extract and blend well. Alternately blend in the flour mixture and figs in 4 or 5 stages, mixing well after each addition.

Scoop the batter into the pan. Use a rubber spatula to smooth and even the top. Bake 55 to 65 minutes, until a wooden pick inserted near the center comes out clean.

Cool in the pan on a rack 15 minutes. Then invert the pan onto the rack and leave for a few minutes for the cake to drop out of the pan. Remove the pan and let the cake cool completely. Dust the top of the cake with powdered sugar before serving.

The cake will keep up to 4 days well wrapped in plastic wrap at room temperature or it can be frozen up to 4 months. If frozen, defrost in the refrigerator for 24 hours before serving.

Anise Nut Tart

A delectable creamy filling, accented with the licoricelike flavor of anise, makes a wonderful textural contrast to the crunchy nuts it holds. This tart is a standout on its own, but it's also great served with Vanilla Bean Ice Cream (page 208).

Makes 1 (8-inch-square) tart, 12 servings.

◆　◆　◆

Pastry

1¾ cups all-purpose flour

¼ cup sugar

1½ sticks (12 tablespoons) unsalted
    butter, chilled, cut into small pieces

1 large egg yolk at room temperature

1 tablespoon plus one teaspoon heavy
    whipping cream

Filling

¼ cup granulated sugar

¼ cup firmly packed golden brown
    sugar

½ cup honey

Pinch of salt

5 tablespoons unsalted butter, melted
    and cooled

1 large egg at room temperature, lightly
    beaten

3 tablespoons anise-flavored liqueur
    (Anisette, Sambuca, Pernod)

2 teaspoons anise seeds, crushed

½ cup pine nuts

½ cup whole unblanched almonds,
    coarsely chopped

Pastry

Place the flour and sugar in the work bowl of a food processor fitted with a steel blade. Add the butter and pulse the mixture until the butter is cut into tiny pieces and the dough is crumbly, about 1 minute. Combine the egg yolk with the cream. With the machine on, add egg yolk mixture through the feed tube. Process until the pastry wraps itself around the blade, about 1 minute. Cover the pastry with plastic wrap and chill at least 1 hour, until firm enough to roll.

Roll out the pastry on a lightly floured work surface to a 10-inch square between ¼ and ⅛ inch thick. Gently drape the pastry around the rolling pin and unroll into an 8-inch-square fluted tart pan with a removable bottom. Carefully lift up the sides of the pastry and fit it into the bottom and against the sides of the tart pan. Trim off the excess pastry at the top of the pan. Chill the pastry shell 30 minutes.

Position a rack in the center of the oven. Preheat oven to 350F (175C). Place the tart pan on a baking sheet. Line the pastry shell with a large piece of foil and fill with tart or pie weights. Bake 10 minutes. Remove the baking sheet from the oven and remove the foil and weights.

Filling

Combine the granulated sugar, brown sugar, honey, salt, and butter in a bowl. Stir in the egg, liqueur, anise seeds, and nuts and blend together thoroughly. Pour the filling into the pastry shell.

Bake the tart 30 to 35 minutes, until the filling is bubbling and golden. Remove from the oven and cool on a rack. The tart will keep 3 days at room temperature, tightly covered with plastic wrap.

Pain d'Epices

Pain d'epices is a classic French spice and honey cake. It is closely related to gingerbread and is descended from ancient spice and honey cakes. Pain d'epices' roots can be traced through the spiced honey cakes of the Middle East encountered by the eleventh-century Crusaders to an ancient Chinese honey bread called *mi-kong*, which was eaten by the followers of Ghengis Khan. This French version of gingerbread evolved during the fifteenth and sixteenth centuries in Rheims and Strasbourg, where it was influenced by contact with bakers from Germany.

Anise is the main spice in *pain d'epices*. Rye flour, which can be found in health food stores and many supermarkets, is also characteristic of this traditional cake. Pain d'epices is delicious served warm, spread with butter, for breakfast or afternoon tea.

Makes 1 (14 × 4-inch) loaf, 18 to 20 servings.

◆　◆　◆

1 tablespoon unsalted butter for pan
　and parchment paper
2 teaspoons all-purpose flour for pan
1¼ cups honey
¾ cup water
¾ cup superfine sugar (see Note, page
　21)
1 tablespoon anise seeds, crushed
1 teaspoon ground cinnamon
¾ teaspoon ground cloves

¼ teaspoon salt
¼ cup dark rum
2½ cups rye flour
1½ cups all-purpose flour
1½ teaspoons baking soda
½ teaspoon baking powder
½ cup finely chopped candied orange
　peel
1 cup finely ground almonds (see Note,
　opposite)

Position a rack in the center of the oven. Preheat oven to 350F (175C). Cut a rectangle of parchment paper to fit the bottom of a 14 × 4-inch loaf pan. (See page 239 for pan equivalents.) Generously butter the inside of the pan and 1 side of the parchment paper. Dust the inside of the pan with flour and tap out the excess. Place parchment paper in the bottom of the pan, buttered side up.

In a heavy-bottomed 2-quart saucepan, combine the honey, water, and sugar, and stir over low heat until the sugar dissolves. Increase heat to medium and bring mixture to a boil. Remove from the heat and transfer to the bowl of a stand mixer or a medium bowl.

Add the spices, salt, and rum, and, using the flat-beater attachment or a hand-held mixer, blend well. Sift together the rye flour, all-purpose flour, baking soda, and baking powder and add to the bowl in 4 or 5 stages, blending well after each addition. The batter will be sticky. Stir in the candied orange peel and ground almonds and blend thoroughly.

Use a rubber spatula to scoop the dough into the loaf pan. Dip the spatula in warm water and smooth and even the top. Bake the cake 45 minutes, until it has risen to the top of the pan and a wooden pick inserted in the center comes out clean. Cool in pan on a cooling rack 15 minutes. Turn the cake out of the pan, remove parchment paper from the back of the cake, and re-invert cake onto the cooling rack. Leave the cake to cool completely.

Store the spice cake, tightly wrapped in plastic wrap, at room temperature up to 1 week or in the refrigerator up to a month. *Pain d'epices* can also be frozen up to 4 months. If frozen, defrost overnight before serving.

Note

Ground almonds are available as almond meal or almond flour in natural foods stores or in nut specialty shops. You can easily make your own ground almonds by pulsing sliced or slivered almonds 30 to 60 seconds, until ground to a powder, in a food processor or in a coffee grinder set aside for grinding nuts.

For each 1 cup of nuts, add 1 tablespoon sugar to absorb the natural oils that are released when the nuts are ground. The amount of sugar is minimal and does not have to be subtracted from that in the recipe.

One cup of sliced or slivered nuts yields 1 cup plus 1 heaping tablespoon ground nuts. Grind almonds and keep them in the freezer until needed.

Springerle

Springerle are classic imprinted German Christmas cookies traditionally flavored with anise seeds. They originated in Swabia, a historic region of Germany, in the fifteenth century. Springerle are formed by either rolling out the dough and imprinting it with a carved rolling pin or rolling the dough into elaborately carved wooden cookie molds. After the cookies are formed, they are dried at room temperature overnight before baking, which helps set the imprinted designs. An ancient tradition is to hand-paint the cookies and use them as ornaments to decorate Christmas trees. Since Springerle mellow with age, they are usually baked a few weeks in advance.

Makes about 36 (2-inch-square) cookies.

◆   ◆   ◆

1 tablespoon unsalted butter, for
  parchment paper

2 teaspoons anise seeds

2 large eggs at room temperature

2 cups powdered sugar, sifted

1 teaspoon anise extract or 1 tablespoon
  dark rum

Zest of 1 medium lemon, finely minced
  or grated

2 cups all-purpose flour

1 teaspoon baking powder

1 teaspoon anise seeds, crushed

Line 2 baking sheets with parchment paper and butter the paper. Scatter anise seeds evenly over paper on each baking sheet.

In the bowl of a stand mixer or in a medium bowl, using the wire-whip attachment or a hand-held mixer, whip the eggs on medium-high speed until frothy. Slowly add powdered sugar and beat until the mixture is pale yellow and holds a slowly dissolving ribbon when the beater is lifted, about 8 minutes. Add the extract or rum and lemon zest and blend thoroughly.

Sift together the flour and baking powder, then toss with the crushed anise seeds. Add the dry ingredients in 3 to 4 stages, blending well after each addition. Stop occasionally to scrape down the sides of the bowl with a rubber spatula.

Roll out the dough between lightly floured sheets of waxed paper to a large rectangle about ¼ inch thick. Trim the edges of the dough evenly. Use a springerle rolling pin to imprint the cookies, then use a sharp knife to separate them. Transfer the cookies to the baking sheets, leaving 1 inch of space between them. If using cookie molds, dust them with flour first, place a ball of dough in the center, and gently roll out the dough into the mold. Then lightly tap the mold on a countertop to release the cookie. Place the cookies on the baking sheets. For plain cookies, use a ruler to score the cookies into 2-inch squares, then use a sharp knife to separate them. Let the cookies stand overnight, uncovered, at room temperature.

The next day, position racks in the upper and lower thirds of the oven. Preheat oven to 300F (150C). Bake the cookies 10 minutes. Switch the baking sheets and bake cookies another 6 to 8 minutes, until set. Cool cookies on baking sheets on cooling racks.

Store the cookies, along with any loose anise seeds from the baking sheets, in an airtight container at room temperature up to 3 months.

Licorice Cake

While this cake sat on the kitchen counter for a couple of days, everyone who walked past it commented on its potent licorice aroma. Anise is the secret ingredient that adds a new flavor dimension to this classic angel food cake. Try serving it with Honey Mace Ice Cream (page 133) or Vanilla Bean Ice Cream (page 208). Softly whipped cream and fresh strawberries, raspberries, or blackberries also make great accompaniments.

Makes 1 (10-inch) tube cake, 14 to 16 servings.

♦ ♦ ♦

4 tablespoons anise seeds

1 cup plus 2 tablespoons sifted cake
    flour

¼ teaspoon salt

1½ cups superfine sugar (see Note, page
    21)

12 large egg whites at room temperature

1 teaspoon cream of tartar

2 teaspoons vanilla extract

½ teaspoon anise extract

1 teaspoon fresh lemon juice

Position a rack in the center of the oven. Preheat oven to 325F (165C).

Use a coffee grinder or a mortar and pestle to lightly crush 2 tablespoons of the anise seeds. In a 1-quart bowl thoroughly blend the flour with the salt, ¾ cup of the superfine sugar, the crushed anise seeds, and the remaining 2 tablespoons of whole anise seeds; set aside. Place the remaining ¾ cup of superfine sugar in a measuring cup near the mixer.

In a greasefree bowl of a stand mixer or in a medium bowl, using the wire-whip attachment or a hand-held mixer, whip the egg whites on low speed until they are slightly frothy. Add the cream of tartar and whip the egg whites until they begin to mound. Increase speed to medium and slowly sprinkle in the remaining ¾ cup of superfine sugar, 2 tablespoons at a time, then continue whipping the whites until they are firm but not dry. Blend in the extracts and lemon juice.

Sprinkle the dry ingredients over the whipped egg whites, 3 tablespoons at a time, and gently fold them into the whites, using a long-handled rubber spatula.

Turn the batter into a 10 × 4-inch tube pan, preferably with a removable bottom. Use the rubber spatula to smooth and even the top. Tap the pan on the countertop gently a few times to eliminate any air bubbles.

Bake the cake 45 to 50 minutes, until it is golden brown, springs back when lightly touched, and a cake tester inserted near the center comes out clean. Remove the pan from the oven and immediately invert it onto its feet, or hang it by the center tube over a funnel or the neck of a bottle. Leave the cake to hang for several hours, until it is completely cool.

To remove the cake from the pan, run a thin-bladed knife around the inside of the pan and around the tube. Gently loosen the cake from the edges and push the bottom of the pan up, away from the sides. Run the knife between the bottom of the cake and the bottom of the pan and invert the cake onto a plate, then re-invert, so it is right side up. Angel food cake is best cut with a serrated knife using a sawing motion.

The cake will keep at room temperature, well wrapped in plastic, 3 days, or it can be frozen up to 3 weeks. If frozen, defrost in the refrigerator 24 hours before serving.

Lebkuchen

Lebkuchen are classic German mixed spice and honey cookies that are traditionally served during the Christmas holiday season. The most famous and most popular Lebkuchen come from Nuremberg. Their flavor actually gets better with age as they become firmer, but I like them still warm and soft, fresh from the oven. They will keep up to three months in an airtight container at room temperature, so they are ideal to bake ahead.

Makes about 60 (2½ × 1½-inch) cookies.

◆　◆　◆

3⅔ cups all-purpose flour
1 teaspoon baking powder
1 teaspoon baking soda
¼ teaspoon salt
2 teaspoons ground cinnamon
1 teaspoon ground cardamom
1 teaspoon ground ginger
1 teaspoon ground cloves
¾ teaspoon ground mace
½ teaspoon crushed anise seeds
Zest of 1 large lemon, finely minced

1 stick (8 tablespoons) unsalted butter, cut into small pieces
⅔ cup honey
½ cup superfine sugar (see Note, page 21)
½ cup firmly packed golden brown sugar
1 cup finely ground almonds (see Note, page 31)
1 large egg at room temperature

Sift together the flour, baking powder, and baking soda, and toss with the salt. Separately sift together the cinnamon, cardamom, ginger, cloves, and mace, and toss with the anise seeds and lemon zest.

In a heavy-bottomed 2-quart saucepan, combine the butter, honey, superfine sugar, and brown sugar and warm over low heat, stirring frequently with a wooden spoon, until the butter is melted and the sugar is dissolved, about 5 minutes.

Remove the saucepan from the heat and transfer the mixture to the bowl of a stand mixer or a medium bowl. Using the flat-beater attachment or a hand-held mixer, blend in the spice mixture. Add the ground almonds in 2 stages, blending well, then add the flour mixture in 4 stages, blending well after each addition. Stop occasionally and scrape down the sides of the bowl with a rubber spatula. Stir in the egg and blend thoroughly.

Gather the dough into a large rectangle and wrap tightly in plastic wrap. Refrigerate at least 3 hours or overnight.

Position racks in the upper and lower thirds of the oven. Preheat oven to 350F (175C). Line 4 baking sheets with parchment paper. Cut the chilled dough in half and keep one half in the refrigerator while rolling out the other half.

Roll out the dough between lightly floured sheets of waxed paper to a large rectangle about 15 × 9 inches and ¼ inch thick. Trim the edges of the dough evenly. Use a ruler to mark rectangles 2½ inches long and 1½ inches wide. Transfer the rectangles to the lined baking sheets, leaving 1 inch of space between them. Gather any scraps together, re-roll, and cut. Repeat with the remaining half of the dough.

Bake the cookies 6 minutes. Switch the baking sheets and bake another 6 minutes, until cookies are very lightly browned and set. Use an offset spatula to transfer the cookies from the baking sheets to racks to cool completely. Store the cookies in an airtight container at room temperature up to 3 months.

Anise Biscotti

The licoricelike flavor of anise perfumes these classic Italian twice-baked cookies. They keep well, although they usually disappear quickly. Biscotti travel well, too, making them ideal for lunch bags or picnics. Try them as an accompaniment to your favorite ice cream.

Makes 36 biscotti.

♦　♦　♦

2 cups all-purpose flour

2 teaspoons baking powder

Pinch of salt

¾ cup sugar

2 large eggs at room temperature,
　lightly beaten

1½ teaspoons pure vanilla extract

1 stick (8 tablespoons) unsalted butter,
　melted and cooled

4 tablespoons anise seeds

Position racks in the upper and lower third of the oven. Preheat oven to 350F (175C). Line 2 baking sheets with parchment paper.

Sift together the flour and baking powder into the bowl of a stand mixer or a medium bowl, then blend in the salt and add the sugar. Using the flat-beater attachment or a hand-held mixer, blend together at low speed 30 seconds. Stir vanilla into the eggs, then add egg mixture and butter to the dry ingredients and mix well. Add the anise seeds and mix 30 seconds, until well blended.

Divide the dough into 2 equal pieces. Take 1 piece and pat it out onto a lined baking sheet to form a mound 8 to 10 inches long, 2 to 3 inches wide, and ½ inch thick. Repeat with the other piece of the dough on the other baking sheet.

Bake the biscotti 25 minutes, until lightly browned and set, switching the baking sheets halfway through baking. Cool the biscotti on the baking sheets on cooling racks 5 minutes. Slice each mound on the diagonal into ½-inch-thick slices. Then place the slices on their sides on the baking sheets. Return the baking sheets to the oven 10 to 15 minutes, until the biscotti are firm. Cool on baking sheets on cooling racks.

Store the biscotti in an airtight container at room temperature up to 3 weeks.

Caraway

[Shallow invites Falstaff to partake of]
"... a last year's pippin of mine own graffing,
with a dish of caraways."

—William Shakespeare, *Henry IV*

Caraway is one of the oldest known spices. Its use has been documented as far back as the Stone Age. The name "caraway" itself is derived from an ancient Arabic word, *karawya*. The first-century epicure Apicius wrote of using caraway to flavor a sauce for fish. During the Middle Ages, caraway was used liberally to flavor many dishes, and in the seventeenth century, herbalists were known to use it in sweet dishes.

Today caraway is widely used in Scandinavian and Eastern European countries to flavor bread, cakes, cookies, confections, cheeses, meats, and vegetables. It is so commonly used in rye bread that many people mistakenly think caraway seeds are rye. Caraway is the main flavoring ingredient in European liqueurs such as *Kümmel, aquavit,* and *schnapps.* Caraway seed oil is used as a flavoring in mouthwash, cough drops, and other medicines, and to scent perfumes.

Lore and Myths

◆　◆　◆

Caraway was considered to be an effective protection from the black arts and capable of warding off the evil eye. In Germany, parents would place the seeds under their child's crib as a protection from witchcraft. Caraway seeds have also been found buried with the Egyptians in their tombs.

Caraway also has been highly valued as a digestive aid. In the Middle Ages, caraway comfits, seeds that were coated with sugar, were chewed to aid digestion and to sweeten breath.

Characteristics

◆　◆　◆

The botanical name for caraway is *Carum carvi*. Caraway is the dried seed (actually, the fruit) of a biennial plant that is a member of the parsley family and is related to anise, cumin, dill, and fennel. The plant has feathery bright green leaves with clusters of tiny off-white flowers. The plant grows to a height of about 2½ feet. The comma-shaped seeds taper at each end and are about ¼ inch long. The outer hard shell is dark brown with five light brown ridges.

Where and How It's Grown

◆　◆　◆

Caraway is native to northern and central Europe and Asia. Holland currently produces the largest quantity, and best-quality, caraway. It is also grown in Germany, Poland, Russia, Morocco, Bulgaria, Canada, and the United States.

Caraway is easily grown from seed in light clay soil. The stems of the plants are cut when the fruit is ripe. The seeds must be harvested early in the day before the sun dries the heads that holds them. If the heads are dry, they will shatter, spreading the seeds at random. The seeds are removed from the plants and sun-dried.

The essential oil, *anethole*, also found in anise and fennel, is extracted from the seeds and is used to impart a licorice flavor to liqueurs, cough drops, and other medicines.

How It Tastes and Smells
◆　◆　◆

Caraway has a mildly sweet, slightly warm flavor that tastes a little like licorice. Caraway gives off a mild licorice scent.

Use and Preparation
◆　◆　◆

In desserts, caraway is used primarily as the whole seed, although occasionally it can be used ground. Grind whole caraway seeds in a spice grinder, a pepper mill, or with a mortar and pestle. To obtain the most flavor, grind the seeds just before use.

Tips for Choosing and Storing
◆　◆　◆

Buy whole caraway seeds from a source with a high turnover to be sure of freshness. Whole caraway seeds should be stored in a tightly sealed glass jar in a cool, dry place where they will last up to 4 years.

Currant and Caraway Scones

Caraway seeds lend their warm, pungent flavor to these scones. They are delicious served warm with afternoon tea or coffee, accompanied by a variety of jams or lemon curd.

Makes 12 (2½-inch) rounds.

◆　　◆　　◆

2¼ cups all-purpose flour
⅓ cup sugar
Pinch of salt
1 teaspoon cream of tartar
1 tablespoon plus 1½ teaspoons baking
　powder

5 tablespoons unsalted butter, chilled,
　cut into small pieces
2 tablespoons caraway seeds
⅓ cup currants
1 cup plus 1 tablespoon buttermilk

Position a rack in the center of the oven. Preheat oven to 425F (220C). Line a baking sheet with parchment paper.

Place the flour, sugar, salt, cream of tartar, and baking powder in the work bowl of a food processor fitted with a steel blade. Pulse for a few seconds to blend the mixture. Add butter and pulse until the butter is cut into tiny pieces, about 1 minute. Add the caraway seeds and currants.

With the machine on, pour 1 cup of buttermilk through the feed tube. Process just until the dough holds together, about 20 seconds. It should be slightly lumpy and may be sticky.

Turn the dough out onto a lightly floured work surface. Roll it out to a rectangle about ½ inch thick. Use a 2½-inch-round cutter to cut circles from the dough. Transfer the scones to the baking sheet, leaving 1 inch of space between them. Brush the tops of the scones with the remaining tablespoon of buttermilk.

Bake the scones 15 minutes, until the tops are lightly browned. Transfer to a rack to cool slightly.

Serve the scones warm or at room temperature. They can be reheated before serving in a 350F (175C) oven. Store the scones at room temperature up to 4 days, tightly covered with foil.

Caraway Seed Cakes

Seed cakes have been popular in England since the Middle Ages. Instead of the traditional loaf or round shape, I bake these in individual fluted-edge tartlet pans. This makes bite-size cakes that are perfect for eating out of hand. Try them for afternoon tea, in the picnic basket, in a bag lunch, or on the buffet table. The reaction I got from a few people who tasted these was very interesting. They said, "The rye in these tastes really good." Well, it wasn't rye, but caraway seeds. I thought it was fascinating that caraway is associated so strongly with rye bread that some people think of the seeds as rye.

Makes 18 (2½-inch-round) cakes.

◆ ◆ ◆

2 tablespoons unsalted butter, melted
    and cooled, for pans
1 stick unsalted butter, softened
⅔ cup sugar
2 large eggs at room temperature,
    lightly beaten

1¼ cups all-purpose flour
3 tablespoons cornstarch
¼ teaspoon baking powder
⅛ teaspoon salt
1 tablespoon caraway seeds
Pinch of ground cloves

Position a rack in the center of the oven. Preheat oven to 350F (175C). Use a pastry brush to butter the insides of 18 (2½-inch-round) fluted tartlet pans. Place the pans on a baking sheet.

Place the stick of butter in the bowl of a stand mixer or in a medium bowl. Using the flat-beater attachment or a hand-held mixer, beat the butter until light and fluffy, about 2 minutes. Add the sugar and beat until well mixed. Add eggs and beat until combined. Stop and scrape down the sides and bottom of the bowl with a long-handled rubber spatula.

Sift together the flour, cornstarch, and baking powder. Then add the salt, caraway seeds, and cloves. Toss the mixture together. Add the dry ingredients to the first mixture in 3 stages, blending well after each addition.

Fill each tartlet pan three-quarters full with the batter. Bake 40 to 45 minutes, until golden brown and set. Cool on a cooling rack 10 minutes, then slip the cakes from the pans and cool completely on a rack.

The cakes will keep up to 1 week at room temperature in an airtight container. They can be warmed before serving in a 300F (150C) oven 10 to 15 minutes.

Pitcaithly Bannock

Bannock is a traditional Scottish sweet bread with a long history. It started out as a flat, primitive, unfermented bread made with a variety of different grains, ground to a meal. Throughout the years, bannock has experienced many changes, depending on the location. With the addition of caraway seeds, toasted almonds, and orange zest, bannock becomes a unique type of shortbread and takes on the name Pitcaithly.

Makes 24 wedges.

◆　　◆　　◆

⅓ cup slivered almonds

2 sticks (16 tablespoons) unsalted
   butter, softened

½ cup superfine sugar (see Note, page
   21)

½ cup rice flour (see Note, opposite)

1½ cups all-purpose flour

⅛ teaspoon salt

1 tablespoon plus 1½ teaspoons
   caraway seeds

Zest of ½ large or 1 small orange,
   finely minced

Position a rack in the oven and preheat to 325F (165C). Place the almonds in a shallow baking pan and toast 5 to 8 minutes, until light golden. Cool slightly, then chop finely.

Position racks in the upper and lower thirds of the oven. Line 2 baking sheets with parchment paper.

In the bowl of a stand mixer or in a medium bowl, using the flat-beater attachment or a hand-held mixer, beat the butter until light and fluffy, about 2 minutes. Add the sugar and continue beating until thoroughly blended.

Blend the rice flour with the all-purpose flour and salt. Add to the butter in 4 stages. Stop and scrape down the sides of the bowl after each addition. Blend in the caraway seeds and orange zest and continue to mix 1 to 2 minutes, until the dough is smooth and soft.

Divide the dough into 3 pieces. Form each piece into a flat circle about 6 inches wide. Place 2 circles on 1 baking sheet and the third on another. Use a fork to press into the outer edge of each circle, making a design. Score each circle into 8 equal wedges.

Place the baking sheets in the oven and reduce the heat to 300F (150C). Bake 25 minutes. Switch the baking sheets and bake another 8 to 10 minutes, until light golden on the bottom and sand colored on top.

Remove the baking pans from the oven and cool slightly on racks. While they are still warm cut the bannock on the scored lines, then cool completely. Store the wedges between layers of waxed paper in an airtight container at room temperature for up to 2 weeks.

Note

Rice flour is available from natural foods stores.

Caraway Ice Cream

Although this sounds like it may be a strange combination, it really is intriguing. The warm, robust flavor of caraway fits perfectly with the rich, creamy quality of this ice cream. Try it. I think you'll be very pleasantly surprised! When some friends tasted this ice cream, it provoked an interesting reaction. They said that it tasted like lunch. I asked what they ate for lunch and they replied that they ate rye bagels. As with the reaction to my Caraway Seed Cakes (page 43), rye and caraway are married so closely that many people think of them as the same.

Makes about 1 quart.

◆　◆　◆

2 cups milk

2 cups heavy whipping cream

½ cup caraway seeds

8 large egg yolks at room temperature

¾ cup sugar

Place the milk and cream in a heavy-bottomed 3- quart saucepan over medium heat. Bring the mixture to just below the boiling point, 10 to 12 minutes. Remove the pan from the heat, stir in the caraway seeds, cover, and let the mixture infuse 30 minutes.

In the bowl of a stand mixer or in a medium bowl, using the wire-whip attachment or a hand-held mixer, whip the egg yolks and sugar together until they are pale yellow and hold a slowly dissolving ribbon when the beater is lifted, about 5 minutes.

Reheat the milk mixture to just below the boiling point. Reduce the mixer speed to low and slowly pour 1 cup of the hot liquid into the egg and sugar mixture. Stir to blend well, then add the egg mixture to the saucepan. Reduce the heat to low and cook, stirring the mixture constantly with a wooden spoon, until the mixture reaches 185F (85C) on a candy thermometer, about 5 minutes. At this point the mixture is thickened, and when a line is drawn through the custard on the back of the spoon, it leaves a clearly defined path.

Strain the mixture through a fine sieve into a bowl. Cover the mixture tightly and chill in the refrigerator for several hours or overnight. Process the mixture in an ice cream maker according to the manufacturer's instructions.

Store the ice cream in a covered container in the freezer for up to 1 month. If it is frozen solid, soften it in the refrigerator for a few hours before serving.

Cardamom

• • • • • • • • • • •

Like saffron and vanilla, cardamom is one of the world's costliest spices. Cardamom can be traced back to Babylonian gardens as well as to Greek and Roman times. Over a thousand years ago the Vikings discovered cardamom during their travels to Constantinople and brought it back to Denmark, where it is still an important ingredient in Danish pastry.

Today cardamom is used extensively in the Scandinavian countries, Russia, and Germany for pastries, cakes, and cookies. It is widely used in the Middle East to flavor coffee, and in India for sweets, curries, pilafs, and as an important ingredient in *garam masala*, a spice mixture. The essential oil extracted from the seeds is used in perfumes.

Lore and Myths

♦ ♦ ♦

Cardamom is thought to be a digestive aid and is chewed to sweeten breath.

Characteristics

◆ ◆ ◆

Cardamom is a pod consisting of an outer shell that contains many tiny seeds. The pods grow on a perennial bush, a member of the ginger family, that reaches heights from 6 to 15 feet. Cardamom's botanical name is *Elettaria cardamomum*.

There are three types of cardamom: green, white, and brown. Green and white cardamom pods are oval, three-sided, and measure about 1/2 inch long. They contain between 12 and 20 three-sided seeds that range in color from brown to black. White cardamom is simply green cardamom that has been bleached because it is thought to be more aesthetically pleasing. Brown cardamom is a relative and is not true cardamom. Brown cardamom pods are longer, about 1 inch, and have a coarse outer texture. They hold between 40 and 50 hard, dark, sticky seeds.

Where and How It's Grown

◆ ◆ ◆

Cardamom is native to India and Southeast Asia, where it grows wild in rain forests. It thrives in hot tropical climates. Guatemala is currently one of the world's biggest producers of cardamom.

Cardamom is harvested every few weeks from September to December just before the fruit is mature. If left on the bush to ripen, the pods split open, spilling out the seeds. The pods are handpicked from the stems, which is why cardamom is so costly. The pods are dried either in special rooms or on large trays in the sun. Pods without cracks are the most valuable because when cracked the seeds are exposed to air and lose their flavor rapidly.

How It Tastes and Smells

◆ ◆ ◆

Green and white cardamom have a mildly sweet, warm, pungent, fresh lemony flavor and aroma. Brown cardamom has a bitter taste and a camphorlike mediciny smell.

Use and Preparation
• • •

In desserts, cardamom is used ground. To get the best flavor, buy whole cardamom pods, crack the pods open, discard the papery outer pods, and grind the seeds with a mortar and pestle just before use.

Tips for Choosing and Storing
• • •

Buy whole cardamom pods without cracks from a source with a high turnover to be sure of freshness. Ground cardamom tends to lose its flavor rapidly.

Whole cardamom pods are best stored in a tightly sealed glass jar in the refrigerator for up to a year. Store ground cardamom under the same conditions no longer than 3 months.

Cardamom Quick Bread

This quick bread is great for serving with brunch. It makes a delightful addition to a buffet and it's perfect for gift-giving. Although delicious on its own, try spreading it with butter, jam, or apple butter. For an elegant touch, serve it for afternoon tea accompanied by sherry or port.

Makes 1 (9-inch) loaf cake, 12 servings.

◆　◆　◆

2 teaspoons unsalted butter, softened, for pan

2 teaspoons all-purpose flour for pan

2 cups all-purpose flour

1 tablespoon finely ground cardamom

2 teaspoons baking powder

½ teaspoon salt

4 tablespoons (½ stick) unsalted butter, softened

1 cup firmly packed golden brown sugar

2 large eggs at room temperature, lightly beaten

1 cup milk

1 teaspoon pure vanilla extract

2 teaspoons lemon extract

Zest of ½ medium lemon, finely minced

½ cup Monukka or Thompson seedless raisins

Position a rack in the center of the oven. Preheat oven to 350F (175C). Use the 2 teaspoons butter to generously butter the inside of a 9 × 5-inch loaf pan. Dust the inside with 2 teaspoons of flour and tap out the excess.

Combine the flour, cardamom, baking powder, and salt in a medium bowl. Toss to blend well, then set aside.

In the bowl of a stand mixer or in a medium bowl, using the flat-beater attachment or a hand-held mixer, beat the butter until light and fluffy, about 2 minutes. Add the sugar and beat until thoroughly combined. Add the eggs and blend well. Stop occasionally and scrape down the sides of the bowl with a rubber spatula.

Combine the milk, vanilla extract, lemon extract, and lemon zest. Add to the mixture and blend thoroughly. Add the flour mixture in 3 stages, blending well after each addition. Beat the mixture until smooth, about 30 seconds, then stir in the raisins.

Transfer the batter to the pan. Use a rubber spatula to smooth and even the top. Bake 50 to 55 minutes, until a wooden pick inserted in the center comes out clean.

Cool bread in the pan on a rack 15 minutes. Turn the bread out of the pan gently and continue to cool on the rack. Cut the bread crosswise into 1-inch slices.

Store the bread, well wrapped in foil, at room temperature up to 5 days or freeze up to 4 months. If frozen, defrost in the refrigerator 24 hours before serving.

Cardamom Butter Nut Balls

These little cookies are quick and easy to make, which is good because they're so scrumptious they disappear quickly.

Makes 48 cookies.
◆   ◆   ◆

1½ cups sliced or slivered almonds

2 cups all-purpose flour

½ cup granulated sugar

1 teaspoon ground cardamom

⅛ teaspoon salt

2 sticks (16 tablespoons) unsalted
    butter, chilled, cut into small pieces

2 teaspoons pure vanilla extract

Finely minced zest of 1 large orange

Powdered sugar

Position a rack in the center of the oven. Preheat oven to 350F (175C). Place the almonds in a cake pan or pie plate and toast 5 minutes. Shake the pan and continue to toast until light golden, about 5 more minutes. Let cool.

Reduce oven temperature to 325F (165C). Line 2 baking sheets, with parchment paper.

Place the almonds, flour, sugar, cardamom, and salt in the work bowl of a food processor fitted with a steel blade. Pulse briefly to blend. Add the butter and pulse until it is cut into tiny pieces. Add the vanilla and orange zest and process the dough until it wraps itself around the blade, 30 to 60 seconds.

Pinch off pieces of the dough and roll them into balls about 1 inch in diameter. Place the balls on the lined baking sheets, leaving 1 inch of space between them.

Bake the cookies about 20 minutes, until lightly golden and set. Cool cookies on baking sheets on racks. Lightly dust the cookies with powdered sugar.

Store the cookies between layers of waxed paper in an airtight container up to 1 week at room temperature.

Pear Crisp

In this baked dessert, the crisp, crunchy topping is an excellent counterpoint to the soft, juicy pears, which get their piquant flavoring from cardamom. This is a great finish for a meal served in the fall, the season when pears are at their peak. Anjou, Bartlett, or Comice pears work very well because they hold their shapes and won't become mushy when baked.

Makes 8 servings.

◆ ◆ ◆

1½ pounds pears (3 to 4), peeled, cored, and cut into ½-inch-thick slices
Zest of ½ large lemon, finely minced
¼ cup whole-wheat flour
½ cup all-purpose flour
¼ cup granulated sugar
⅓ cup firmly packed golden brown sugar

¾ teaspoon ground cardamom
Pinch ground cloves
6 tablespoons (¾ stick) unsalted butter, chilled, and cut into small pieces
¾ cup heavy whipping cream
½ teaspoon pure vanilla extract
¼ teaspoon ground cardamom

Position a rack in the center of the oven. Preheat oven to 375F (190C). In a large bowl, combine the sliced pears and lemon zest. Toss to mix well. Transfer the pears to the bottom of a 9-inch pie plate or cake pan.

Combine the whole-wheat flour, all-purpose flour, granulated sugar, brown sugar, cardamom, and cloves in the work bowl of a food processor fitted with a steel blade and pulse for several seconds to blend. Add the butter and pulse until it is cut into very tiny pieces. Sprinkle the mixture evenly over the pears.

Bake the crisp 40 minutes, until the topping is lightly browned, the pears are tender, and their juices are bubbling around the edges. Transfer the crisp to a rack to cool slightly.

In the bowl of a stand mixer or in a medium bowl, using the wire-whip attachment or a hand-held mixer, whip the cream on medium speed until it begins to thicken. Add the vanilla and cardamom, and continue to whip until the cream holds soft peaks.

Serve slices of the crisp with a large dollop of whipped cream. It is best to serve the crisp within 2 hours of preparation or it will become soggy.

Summer Fresh Fruit Salad

Cardamom lends its pungent fragrance and sweet, lemony flavor to this refreshing summer fruit salad. Try it for breakfast, a snack, or part of a summer afternoon tea.

Makes 3½ cups, 4 servings.

◆　◆　◆

½ cup fresh raspberries

½ cup fresh blackberries

½ cup fresh blueberries

1 kiwi fruit, skinned and diced

½ large peach, peeled, pitted, diced

1 cup fresh strawberries, hulled and
  thinly sliced

½ teaspoon ground cardamom

Combine the fruit in a large bowl. Sprinkle on the cardamom and toss to mix well. Cover tightly with plastic wrap and refrigerate until ready to serve. Make the fruit salad no more than 3 hours before serving.

Summer Fruit Salad Tartlets

During a conversation with my good friend and fellow food writer Deborah Krasner, I told her about the delicious fruit salad I had created. She suggested serving it in a tart shell with lemon cream. Here's the result——a simply scrumptious variation of Summer Fresh Fruit Salad.

Makes 16 (2¹/₂-inch) tartlets.

♦ ♦ ♦

Tartlet Shells

1¹/₄ cups all-purpose flour

¹/₃ cup plus 1 tablespoon sifted powdered sugar

Pinch of salt

Pinch of ground cardamom

1 stick plus 2 tablespoons (10 tablespoons) unsalted butter, chilled, cut into small pieces

1 large egg yolk at room temperature, lightly beaten

2 teaspoons heavy whipping cream

¹/₂ teaspoon lemon extract

Lemon Topping

¹/₂ recipe Lemon Curd (page 136)

¹/₂ cup heavy whipping cream

¹/₄ teaspoon ground cardamom

Filling

1 recipe Summer Fresh Fruit Salad (page 53)

Tartlet Shells

Combine the flour, powdered sugar, salt, and cardamom in the work bowl of a food processor fitted with a steel blade. Pulse 5 seconds to mix. Add butter to flour mixture. Pulse until the butter is cut into very tiny pieces, about 1 minute.

In a small bowl, beat the egg yolk with the cream and lemon extract, then pour this mixture through the feed tube while the food processor is running. Process the dough until it wraps itself around the blade, about 1 minute. Wrap the pastry dough in plastic wrap and chill 3 to 4 hours before using.

This pastry dough will keep 4 days in the refrigerator or can be frozen for up to 4 months, if very well wrapped. If frozen, defrost at least 24 hours in the refrigerator before using.

If the pastry dough is very cold, let it sit at room temperature until it is pliable, but not soft, then knead it briefly on a lightly floured surface before using.

Position a rack in the center of the oven. Preheat oven to 400F (205C). Roll out the pastry dough on a lightly floured work surface to about a ⅛-inch thickness. Using a 3-inch-round cutter, cut out circles of dough. Carefully place each dough circle into a 2½-inch fluted-edge tartlet shell and fit it into the bottom and against the sides. Pinch off any excess dough at the top. Place another tartlet pan on top of the pastry dough to act as a weight and place tartlet pans on a baking sheet.

Bake the tartlet shells 10 minutes. Remove the top tartlet pans, pierce the bottom of each tartlet shell with a fork, and bake another 10 to 12 minutes, until golden brown and set. Remove the baking sheet from the oven and cool on a rack. (The tartlet shells can be baked up to 2 days before they are used and held at room temperature wrapped in foil.)

Lemon Topping

Prepare lemon curd as directed on page 136. Pour the lemon curd into a bowl and cover it with plastic wrap. Cool slightly, then refrigerate until chilled thoroughly. Lemon curd will keep for up to 1 month in a tightly covered container in the refrigerator.

Pour the whipping cream into the bowl of a stand mixer or into a medium bowl. Using the wire-whip attachment or a hand-held mixer, whip the cream on medium speed until it is frothy. Add the cardamom and continue to whip until cream holds soft peaks. Fold the whipped cream into the lemon curd and blend together thoroughly.

Slip the tartlet shells from the pans. Mound 2 to 3 tablespoons of fruit salad into each tartlet shell and top with a spoonful of lemon cream. Refrigerate the tartlets until ready to serve, but assemble no more than 2 hours before serving.

Very Fudgy Brownies

Cardamom adds an unusual yet delicious twist to these classic fudgy brownies.

Makes 25 (1½-inch-square) brownies.

◆　◆　◆

1 tablespoon unsalted butter for pan
　and parchment paper
2 teaspoons all-purpose flour for pan
7 ounces bittersweet or semisweet
　chocolate, finely chopped
1½ sticks unsalted butter, cut into small
　pieces
4 large eggs at room temperature

1 cup sugar
1 teaspoon pure vanilla extract
½ teaspoon lemon extract
Zest of 1 large lemon, finely minced
⅓ cup all-purpose flour
1½ teaspoons finely ground cardamom
Pinch of salt
1 cup walnuts, finely chopped

Position a rack in the center of the oven. Preheat oven to 350F (175C). Cut a square of parchment paper to fit the bottom of an 8-inch-square baking pan. Use the 1 tablespoon butter to generously butter the inside of the baking pan and the square of parchment paper. Dust the inside of the pan with the 2 teaspoons flour, then shake out the excess. Line the bottom of the pan with the buttered square of parchment paper and set aside.

Place the chocolate and butter together in the top of the double boiler over hot, not simmering, water. Stir frequently with a rubber spatula so they melt evenly.

In the bowl of a stand mixer or in a medium bowl, using the wire-whip attachment or a hand-held mixer, beat the eggs and sugar together until they are very thick, pale yellow, and hold a ribbon when the beater is lifted, about 5 minutes. Blend in the vanilla and lemon extracts and the lemon zest.

Combine the flour with the cardamom and salt and add slowly to the egg mixture with the mixer at low speed. Stop and scrape down the sides of the bowl with a rubber spatula and mix again.

Take the double boiler off the heat, remove the top pan from the water, and wipe the bottom dry. Pour the melted chocolate and butter into the batter and blend thoroughly. Then add the nuts and mix briefly to combine.

Pour the batter into the prepared pan. Bake the brownies 30 to 35 minutes, until a wooden pick inserted 2 inches in from the edge still has moist crumbs clinging to it. The center will be very moist. Remove the pan from the oven and cool completely on a rack.

Cut the brownies into 1½-inch squares, 5 rows in each direction, using a knife dipped in hot water and dried. The brownies can be stored 3 days at room temperature in an airtight container or 1 week in a well-covered container in the refrigerator. If refrigerated, they will firm up slightly, but still remain very fudgy.

Speculaas

Speculaas are classic Dutch and Belgian Christmas spice cookies. They are traditionally imprinted with decorative wooden molds of various shapes like animals and figures, like that of St. Nicholas, which is made almost 2 feet tall. Even if you don't have any special molds, you can shape these cookies with any cutter or simply cut them into rectangular bars. Like many other spice cookies, their flavor improves with age.

Makes about 42 (3 X 2-inch) cookies.

◆　◆　◆

2 cups all-purpose flour

1 teaspoon baking powder

1¼ teaspoons ground cinnamon

½ teaspoon ground cardamom

½ teaspoon ground cloves

¼ teaspoon freshly grated nutmeg

¼ teaspoon salt

½ cup finely ground almonds (see Note, page 31)

1 stick plus 1 tablespoon (9 tablespoons) unsalted butter, softened

¼ cup superfine sugar (see Note, page 21)

⅓ cup firmly packed golden brown sugar

1 large egg at room temperature, lightly beaten

Zest of 1 large lemon, finely minced or grated

½ cup sliced or slivered almonds

Position racks in the upper and lower thirds of the oven. Preheat oven to 350F (175C). Line 4 baking sheets with parchment paper.

Sift together the flour, baking powder, cinnamon, cardamom, and cloves into a medium bowl and toss with the nutmeg, salt, and ground almonds.

In the bowl of a stand mixer or in a medium bowl, using the flat-beater attachment or a hand-held mixer, beat the butter until soft and fluffy. Add the superfine sugar and brown sugar and beat until thoroughly blended. Add the egg to the mixture, then blend in the lemon zest. Stop occasionally and scrape down the sides of the bowl with a rubber spatula.

Add the dry ingredients in 3 to 4 stages, blending well after each addition. Divide the dough in half, wrap one half in plastic wrap, and refrigerate while working with the other half.

Roll out the dough between lightly floured sheets of waxed paper to a large rectangle about ¼ inch thick. Trim the edges of the dough evenly. Use a ruler to mark rectangles 2 inches long and 3 inches wide. Or use cookie cutters, dipping them in flour occasionally to keep them from sticking. If using cookie molds, dust them with flour first, place a ball of dough in the center, and gently roll out the dough into the mold. Then lightly tap the mold on a countertop to release the cookie. Transfer the cookies to the lined baking sheets, leaving 1 inch of space between them. Gather any scraps together, re-roll, and cut. Repeat with the remaining half of the dough. Sprinkle a few sliced or slivered almonds on each cookie and press gently so they will stick.

Bake the cookies 6 minutes. Switch the baking sheets and bake another 3 to 5 minutes, until lightly colored and set. Cool cookies on baking sheets on racks. Store the cookies up to 3 months in an airtight container at room temperature.

Brune Kager

Brune kager, pronounced BROO-neh KAH-gher, are Danish specialty spice cookies that translate as "little brown cakes." Brune kager are traditionally served during the Christmas holiday season. They can be stored for several weeks in airtight containers at room temperature, making them very easy to prepare in advance.

Makes 36 cookies.

◆　◆　◆

¾ stick (6 tablespoons) unsalted butter, softened

½ cup firmly packed golden brown sugar

½ cup dark corn syrup

1½ cups all-purpose flour

½ teaspoon baking powder

½ teaspoon baking soda

1½ teaspoons ground cardamom

½ teaspoon finely ground cloves

¼ teaspoon ground ginger

¼ teaspoon salt

Zest of 1 large lemon, finely minced

36 whole unblanched, raw almonds

Place the butter in the bowl of a stand mixer or in a medium bowl. Using the flat-beater attachment or a hand-held mixer, beat the butter until light and fluffy, about 2 minutes. Add the brown sugar and beat well. Add the corn syrup and blend thoroughly.

Sift together the flour, baking powder, baking soda, cardamom, cloves, ginger, and salt into a medium bowl. Add lemon zest and stir to blend well. Add this mixture in 3 stages to the butter mixture, stopping occasionally to scrape down the bottom and sides of the bowl with a rubber spatula. Shape the dough into a flat round, wrap tightly in plastic wrap, and refrigerate at least 2 hours, until firm enough to roll.

Cut the dough into 2 equal pieces and work with 1 piece while keeping the other piece in the refrigerator. Between sheets of lightly floured waxed paper, roll out the dough to about a ⅛-inch thickness. Transfer the dough, still in the waxed paper, to a baking sheet and chill in the freezer 15 minutes.

Line 2 baking sheets with parchment paper. Cut the dough into 2-inch circles using a 2-inch-round cutter. Chill the dough in the freezer another 15 minutes.

Position a rack in the center of the oven. Preheat oven to 375F (190C).

Using a small offset spatula, transfer the circles to the lined baking sheets, leaving 2 inches of space between them. Press an almond into the center of each round. Bake 1 sheet of cookies at a time 8 minutes, until golden brown. Cool cookies on the baking sheets on racks. Gently peel the parchment paper off the back of the cookies. Store the cookies up to 2 months in an airtight container at room temperature.

Cassia

• • • • • • • • • • •

Cassia, also called Chinese cinnamon or false cinnamon, is often confused with true cinnamon, which is its close relative. Its use has been recorded in China as far back as 2500 B.C. Cassia is mentioned in Sanskrit texts and there are several Biblical references to it. Cassia reached Europe by way of the old spice caravans, which made it available to the ancient Greeks and Romans.

In the United States, cassia is commonly referred to as cinnamon. Its primary use is to flavor pastries, cakes, cookies, and sweet rolls. In China, cassia is one of the main ingredients in Chinese five-spice powder. In the Middle East it is used in savory cooking.

Lore and Myths

• • •

The Chinese believed the cassia tree was the tree of life. To them, it had always grown in Paradise, which they thought was a fabulous garden at the headwaters of the Yellow River. It was believed that if upon entering Paradise, the fruit of the cassia tree was eaten, immortality was guaranteed.

Cassia is thought to be a cure for intestinal and stomach disorders.

Characteristics

◆ ◆ ◆

Cassia, like its cousin cinnamon, is a member of the laurel family. Its botanical name is *Cinnamomum cassia.* Cassia is the dried bark of a tropical evergreen tree that has shiny, large leaves and lacy, small, pale yellow flowers. The trees reach heights of about 3 feet. The outer side of the bark is roughly textured and dull gray-brown. The inner side is smoother and more reddish-brown. The bark is usually ground to a fine powder. Ground cassia is dark reddish-brown, making it easy to distinguish from true cinnamon's light tan color.

Similar in size to cloves, the round, smooth cassia buds are dark brown. They are often used in pickling mixtures.

Where and How It's Grown

◆ ◆ ◆

Cassia trees are native to Burma, southern China, and northern Vietnam. Today they are also grown in Indonesia, Cambodia, and Laos. The trees have been known to produce for as long as 200 years.

The bark is stripped from thin branches of the trees during the rainy season, because the humidity makes this easier to manage. The bark is air-dried and during drying often curls into quills, known as cinnamon sticks. Pieces of the bark are sometimes available in small, flat sections.

How It Tastes and Smells

◆ ◆ ◆

Cassia has a strong, rich, sweet taste and aroma. It is much sweeter and stronger than true cinnamon. Cassia buds have a cinnamonlike aroma with a warm, pungent, sweet taste.

Use and Preparation

◆ ◆ ◆

In desserts, cassia is primarily used ground. Sticks or quills of cassia are often used to flavor hot drinks such as apple cider and hot chocolate, and dessert sauces, jams, and spiced fruits. Because cassia has such a powerful fragrance and taste, it is best to use slightly less of it than true cinnamon. Cassia quills can be ground to a powder in a spice or coffee grinder.

Tips for Choosing and Buying

◆ ◆ ◆

Buy ground cassia from a source with a high turnover to be sure of freshness. Ground cassia is best stored in a tightly sealed glass jar in a cool, dark, dry place for up to 1 year. Store cassia quills under the same conditions for up to 2 years.

Phyllo Caramel Cups

This special dessert features a variety of textural contrasts. Crisp phyllo pastry cups hold a creamy caramel filling accented with cassia cinnamon. Mascarpone, a tangy Italian cream cheese, is used for the creamy filling. It is available in shops that sell imported and gourmet foods. If mascarpone is unavailable, use low-fat or Neufchâtel cream cheese.

Makes 8 servings.

◆　◆　◆

Phyllo Pastry Cups

3 tablespoons granulated sugar
½ teaspoon ground cassia cinnamon
8 sheets phyllo pastry dough at room
　　temperature
6 tablespoons (¾ stick) unsalted butter,
　　melted

Caramel Filling

½ cup granulated sugar
½ teaspoon fresh lemon juice
⅓ cup heavy whipping cream
8 ounces mascarpone
2 tablespoons superfine sugar (see Note,
　　page 21)
1 teaspoon ground cassia cinnamon

Assembly

Powdered sugar

Phyllo Pastry Cups

Position a rack in the center of the oven. Preheat oven to 375F (190C). Spray the inside of 8 (¾-cup) custard cups with nonstick spray. In a small bowl, thoroughly stir together the sugar and cassia.

Stack together 8 sheets phyllo pastry dough. Trim the phyllo dough to a 12-inch square. Then cut the phyllo dough into 4 (6 × 6-inch) squares. Stack the phyllo squares and cover with a damp cloth. Place 1 phyllo dough square on a smooth work surface and brush with melted butter, then sprinkle lightly with the cassia and sugar mixture. Fit the phyllo square into one of the custard cups with a pointed end over the top edge. Repeat with 3 more phyllo squares, arranging the points at alternate corners. Use 4 phyllo squares for each remaining custard cup.

Place the custard cups on a baking sheet and bake until golden brown, 15 to 18 minutes. Cool pastry in cups on a rack. Gently slip the pastry from the custard cups. (The pastry cups can be baked 1 day in advance and held, covered with foil, at room temperature.)

Caramel Filling

Heat the granulated sugar in a heavy-bottomed 1-quart or unlined copper pan over medium heat, stirring frequently with a long-handled wooden spoon. As the sugar melts, stir constantly to remove any lumps. Stir in the lemon juice; be careful as it will splatter. Cook the mixture until it turns light amber, 3 to 4 minutes. Remove from the heat and immediately pour in the cream; be careful as it will splatter. Stir until the mixture is smooth. Pour the caramel into a ½-quart bowl, cover tightly with plastic wrap, and cool to room temperature. Chill the caramel until it is thick, 3 hours or overnight. (The caramel can be prepared up to 1 week in advance and kept in the refrigerator.)

To complete the filling, place the mascarpone in the bowl of a stand mixer or in a medium bowl. Using the flat-beater attachment or a hand-held mixer, beat the mascarpone with the superfine sugar and cassia at low speed until it holds firm peaks, about 2 minutes. Add the caramel and stir until thoroughly blended.

To assemble

Place 2 to 3 tablespoons of filling in the center of each pastry cup, then dust the tops generously with powdered sugar. Serve the cups immediately or refrigerate until 20 minutes before serving. Do not assemble more than 2 hours before serving.

Tarte Tatin

This classic caramelized upside-down apple tart is made even better with the addition of pungent cassia cinnamon. It's the perfect ending for a fall meal. For a real knockout, serve it with Vanilla Bean Ice Cream (page 208).

Makes 1 (10-inch) tart, 8 to 10 servings.

◆ ◆ ◆

Pastry

1 cup all-purpose flour
⅛ teaspoon salt
¼ teaspoon granulated sugar
¼ teaspoon ground cassia cinnamon
6 tablespoons (¾ stick) cold unsalted
    butter, cut into pieces
3 tablespoons cold water

Filling

½ cup granulated sugar
⅓ cup water
4 tablespoons unsalted butter, cut into
    1-inch cubes
8 medium Granny Smith or Golden
    Delicious apples, peeled, cored,
    halved, and thickly sliced
⅓ cup superfine or granulated sugar
Zest of 1 large lemon, finely minced
3 teaspoons ground cassia cinnamon

Pastry

Place the flour, salt, sugar, and cassia in the work bowl of a food processor fitted with a steel blade. Pulse 5 seconds to blend, then add the butter and pulse until it is cut into tiny pieces, about 1 minute. With the machine on, add the cold water through the feed tube and process until the dough forms a ball around the blade, about 30 seconds. Wrap the pastry dough in plastic and chill in the refrigerator for at least 1 hour, until firm enough to roll.

Filling

Combine the ½ cup granulated sugar and ⅓ cup water in a heavy-bottomed 1-quart saucepan and bring to a boil over high heat. Cook the sugar syrup to a golden caramel color, about 8 minutes, occasionally washing down the sides of the pan with a pastry brush dipped in warm water. Pour the caramel into a 10-inch glass pie plate or round metal cake pan and tilt the pan to completely cover the bottom with the caramel. Set the pan aside while preparing the apples.

Melt butter in a large skillet over medium heat until foamy. Add the apples, the 1/3 cup sugar, and lemon zest. Cook the apples over medium heat, stirring them frequently with a wooden spoon, until they are golden and soft, but still hold their shape, about 15 minutes. Sprinkle with 2 teaspoons of the cassia and stir to blend well. Transfer the apples to a baking sheet to cool briefly.

To assemble

Arrange the apple slices in tight concentric circles over the caramel in the pie plate or cake pan. Sprinkle the remaining teaspoon of cassia evenly over the apples.

Position a rack in the center of the oven and preheat to 400F (205C). Roll out the dough on a lightly floured surface to about a 1/4-inch thickness. Loosely roll the dough around the rolling pin, then unroll it onto the apples. Trim off any excess dough and tuck the dough around the edges into the pan to completely cover the apples. Pierce the dough in several places. Bake the tart 45 minutes, until the crust is browned. Remove the tart from the oven and run a knife around the edges to loosen the crust. Cool tart on a rack about 10 minutes.

Place a serving plate over the top of the tart and carefully invert the tart onto the serving plate. Gently remove the pan. Serve the tart warm or at room temperature.

Pumpkin-Walnut Cheesecake

This recipe first appeared on the electronic Gourmet Guide (the eGG) in my column, "The Pastry Chef." This unusual cheesecake is perfect for the fall and winter season. Try it in place of pumpkin pie!

Makes 1 (9½-inch) cake, 14 servings

◆   ◆   ◆

Crust

1 tablespoon unsalted butter, softened, for pan

8½ ounces (about 22) small butter cookies

½ cup walnuts, finely chopped

2 tablespoons sugar

1 teaspoon ground cassia cinnamon

3½ tablespoons unsalted butter, melted

Filling

3 (8-oz.) packages cream cheese, softened

½ cup firmly packed golden brown sugar

2 tablespoons all-purpose flour

4 large eggs at room temperature

1 large egg yolk at room temperature

1¼ cups pumpkin puree

½ cup heavy whipping cream

2 teaspoons pure vanilla extract

1½ teaspoons ground cassia cinnamon

¾ teaspoon ground cloves

¾ teaspoon ground ginger

¾ teaspoon freshly grated nutmeg

¾ cup walnuts, coarsely chopped

Decoration

¼ cup heavy whipping cream

14 walnut halves

Crust

Position a rack in the center of the oven and another rack in the bottom of the oven. Preheat oven to 350F (175C).

Use the tablespoon of butter to heavily butter the inside of a 9½-inch-round spring-form pan. In the work bowl of a food processor fitted with a steel blade, combine the cookies, walnuts, sugar, and cassia. Pulse the mixture until it is finely ground, about 2 minutes. With the machine on, pour the melted butter through the feed tube. Continue to process until the mixture holds together, about 30 seconds. Transfer the crust to the springform pan and press it evenly into the bottom and up the sides. Chill the crust while preparing the filling.

Filling

In the bowl of a stand mixer or in a medium bowl, using the flat-beater attachment or a hand-held mixer, beat the cream cheese until fluffy, about 2 minutes. Add the brown sugar and flour and blend well. Scrape down the bottom and sides of the bowl with a rubber spatula as necessary. One at a time, add the eggs and egg yolk, beating well after each addition. Add the pumpkin, whipping cream, and vanilla and blend thoroughly. Combine the spices and add, blending well, then stir in the walnuts.

To assemble

Place a shallow cake or pie pan with hot water on the lower rack of the oven. Place the springform pan on a baking sheet and pour the filling into the crust. Bake the cake 20 minutes. Reduce oven temperature to 250F (120C) and continue to bake the cake 1 hour and 30 minutes, until the top is no longer wet and the center moves slightly when the cake is shaken. Turn off the oven and hold the door ajar with a wooden spoon. Leave the cake in the oven for 1 hour. Remove the cake from the oven and place on a rack to cool to room temperature.

Tent the cake loosely with foil and chill in the refrigerator at least 4 hours or overnight before serving. The cake will keep, well covered, up to 5 days in the refrigerator or up to 3 months in the freezer. To unmold the cake, dip a thin-bladed knife in hot water and dry, then run it around the inner edge of the pan and gently remove the outside rim.

To decorate

Pour cream into the bowl of a stand mixer or into a medium bowl. Using the wire-whip attachment or a hand-held mixer, whip the cream on medium speed to soft peaks. Fit a pastry bag with a large open-star tip (number 3) and fill with the cream. Mark the top outside edge of the cake into serving pieces. Pipe a rosette of cream in the center and at the outside edge of each piece, then top each rosette with a walnut half.

Hazelnut Wafers

Although these elegant cookies are made in three stages, they are easy to assemble because each part can be prepared separately. These were inspired by cookies I ate in Vienna, Austria, and Switzerland.

Makes 48 sandwiched wafers.

◆　◆　◆

2 cups shelled raw hazelnuts, toasted
　(see Note opposite)
¼ cup sugar
2 sticks plus 2 tablespoons unsalted
　butter, at room temperature
⅔ cup sugar
1 cup finely ground hazelnuts (from
　above)
1¼ teaspoons ground cassia cinnamon
4 large egg yolks at room temperature

½ teaspoon pure vanilla extract
3 cups all-purpose flour

Assembly

½ cup apricot preserves
8 ounces bittersweet or semisweet
　chocolate, finely chopped
½ cup finely ground hazelnuts (from
　above)

Position racks in the upper and lower thirds of the oven. Preheat oven to 375F (190C). Line 4 baking sheets with parchment paper.

To grind hazelnuts, place the cooled nuts and sugar in the work bowl of a food processor fitted with a metal blade. Pulse the mixture until it is finely ground, about 30 seconds. Use 1 cup of the ground hazelnuts in the cookie dough and ½ cup for assembly.

Wafers

In the bowl of a stand mixer or in a medium bowl, using the flat-beater attachment or a hand-held mixer, beat the butter until it is soft, about 1 minute. Add the sugar and blend together until fluffy, about 2 minutes. Add 1 cup of the ground hazelnuts and blend well, then blend in the cassia. One at a time, add the egg yolks, blending thoroughly after each addition, then blend in the vanilla. Add the flour in 3 stages, blending thoroughly after each addition. Stop occasionally and scrape down the sides and bottom of the bowl with a rubber spatula.

Divide the dough into 2 equal pieces. Cover and refrigerate 1 piece of the dough while working with the other piece. Roll out the dough between 2 sheets of waxed paper to about ⅛-inch thickness. Peel off the top sheet of waxed paper and lay it loosely back on the dough, then turn the dough over and peel off and replace the second piece of waxed paper, repeating this procedure once more while rolling out the dough to ⅛-inch thickness. Use a 2½-inch-round plain-edge cookie cutter to cut out the dough. Then use a sharp thin-bladed knife to cut each circle in half. Transfer the wafers to the baking sheets. Gather up the scraps of dough and re-roll between the sheets of waxed paper, then cut out the same as previous batch.

Bake the wafers 6 minutes. Switch the baking sheets and bake another 6 to 8 minutes, until lightly browned. Remove from the oven and cool on a rack.

To assemble

Place a teaspoon of preserves on the flat side of half of the wafers and top each with another wafer, forming sandwiches.

To prepare the chocolate, melt two-thirds of it in the top of a double boiler over hot, not simmering water, stirring frequently with a rubber spatula until smooth. Remove the double boiler from the heat, then remove the top pan of the double boiler and wipe it completely dry. Stir in the remaining chocolate in three batches, making sure that each batch is completely melted before adding the next. When all the chocolate has been added, the chocolate will be at the correct temperature. To test for this, place a dab of chocolate under your lower lip. It should feel comfortable, not hot and not cool.

Place the pan of chocolate over a shallow pan of water slightly warmer than the chocolate. Line 2 baking sheets with waxed paper. Place the ground hazelnuts in a small bowl. Dip the ends of each sandwiched wafer in the chocolate. Gently shake off the excess chocolate and dip the chocolate ends into the ground hazelnuts. Place the wafers on the baking sheets. Place the baking sheets in the refrigerator 20 minutes to set the chocolate.

The wafers will keep for 3 to 4 days in a well-sealed container at room temperature.

Note

To toast hazelnuts, position a rack in the center of the oven. Preheat oven to 350F (175C). Spread the hazelnuts in a single layer on a jelly-roll pan and toast 15 to 18 minutes, until the skins are split and the nuts are a light golden color. Cool nuts in the pan on a rack 10 minutes. Rub the nuts in your hands or a towel to remove as much of the skins as possible.

Apple and Dried Cherry Pie

I created this recipe for my column, "The Pastry Chef," which I wrote for the electronic Gourmet Guide (eGG) on America Online®. The pie has a wonderful balance of sweet and tart, with a good measure of spice. Here I use a classic pie crust made with a combination of vegetable shortening and butter.

Makes 1 (10-inch) pie, 8 to 10 servings.

◆   ◆   ◆

Pastry

2¼ cups all-purpose flour

½ teaspoon salt

1 stick (8 tablespoons) unsalted butter, chilled, cut into small pieces

4 tablespoons solid vegetable shortening, chilled

5 to 7 tablespoons cold water

Filling

½ cup dried Montmorency cherries

Zest and juice of 1 large orange

2½ pounds (5 to 7) tart green apples, such as Granny Smith

½ cup firmly packed golden brown sugar

2 tablespoons all-purpose flour

1¼ teaspoons ground cassia cinnamon

½ teaspoon freshly grated nutmeg

½ teaspoon ground allspice

⅛ teaspoon ground cloves

Glaze

1 egg at room temperature

1 tablespoon water

Pastry

Combine the flour and salt in the work bowl of a food processor fitted with a steel blade. Pulse briefly to blend. Add butter and shortening and pulse until it is cut into tiny pieces, about 1 minute. With the machine on, add the water through the feed tube, 1 tablespoon at a time, adding a total of 5 tablespoons. If necessary add 1 or 2 more tablespoons water. Process until the dough wraps itself around the blade, about 30 seconds. Wrap dough in plastic wrap and refrigerate 30 minutes. The dough can be kept in the refrigerator up to 3 days or it can be frozen up to 2 months. If frozen, defrost in the refrigerator at least 24 hours before using.

Filling

Place the dried cherries in a small bowl. Zest the orange and finely mince the zest. Cover with plastic wrap and set aside. Squeeze the juice from the orange and pour over the dried cherries. Cover the bowl tightly with plastic wrap and let stand 30 minutes.

Peel, quarter, and core the apples, then cut into ½-inch-thick slices and place in a medium bowl. Add the brown sugar, dried cherries and orange juice, orange zest, flour, and spices and toss to blend together well.

To assemble

Position a rack in the center of the oven. Preheat oven to 375F (190C). Roll out half of the dough on a lightly floured work surface to a large circle, about 12 inches in diameter. Carefully roll the dough around the rolling pin, then gently unroll the dough into a 10-inch-round pie pan. Gently lift up the edges of the pie dough and fit it into the bottom and against the sides of the pan. Transfer the filling to the pie shell.

Roll out the remaining half of the pie dough on a lightly floured work surface to a large circle, about 13 inches in diameter. Use a pastry brush to dampen the edges of the lower crust. Transfer the top crust to the pie and trim off any large edges. Pinch the edges of both crusts together and shape them into a fluted edge. Use a sharp knife to make several slits in the top crust.

Lightly beat the egg with the water, then brush the top of the pie with the glaze. Place the pie on a jelly-roll pan and bake 45 to 60 minutes, until the crust is golden and the filling is bubbling. Cool on a rack. The pie will keep for 3 days at room temperature wrapped in foil.

Spicy Shortcake

This shortcake is a perfect foil for a mixture of fresh summer berries. If berries are not in season, use frozen berries packaged without syrup.

Makes 1 (8-inch-square) or (9-inch-round) shortcake, 8 or 9 servings.

◆   ◆   ◆

Shortcake

1 tablespoon unsalted butter, softened,
    for pan
1¾ cups all-purpose flour
1 tablespoon baking powder
¼ teaspoon salt
1 teaspoon ground cassia cinnamon
½ teaspoon freshly grated nutmeg
⅛ teaspoon ground allspice
¼ cup plus 1 teaspoon sugar
1 cup heavy whipping cream

Topping

3 cups mixed fresh berries
Zest of 1 lemon, finely minced
2 tablespoons sugar
2 tablespoons Grand Marnier or other
    orange liqueur
1 cup heavy whipping cream
2 tablespoons sugar

Shortcake

Position a rack in the center of the oven. Preheat oven to 400F (205C). Generously coat the inside of an 8-inch-square baking pan or a 9-inch-round pie pan with the butter.

In a 2-quart bowl, sift together the flour, baking powder, salt, and spices. Stir in sugar. Gradually pour the cream into the dry ingredients while tossing the mixture lightly with a rubber spatula. Mix the dough just until it comes together; it should be slightly lumpy. If it is mixed too much, it becomes tough.

Turn the dough into the pan and pat gently with floured fingertips until it is evenly distributed. Bake about 25 minutes, until golden brown and the edges are crisp. Cool slightly on a rack, then cut into squares if using the square pan or wedges if using the pie pan.

Topping

Combine the berries, lemon zest, sugar, and Grand Marnier in a medium bowl. Toss to blend well. Place half the mixture in the work bowl of a food processor fitted with a steel blade and pulse until it is liquid, 30 to 60 seconds.

Place the whipping cream in the bowl of a stand mixer or in a medium bowl. Using the wire-whip attachment or a hand-held mixer, whip the cream until it is frothy. Add the sugar and continue to whip the cream until it holds soft peaks.

To serve

Spoon a tablespoon of berry sauce on each serving plate. Place a piece of shortcake on the sauce and top with a scoop of the berry mixture. Top the berry mixture with a dollop of whipped cream and serve immediately.

The shortcake can be made up to 2 days in advance and held at room temperature tightly covered with plastic wrap. The berry topping and sauce can also be made 2 or 3 days in advance and kept in tightly covered containers in the refrigerator. Whip cream just before serving.

Chocolate Nut Purses

These unusual pastries are deceptively easy to prepare. Use top-quality chocolate and store-bought puff pastry and you will have a winner every time! By mixing and matching the types of chocolate and nuts, you can let your imagination go and create an almost unlimited variety of this dessert.

Makes 8 purses.

◆   ◆   ◆

6 ounces top-quality chocolate
    (bittersweet, semisweet, milk, or
    white)
1/3 cup walnuts, hazelnuts, or almonds,
    toasted (see Note, page 71)

1 teaspoon ground cassia cinnamon
2 sheets frozen puff pastry, thawed
Powdered sugar for decorating

Position racks in the upper and lower thirds of the oven. Preheat oven to 425F (220C). Line 2 baking sheets with parchment paper.

Use a large chef's knife and a cutting board to finely chop the chocolate. Transfer the chocolate to a medium bowl. Chop the nuts finely and mix with the chocolate. Add the cassia and toss to blend well.

Roll out each sheet of puff pastry on a lightly floured work surface to a 12-inch square. Cut the square in half lengthwise and again in half horizontally, creating 4 smaller squares. Place about 2 tablespoons of chocolate filling in the center of each square. Bring the points of the square together in the center above the filling. Squeeze the pastry together just above the filling, then spread out the top edges. Place the purses on the lined baking sheets with a few inches of space between them.

Bake purses 15 minutes, until golden brown. Cool on baking sheets on a rack. Dust the purses with powdered sugar before serving. The purses are best served while slightly warm.

These pastries can be prepared up to 2 days in advance and kept at room temperature tightly covered with foil. Warm them in a 325F (165C) oven 10 minutes before serving.

Cinnamon

Nose, nose, nose, nose
And who gave thee this jolly red nose?
Nutmegs and ginger, cinnamon and cloves
And they gave me this jolly red nose.

—Thomas Ravenscroft, "Deuteromelia"

Cinnamon, often called true cinnamon, is possibly the world's oldest spice. In ancient times, cinnamon was used during religious ceremonies, when it was burned like incense and the Egyptians used it to embalm their dead. Cinnamon is mentioned in Sanskrit texts and there are several references to it in Biblical writings. There have been times in history when cinnamon was more highly valued than gold. Cinnamon first reached Europe by way of the old overland spice caravans.

The Portuguese controlled the first monopoly on cinnamon until The Dutch East India Company drove them out of Sri Lanka. The Dutch began cultivation of cinnamon, which until then had been gathered in the wild. They held a strong monopoly on the cinnamon trade that was not broken until the late eighteenth century, when the English East India Company gained control.

In Europe, true cinnamon is the only recognized cinnamon. It is used to flavor both sweet and savory dishes, and mulled wine. It is also widely used in Middle Eastern cuisines, and in Mexico cinnamon is traditionally mixed with chocolate. In the United States, cinnamon is a popular flavoring in desserts and baked goods.

Lore and Myths
◆　◆　◆

Cinnamon was thought to clear the eyes, sweeten breath, and when mixed with honey it has been used as a cosmetic. Cinnamon was also thought to be a digestive aid and an extracted form was used to aid stings and venomous snakebites.

Characteristics
◆　◆　◆

Cinnamon, like its close relative cassia, is a member of the laurel family. Its botanical name is *Cinnamomum zelyanicum*. Cinnamon is the dried bark of the tropical evergreen laurel tree. The tree has shiny, large oblong leaves and lacy, small, off-white flower clusters with dark blue berrylike fruit. In the wild the trees range in height from 9 to 15 feet. When cultivated, they are kept to a maximum height of 8 feet.

The bark is tan colored and fairly smooth. When ground, cinnamon's tan color makes it easy to distinguish from the dark reddish-brown color of cassia.

Where and How It's Grown
◆　◆　◆

True cinnamon is native to the tropical climate of Sri Lanka, which is reputed to produce the highest quality. Cinnamon is also cultivated in Indonesia, India, the Seychelle Islands, and Brazil.

Cinnamon is a very labor-intensive spice. All the work is done by hand. The bark is stripped from thin branches of the trees during the twice-yearly rainy season, because the humidity makes this operation easier to accomplish. Each successive stripping yields better-quality bark with the very best quality coming from the young, thin inner shoots. The bark is removed in two strips from each side of a shoot. These pieces are placed together, back side to front side, and left to ferment for about 24 hours. A curved knife is used to remove the outer bark and then the bark pieces are placed inside of each other to air-dry in the shade. During this process the bark curls inward, forming quills, known as cinnamon sticks. The quills are rolled daily to be sure they are curling correctly, which produces a smooth outer texture. The longest and best-quality pieces of bark are used for the quills. Smaller broken bark pieces are called quillings.

The bark is finely ground to produce ground cinnamon. Cinnamon oil is extracted from the bark through a distillation process.

How It Tastes and Smells

◆ ◆ ◆

True cinnamon has a woody, warm, aromatic aroma with a citrus overtone. Its flavor is not as pungent as cassia but more delicate and complex.

Use and Preparation

◆ ◆ ◆

In desserts, cinnamon is used primarily ground. However, cinnamon quills are often used to flavor hot drinks and for slow cooking.

No special preparation is needed if cinnamon is bought in the form in which it will be used. However, if you need ground cinnamon and you only have cinnamon sticks available, they can be finely ground using a spice or coffee grinder. Break the sticks into small pieces before placing them in the grinder. Cinnamon sticks can also be grated with a nutmeg grater, which will produce coarser results than a grinder.

Tips for Choosing and Storing

◆ ◆ ◆

Buy ground cinnamon and cinnamon sticks from a source with a high turnover to be sure of freshness. Ground cinnamon is best stored in a tightly sealed glass jar in a cool, dark, dry place for up to 1 year. Store cinnamon sticks under the same conditions for up to 2 years.

Chocolate-Hazelnut Crostata

The combination of chocolate and hazelnut is often found in Northern Italy. *Crostata* is the Italian word for a tart. My husband and I love Italy and Italian food, so it's no surprise that this is our very favorite recipe in the book. When I made this we both had a difficult time holding ourselves back from eating a second and even a third piece. The yield is large, which is a good thing, making it a great dessert for a party.

Makes 1 (11-inch) tart, 14 to 16 servings.

◆　◆　◆

Pastry

1¾ cups all-purpose flour
½ teaspoon baking powder
Pinch of salt
⅓ cup plus 1 teaspoon sugar
½ teaspoon ground cinnamon
Zest of ½ orange, finely minced
1 stick plus 2 tablespoons (10 tablespoons) unsalted butter, chilled, cut into small pieces
1 large egg at room temperature, lightly beaten
1 teaspoon fresh orange juice
½ teaspoon pure vanilla extract

To serve

1 cup heavy whipping cream
1 teaspoon orange liqueur
1 teaspoon pure vanilla extract
¼ teaspoon ground cinnamon

Filling

1¾ cups raw hazelnuts, toasted (see Note, page 71)
¾ cup plus 2 tablespoons sugar
6 tablespoons (¾ stick) unsalted butter, softened
2 large eggs at room temperature, lightly beaten
Zest of ½ orange, finely minced
1 tablespoon all-purpose flour
¾ teaspoon ground cinnamon
3 ounces bittersweet chocolate, finely chopped
1 tablespoon orange liqueur
1 teaspoon pure vanilla extract

Pastry

Place the flour, baking powder, salt, sugar, cinnamon, and orange zest in the bowl of a food processor fitted with a steel blade. Add butter and pulse the mixture until the butter is cut into tiny pieces and the dough is crumbly, about 1 minute. Combine the egg with the orange juice and vanilla. With the machine on, add egg mixture through the feed tube. Process until the pastry wraps itself around the blade, about 1 minute.

Roll out the pastry dough on a lightly floured work surface to a 14-inch circle, about ⅛ inch thick. Gently drape the pastry around the rolling pin and unroll into an 11-inch fluted tart pan with a removable bottom. Carefully lift up the sides of the pastry and fit it into the bottom and against the sides of the tart pan. Trim off the excess pastry at the top of the pan leaving a ½-inch border. Turn this to the inside, doubling the outside edge of the pastry. Pierce the bottom of the pastry and chill the shell for at least 30 minutes.

Filling

Position a rack in the center of the oven. Preheat oven to 400F (205C). Place the hazelnuts in the work bowl of a food processor fitted with the steel blade. Add the 2 tablespoons sugar and pulse until the nuts are very finely ground, about 1 minute; set aside.

In the bowl of a stand mixer or in a medium bowl, using the flat-beater attachment or a hand-held mixer, beat the butter until light and fluffy, about 2 minutes. Add the ¾ cup sugar and beat until thoroughly blended. Add eggs and orange zest and blend well. Stop occasionally and scrape down the sides of the bowl with a rubber spatula. Add the flour, cinnamon, hazelnuts, and chocolate and blend thoroughly. Add orange liqueur and vanilla and blend the mixture thoroughly.

To assemble

Place the tart pan on a jelly-roll pan and pour the filling into the pastry shell. Bake 25 to 30 minutes, until filling is puffed, golden, and set. Cool on a rack.

To serve

In the bowl of a stand mixer or in a medium bowl, using the wire-whip attachment or a hand-held mixer, whip the cream until frothy. Add the orange liqueur, vanilla, and cinnamon and continue to whip the cream until it holds soft peaks. Serve slices of the tart with a dollop of whipped cream.

The tart will keep at room temperature, tightly covered with foil, up to 3 days.

Cinnamon-Hazelnut Pound Cake

This recipe combines classic pound cake ingredients with the pungent flavor of cinnamon and coarsely chopped, toasted hazelnuts. The cake has a moist, dense texture and a rich, full-bodied flavor. It is made in a loaf pan and needs no special decoration. This cake keeps very well and travels easily, making it perfect to take along on a picnic.

Makes 1 (10-inch) loaf cake, 12 to 14 servings.

◆ ◆ ◆

1 tablespoon unsalted butter, softened, for the pan

¾ cup raw hazelnuts, toasted (see Note, page 71)

2 sticks (16 tablespoons) unsalted butter, softened

1⅓ cups sugar

4 large eggs at room temperature, separated

¼ teaspoon cream of tartar

2 cups all-purpose flour

2 teaspoons ground cinnamon

½ teaspoon salt

Position a rack in the center of the oven. Preheat oven to 350F (175C). Use the 1 tablespoon butter to generously butter the inside of a 10 × 5-inch loaf pan. (See page 239 for pan equivalents.)

Coarsely chop the hazelnuts in the work bowl of a food processor fitted with a steel blade or with a chef's knife on a cutting board; set aside.

In the bowl of a stand mixer or in a medium bowl, using the flat-beater attachment or a hand-held mixer, beat the butter until light and fluffy, about 2 minutes. Add ⅓ cup of the sugar and beat until thoroughly blended. Add the egg yolks, one at a time, beating well after each addition. Stop occasionally and scrape down the sides of the bowl with a rubber spatula.

In a separate greasefree bowl, whip the egg whites with the cream of tartar until they hold soft peaks. Add the remaining 1 cup sugar, a little at a time, continuing to beat until glossy and stiff but not dry.

Fold one-quarter of the beaten egg whites into the butter mixture. Fold in remaining egg whites in 2 or 3 stages. Toss the flour with the cinnamon and salt, then sprinkle the flour mixture and hazelnuts over the butter mixture in 3 stages, folding together until well blended.

Pour the batter into the pan. Use a rubber spatula to smooth and even the top. Bake 55 to 60 minutes, until a wooden pick inserted in the center of the cake comes out clean.

Cool cake in pan on a rack 15 minutes. Turn cake out of the pan and cool on the rack. Cut the cake crosswise into 1-inch slices.

Store the cake up to 5 days at room temperature, well wrapped in foil, or it can be frozen up to 4 months. If frozen, defrost in the refrigerator 24 hours before serving.

Almond Cinnamon Stars

These cookies always disappear quickly, so you might want to consider making a double batch. Slip a few into the lunch box of someone you love and he or she will be yours forever.

Makes 48 (2¹/₂-inch) stars.

◆　◆　◆

1 stick plus 2½ tablespoons (10½ tablespoons) unsalted butter, softened
½ cup granulated sugar
1 cup finely ground almonds (see Note, page 31)
½ teaspoon ground cinnamon

½ teaspoon pure vanilla extract
1 large egg at room temperature, lightly beaten
2 cups all-purpose flour
Pinch of salt
Powdered sugar

In the bowl of a stand mixer or in a medium bowl, using the flat-beater attachment or a hand-held mixer, beat the butter until light and fluffy, about 2 minutes. Add the sugar and beat until thoroughly blended, about 2 more minutes. Scrape down the sides of the bowl with a long-handled rubber spatula. Add the finely ground almonds in 2 stages, blending well after each addition. Beat in the cinnamon and vanilla, add the egg, and blend well.

Combine the flour and salt and add to the almond mixture in 3 stages, stopping to scrape down the sides of the bowl often. Beat the dough until smooth, about 2 minutes. Gather the dough together, wrap in plastic wrap, and chill in the refrigerator at least 3 hours, or until firm before using. (The dough can be kept in the refrigerator up to 3 days or it can be frozen. If frozen, defrost overnight in refrigerator before using.)

Position the racks in the upper and lower thirds of the oven. Preheat oven to 350F (175C). Line 3 baking sheets with parchment paper.

Roll out the dough on a lightly floured work surface to a ¼-inch thickness. Using a 2½-inch star-shaped cookie cutter, cut out stars from the dough.

Place the stars on the lined baking sheets, leaving 1 inch of space between them. Bake 2 sheets of cookies at a time 6 minutes, then switch the baking sheets. Bake another

6 to 8 minutes, until the cookies are light golden and set. Cool cookies on baking sheets on racks. Repeat with the remaining cookies.

Lightly dust the tops of the cookies with powdered sugar. The cookies will keep 5 days at room temperature, stored between layers of waxed paper in an airtight container.

Streusel Apple Pie

I hadn't made this pie for many years, but I remembered that it was delicious. When my husband took a bite, his eyes lit up and his whole face turned into a smile. I think he ate almost the entire pie himself. The crunchy streusel topping makes a perfect foil for the soft, juicy apples. If you're looking for a great apple pie recipe, this is it. I prefer to use Granny Smith apples, but Pippins work well, too.

Makes 1 (9½-inch) pie, 8 servings.

◆　◆　◆

Pastry

1½ cups all-purpose flour
Pinch of granulated sugar
¼ teaspoon salt
1 stick plus ½ tablespoon (8½ tablespoons) unsalted butter, chilled, cut into small pieces
5 tablespoons cold water

Filling

2 pounds tart apples (5 to 6), such as Granny Smith, peeled, cored, and cut into ½-inch-thick slices
½ cup sour cream
2 tablespoons all-purpose flour

¾ teaspoon ground cinnamon
½ teaspoon freshly grated nutmeg
¼ cup granulated sugar

Topping

½ cup all-purpose flour
½ cup firmly packed golden brown sugar
¼ teaspoon ground cinnamon
5 tablespoons unsalted butter, softened, cut into pieces

To serve

¾ cup heavy whipping cream or 1 pint vanilla ice cream

Pastry

Combine the flour, sugar, and salt in the work bowl of a food processor fitted with a steel blade. Pulse briefly to blend. Add butter and pulse until butter is cut into very tiny pieces. With the machine on, pour the water through the feed tube and process just until the dough forms a ball, about 30 seconds. Wrap the dough in plastic wrap and chill 2 hours or until firm before using.

Preheat the oven to 400F (205C). Roll out the dough on a lightly floured work surface to a ¼-inch thickness. Very gently roll the pastry dough up around the rolling pin, then lift the rolling pin over a 9½-inch pie plate and gently unroll the dough. Carefully lift up the sides of the pastry dough and fit it into the bottom and sides of the pan. Trim off any excess dough with a sharp knife, then flute the top edges. Chill the pastry shell while preparing the filling and topping.

Filling

Toss the sliced apples with the sour cream in a medium bowl. Combine the flour, cinnamon, nutmeg, and sugar in a small bowl, then stir mixture into the apples. Transfer the apples to the chilled pastry shell.

Topping

Combine the flour, brown sugar, and cinnamon in a small bowl. Add the butter and mix thoroughly. Crumble the topping evenly over the apples.

Place the pie on a baking sheet and bake 50 minutes, until the apples are tender, the juices are bubbling, and the pastry is light golden brown. Transfer to a rack to cool slightly.

To serve

If using, place the whipping cream in the bowl of a stand mixer or in a medium bowl. Using the wire-whip attachment or a hand-held mixer, whip the cream on medium speed until it holds soft peaks, 2 to 3 minutes.

Serve slices of the pie with a dollop of whipped cream or a scoop of ice cream. The pie will keep 3 days at room temperature, tightly wrapped in foil.

Linzertorte

Cinnamon mixed with a small amount of cloves is what gives this classic Austrian tartlike pastry its distinctive spicy flavor. Variations are easy to make by using different jams for the filling or substituting hazelnuts for almonds in the pastry dough.

Makes 1 (9½-inch) torte, 12 servings.

♦ ♦ ♦

1 cup all-purpose flour
1½ cups finely ground almonds (see Note, page 31)
1½ teaspoons ground cinnamon
¼ teaspoon ground cloves
½ cup sugar

2 sticks (16 tablespoons) unsalted butter, cut into small pieces, softened
2 large egg yolks at room temperature
1¼ cups red raspberry preserves
Powdered sugar

Combine flour, almonds, cinnamon, cloves, and sugar in the bowl of a stand mixer, a medium bowl, or a food processor. Add the butter and egg yolks. Using the flat-beater attachment or a hand-held mixer, blend all the ingredients until the dough forms a ball and is smooth, 2 to 4 minutes. If using the food processor, use the steel blade and pulse the mixture until it is smooth and forms a ball, about 1 minute. Cover the dough with plastic wrap and chill for at least 4 hours or overnight. (At this point the dough may be frozen for several months. If it is frozen, be sure to defrost it in the refrigerator at least 24 hours before using.)

Before rolling the dough, knead it slightly to soften. It can be difficult to work with and may crack. Cut off one-fourth of the dough and keep it chilled while working with the remaining dough. Roll out the dough between sheets of lightly floured waxed paper to a ¼-inch thickness. Remove the top sheet of waxed paper. Grasp the outer edges of the bottom piece of waxed paper and turn the dough upside down over the top of a 9½-inch-round tart pan. Carefully place the dough into the pan and peel off the waxed paper. Use your hands to help fit the dough into the pan, making sure it fits snugly against the bottom and sides. If necessary, patch any cracks. Trim off the excess pastry dough at the top edge of the tart pan. Spread the bottom of the pastry shell evenly with the raspberry preserves.

Between sheets of lightly floured waxed paper roll out the remaining pastry dough to the same thickness as the first dough. Using a fluted-edge cutter, cut this dough into ½-inch-wide strips. Using an offset spatula, transfer the strips to the tart pan. Form a lattice on the top of the torte by arranging the strips in a woven pattern. With any remaining pastry dough roll a long rope about ¼ inch in diameter. Place this around the outer top edge of the tart where the ends of the strips and edges of the shell meet. Use a fork to press this rope into the edge of the tart to give it a finished look.

Chill the pastry in the refrigerator 15 minutes. Position a rack in the center of the oven. Preheat oven to 375F (190C). Place the torte on a baking sheet and bake 30 minutes, until crust is golden brown and the preserves are bubbling. Cool on a rack 15 minutes.

Serve the Linzertorte at room temperature. Store it, tightly wrapped in foil, at room temperature for up to 4 days.

Sour Cream Coffee Cake

Serve this traditional yummy cake for breakfast, afternoon coffee, or after-dinner dessert. It's a classic that gets better a day or two after it's baked. I developed this from two recipes I had in my files: one came from my mother and the other from an aunt. My husband tasted the cake several times over three days (all in the name of research, of course) and kept talking about how much he liked it.

Makes 1 (9½-inch) cake, 12 to 14 servings.

◆ ◆ ◆

Cake

1 tablespoon unsalted butter, softened, for pan

1½ sticks (12 tablespoons) unsalted butter, softened

1½ cups granulated sugar

3 large eggs at room temperature

1 cup sour cream

2 teaspoons pure vanilla extract

3 cups all-purpose flour

1 tablespoon baking powder

½ (scant) teaspoon salt

Topping

¼ cup granulated sugar

¼ cup firmly packed golden brown sugar

2 teaspoons ground cinnamon

½ cup walnuts, finely chopped

Position a rack in the center of the oven. Preheat oven to 350F (175C). Use the 1 tablespoon butter to butter the inside of a 9½-inch-round springform pan.

Place the butter in the bowl of a stand mixer or in a medium bowl. Using the flat-beater attachment or a hand-held mixer, beat the butter until it is light and fluffy, about 2 minutes. Add the sugar and beat until thoroughly combined. Add the eggs, one at a time, blending well after each addition. Blend in the sour cream and vanilla.

Combine the flour, baking powder, and salt in a small bowl. Add to the butter mixture in 3 stages, stopping to scrape down the bottom and sides of the bowl with a rubber spatula after each addition.

Topping

Combine the granulated sugar, brown sugar, cinnamon, and walnuts in a medium bowl. Toss to combine.

To assemble

Pour half of the cake batter into the prepared pan. Evenly sprinkle half of the topping over the batter. Pour the remaining half of the batter over the topping. Use the rubber spatula to smooth and even the top. Evenly sprinkle the remaining half of the topping over the top of the batter.

Bake the cake 35 to 40 minutes, until a cake tester inserted near the center comes out with moist crumbs barely clinging to it. Cool completely in the pan on a rack.

The cake will keep 5 days at room temperature, tightly wrapped in foil. It can be frozen up to 3 months.

Ischl Tartlets

These traditional Austrian treats aren't tartlets at all; they're double-decker cookies. Ischl tartlets can be made in many shapes, depending on the cutter you use. My favorite is heart-shaped. Apricot and raspberry preserves are the classic fillings, but you can try using different preserves for variety.

Makes 42 tartlets.

◆　◆　◆

1¾ cups all-purpose flour, sifted
1 cup (scant) granulated sugar
1½ cups finely ground almonds (see
　　Note, page 31)
1 teaspoon ground cinnamon

2½ sticks (20 tablespoons) unsalted
　　butter, cut into small pieces, softened
1 cup apricot or raspberry preserves
Powdered sugar for garnish

Place the flour, granulated sugar, ground almonds, and cinnamon in the work bowl of a food processor fitted with a steel blade. Pulse the mixture 10 seconds. Add the butter and pulse the mixture to cut the butter into tiny pieces, then process until the dough forms a ball, another 30 seconds. Shape the dough into a flattened disc, cover tightly with plastic wrap, and chill 1 hour.

Position the racks in the upper and lower thirds of the oven. Preheat oven to 350F (175C). Line 4 baking sheets with parchment paper.

Roll out the dough on a lightly floured work surface into a large rectangle about ⅛ inch thick. Using a 2-inch-diameter heart-shaped cutter, cut out shapes. In half of the hearts, cut out the center with a 1-inch-round cutter. Place the shapes on the lined baking sheets with at least 2 inches of space between them. Bake 8 minutes. Switch the baking sheets and bake another 7 minutes, until hearts are lightly colored and set. Cool on baking sheets on racks.

When the hearts are cool, place a teaspoonful of preserves on the solid hearts. Heavily dust the hearts with the hole in the center with powdered sugar and place these on top of the preserves.

The filled hearts will keep 1 day at room temperature, covered with foil. The hearts can be baked up to 3 days in advance of assembly. Store them at room temperature, tightly covered with foil.

Fresh Plum Custard Tart

This tart received rave reviews from my tasting panel (actually my neighbors, whom I invited for dessert). It's a classic tart typically available in pastry shops in Austria, Switzerland, or Germany. Be sure to use fresh, fragrant plums for the best flavor.

Makes 1 (9½-inch) tart, 14 servings.

◆　◆　◆

2½ cups all-purpose flour

⅓ cup plus 2 tablespoons sugar

2 sticks (16 tablespoons) unsalted
　　butter, chilled, cut into small pieces

1 large egg yolk at room temperature

1 teaspoon pure vanilla extract

½ cup raw hazelnuts, toasted (see Note,
　　page 71)

½ recipe Vanilla Custard (page 209)

6 to 7 large, or 12 to 14 small, ripe
　　plums

2 teaspoons ground cinnamon

Place the flour and ⅓ cup sugar in the work bowl of a food processor fitted with a steel blade. Add butter and pulse the mixture until the butter is cut into tiny pieces and the dough is crumbly, about 1 minute. Lightly beat the egg with the vanilla. With the machine on, add egg yolk mixture through the feed tube. Process until the pastry wraps itself around the blade, about 1 minute. Cover the pastry with plastic wrap and chill at least 2 hours, until firm enough to roll.

Position a rack in the center of the oven. Preheat oven to 350F (175C). Roll out the pastry on a lightly floured work surface to an 11-inch circle, about ⅛ inch thick. Gently drape the pastry around the rolling pin and unroll into a 9½-inch-round springform pan. Carefully lift up the sides of the pastry and fit it into the bottom and against the sides of the pan. Trim the pastry evenly to 1 inch below the top of the pan.

Place the springform pan on a jelly-roll pan. Stir the custard to remove any lumps, then spread it evenly in the bottom of the pastry shell. Sprinkle the ground hazelnuts evenly over the custard. Cut the plums in half and remove the pits. Cut each plum half into 4 or 5 equal slices, leaving them intact at the bottom. Fan the plums out in tight concentric circles over the filling.

Combine the remaining tablespoon of sugar and the cinnamon in a small bowl. Sprinkle cinnamon-sugar evenly over the plums. Bake the tart 40 to 45 minutes, until the crust is golden and the plums are soft. Cool in pan on a rack at least 20 minutes before removing the sides of the pan.

The tart is best eaten within 5 hours of preparation, but will last up to 3 days in the refrigerator, tightly covered with plastic wrap.

Spicy Pumpkin Roulade

A classic spice blend of cinnamon, ginger, and nutmeg enhances the earthy taste of pumpkin in this cake. Walnuts and candied orange peel add to the rich mosaic of flavors. Since canned pumpkin is readily available, this cake can be made year-round.

Makes 1 (15-inch) rolled cake, 12 to 14 servings.

◆ ◆ ◆

Cake

1 tablespoon unsalted butter, for
   parchment paper

4 large eggs at room temperature

1⅓ cups granulated sugar

¾ cup canned pumpkin

1¼ teaspoons fresh lemon juice

1 cup all-purpose flour

1½ teaspoons baking powder

½ teaspoon salt

2½ teaspoons ground cinnamon

1½ teaspoons ground ginger

¾ teaspoon freshly ground nutmeg

1⅓ cups finely chopped walnuts

Powdered sugar

Filling and Decorating

2 cups heavy whipping cream

2 tablespoons powdered sugar, sifted

1½ teaspoons pure vanilla extract

½ teaspoon ground cinnamon

¼ teaspoon ground ginger

¼ teaspoon freshly ground nutmeg

12 walnut halves

Candied orange peel for garnish,
   optional

Position a rack in the center of the oven. Preheat oven to 375F (190C). Line a jelly-roll pan with a sheet of parchment paper and butter the paper evenly with the 1 tablespoon butter.

In the bowl of a stand mixer or in a large bowl, using the wire-whip attachment or a hand-held mixer, whip the eggs on medium-high speed until they are very thick, pale yellow, and hold a slowly dissolving ribbon as the beater is lifted, about 5 minutes. Gradually beat in the granulated sugar, then blend in the pumpkin and lemon juice thoroughly.

In a separate medium bowl, combine the flour, baking powder, salt, cinnamon, ginger, and nutmeg. Fold this mixture into the pumpkin mixture in 3 stages, blending thoroughly after each addition. Fold in 1 cup of the walnuts.

Turn the mixture into the prepared pan, and using an offset spatula, spread it smoothly and evenly on the parchment paper. Sprinkle the remaining ⅓ cup of walnuts over the top of the cake. Bake 15 to 18 minutes, until the cake is evenly colored and the top springs back when touched.

Remove cake from the oven and use a sharp knife to loosen the edges. Lay a kitchen towel on a smooth surface, cover it with a sheet of parchment paper, and dust the parchment paper lightly with powdered sugar. Quickly turn the cake out onto the sugared parchment paper and gently peel the parchment paper off the back of the cake. Immediately roll up cake and parchment paper tightly in the towel, starting from one long side. Let cake cool completely, rolled in the towel.

Filling and Decorating

Whip the cream in a chilled bowl with a chilled beater until it holds soft peaks. Add the powdered sugar, vanilla, and spices. Continue to whip the cream until it holds firm, but not stiff, peaks.

Unroll the cake and remove the towel. Trim off any rough ends or edges. Using an offset spatula, evenly spread one-fourth of the cream over the cake. Roll up the cake, using the parchment paper as a guide. To make a tight roll, pull part of the parchment paper over the top of the cake, leaving a piece to hold from underneath. Wedge a ruler against the cake and push away from yourself, while pulling the bottom piece of parchment paper toward yourself.

Carefully place the rolled cake on a rectangular serving plate, seam side down, and discard the parchment paper. Fit a 14-inch pastry bag with a large closed-star tip (number 3) and partially fill with whipped cream. Pipe parallel rows of cream from one end of the rolled cake to the other, starting from the bottom and moving toward the top. Turn the serving plate around and repeat piping the cream on the other side. With the remaining whipped cream, pipe a row of rosettes on top of the rolled cake. Place walnut halves in the center of the rosettes and use the candied orange peel to decorate around the rosettes.

Refrigerate the cake until ready to serve or up to 3 hours. Slice crosswise into serving pieces.

Cloves

◆ ◆ ◆ ◆ ◆ ◆ ◆ ◆ ◆ ◆ ◆

Color of cinnamon
Clove's sweet smell . . .

—Jorge Amado, *Gabriela, Clove and Cinnamon*

Cloves are one of the oldest known and most sought after spices. The history of cloves involves intrigue, mystery, villains, and heroes—all the elements of a good novel. About 300 B.C., Chinese courtiers were required to chew cloves to sweeten their breath before an audience with the emperor. The Chinese obtained their cloves from India, where it is referred to in Sanskrit texts.

Arab traders brought cloves to ancient Greece and Rome. Apicus, the first-century gourmet, mentions cloves in several recipes. The ancient Egyptians were using cloves about A.D 200. Cloves were highly valued during the reign of the Emperor Constantine, about A.D 350. As a newly converted Christian, he gave 150 pounds of cloves, worth a substantial fortune, to Pope Sylvester as a gesture of respect to the church.

Cloves were one of the most heavily used spices during the Middle Ages, when spices were in great demand in Europe. Even as the use of many other spices subsided to a minimum, cloves remained the most popular spice next to pepper.

The Portuguese dominated the clove trade in the sixteenth century. It wasn't until the early seventeenth century that the Portuguese lost their monopoly when they were forced out by the Dutch, who maintained their monopoly by ruthlessly restricting the growth of clove trees to only one island in the Moluccas in the South Seas. They burned the trees if they produced too much, keeping the supply low and the demand high.

It was the Frenchman Pierre Poivre (pepper) who broke the Dutch monopoly on the clove trade by smuggling some young trees out of the Moluccas and planting them on Mauritius and Bourbon. After this, plantations were set up in Madagascar and Zanzibar, which is now part of Tanzania. Today these two countries are the biggest producers of cloves.

Cloves are used in both sweet and savory dishes in many cuisines of the world. In Europe and the United States, cloves are primarily used to flavor sweet dishes and chewing gum. In China and India cloves are used more extensively in both sweet and savory dishes and in mixtures with other spices.

Lore and Myths

◆ ◆ ◆

Cloves were thought to be a breath freshener from earliest times. They were also used to preserve meat. Clove pastilles were made in Naples and used as an aphrodisiac. During the Middle Ages, cloves had many medicinal uses. A clove-studded orange was thought to ward off the plague and oil of cloves was used to ease toothache.

Characteristics

◆ ◆ ◆

Cloves have two botanical names, *Eugenia aromatica* and *Syzygium aromaticus*. Cloves are the dried unopened flower buds of a tropical evergreen tree that is a member of the myrtle family. In the wild, the trees can reach heights of 30 feet. From ten to twenty buds grow in clusters on the branches surrounded by shiny large green leaves. Whole cloves resemble their Latin name, which means "nail." They are about ½ inch long, with small, pointed, dark brown stems crowned by a lighter reddish-brown round bud. The outer texture is rough. Ground cloves are a rich, dark reddish-brown. Cloves have a high natural oil content of about 17 percent.

Where and How It's Grown

* * *

Cloves are native to the Moluccas, the Spice Islands of Indonesia. They grow only in tropical climates near the ocean. Today they are successfully cultivated in Tanzania, Madagascar, Grenada, Malaysia, and Sri Lanka. Tanzania exports about 80 percent of the world's supply of cloves.

To make harvesting easier the trees are kept to a height of no more than 15 feet. Harvesting takes place twice a year, in late summer and in midwinter. The pink flower buds are picked before they open, then they are sun-dried for several days. The buds lose up to two-thirds of their weight as they dry and turn dark reddish-brown.

The essential oil, eugenol, is extracted from the clove buds.

How It Tastes and Smells

* * *

Cloves are the most fragrant of the spices. They have a sweet, rich, warm, pungent flavor and aroma. A whole clove is biting, hot, and almost bitter. It can numb the mouth temporarily.

Use and Preparation

* * *

Cloves are used both whole and ground in making many desserts, pastries, and confections. Cloves are more pungent and flavorful if ground just before use.

No special preparation is needed if cloves are bought in the form in which they will be used. Whole cloves can be ground to a powder in a spice or coffee grinder or with a mortar and pestle just before use.

Tips for Choosing and Storing

* * *

Good-quality cloves should have a bright, uniform color and a pungent, fragrant aroma.

Whole cloves should be stored in a tightly sealed container in a cool, dark, dry place up to 4 years. Store ground cloves under the same conditions for up to 2 years.

Raisin and Walnut Tart

Years ago I used to bake a succulent tart with raisins and chopped walnuts, but had lost my recipe. I found it again after an extensive hunt that I think you will agree was well worth the effort.

Makes 1 (12 × 8½-inch) tart, 12 to 16 servings.

◆   ◆   ◆

Pastry

2½ cups all-purpose flour

⅓ cup sugar

¼ teaspoon ground cloves

Pinch of freshly grated nutmeg

2 sticks (16 tablespoons) unsalted
    butter, chilled, cut into small pieces

1 large egg at room temperature, lightly
    beaten

1 teaspoon pure vanilla extract

Filling

1½ sticks (12 tablespoons) unsalted
    butter, melted and cooled

2 cups firmly packed golden brown
    sugar

3 large eggs at room temperature,
    lightly beaten

1 teaspoon pure vanilla extract

¾ teaspoon ground cloves

¼ teaspoon freshly grated nutmeg

3 cups Monukka or Thompson seedless
    raisins

1 cup walnuts, finely chopped

To serve

1 cup heavy whipping cream

1 teaspoon pure vanilla extract

½ teaspoon ground cloves

Pinch of freshly grated nutmeg

Pastry

Place the flour, sugar, cloves, and nutmeg in the work bowl of a food processor fitted with a steel blade. Add butter and pulse the mixture until the butter is cut into tiny pieces and the dough is crumbly, about 1 minute. Lightly beat the egg with the vanilla. With the machine on, add egg mixture through the feed tube. Process until the pastry wraps itself around the blade, about 1 minute. Cover the pastry with plastic wrap and chill at least 2 hours, until firm enough to roll.

Position a rack in the center of the oven. Preheat oven to 350F (175C). Roll out the pastry on a lightly floured work surface to a 15 × 10-inch rectangle, about ⅛ inch thick. Gently drape the pastry around the rolling pin and unroll it into a 12 × 8½-inch fluted tart pan with a removable bottom. Carefully lift up the sides of the pastry and fit it into the bottom and against the sides of the tart pan. Trim off the excess pastry at the top of the pan. Chill the pastry shell while preparing the filling.

Filling

Combine the butter and sugar in a medium bowl. Using a wooden spoon or rubber spatula, blend together thoroughly. Add the eggs, vanilla, cloves, and nutmeg and blend until smooth, about 1 minute. Stir in the raisins and blend thoroughly.

Place the tart pan on a jelly-roll pan and pour the filling into the pastry shell. Sprinkle the chopped walnuts over the top of the tart. Bake the tart 45 to 50 minutes, until the filling is puffed, golden, and set. Cool in pan on a rack.

To serve

Pour whipping cream into the bowl of a stand mixer or into a medium bowl. Using the wire-whip attachment or a hand-held mixer, whip the cream until it is frothy. Add the vanilla, cloves, and nutmeg and continue to whip the cream until it holds soft peaks, 2 to 3 minutes.

Serve slices of the tart with a dollop of whipped cream. The tart will keep at room temperature up to 4 days, tightly covered with foil.

Bread Pudding

Bread pudding is a true comfort food. Although it's usually made from leftover bread, this one is dressed up by using a fresh baguette or another type of good-quality white bread, giving it a sophisticated flavor. Next time you feel blue, eat this, and watch the blues fade away.

Makes 6 to 8 servings.

◆　◆　◆

¾ fresh baguette or ½ loaf fresh, good-quality white bread

1 tablespoon unsalted butter for pan

1 tablespoon superfine sugar for pan

½ cup raisins

2 cups milk

1 cup heavy whipping cream

5 large eggs at room temperature, lightly beaten

2 teaspoons pure vanilla extract

½ cup superfine sugar (see Note, page 21)

½ cup firmly packed golden brown sugar

¼ teaspoon salt

2 teaspoons freshly ground cloves

¼ teaspoon freshly grated nutmeg

To serve

1 cup heavy whipping cream

2 tablespoons powdered sugar, sifted

Position a rack in the center of the oven. Preheat oven to 400F (205C). Cut the crusts off the bread and cut the bread into 1-inch cubes. Place the cubes in a shallow layer in a baking pan and dry in the oven 15 minutes.

Use the 1 tablespoon butter to coat the inside of a 2-quart baking pan. Sprinkle the 1 tablespoon sugar over the butter. Transfer the bread cubes to the prepared baking pan. Sprinkle the raisins over the bread.

In a 2-quart bowl, combine the milk, cream, eggs, vanilla, superfine sugar, brown sugar, salt, cloves, and nutmeg. Blend together well. Pour the milk mixture over the bread and raisins. Cover the pan with plastic wrap and let the mixture stand in the refrigerator 30 minutes.

Preheat oven to 350F (175C). Remove the plastic wrap and place the baking pan in a larger baking pan. Place the pan on the oven rack and pour boiling water into the bottom pan until it reaches halfway up the sides. Bake the pudding 35 to 45 minutes, until it is puffy and a knife inserted near the center comes out almost clean.

Remove the pudding from the water bath and cool on a rack.

To serve

Pour whipping cream into the bowl of a stand mixer or into a medium bowl. Using the wire-whip attachment or a hand-held mixer, whip the cream until it is frothy. Sprinkle the powdered sugar over the cream and continue to whip until the cream holds soft peaks. Serve the pudding warm or at room temperature with a large spoonful of the whipped cream.

The pudding will keep 3 days in the refrigerator, tightly covered with plastic wrap.

Clove Ice Cream

The flavor of cloves may seem unusual for ice cream, but I think you'll be delightfully surprised by the taste. To get the best flavor, I highly recommend grinding the cloves just before use.

Makes about 3 cups, 6 servings.

◆　　◆　　◆

1 cup milk

1½ cups heavy whipping cream

1½ teaspoons freshly ground cloves

¼ teaspoon freshly ground nutmeg

5 large egg yolks, at room temperature

½ cup sugar

Combine the milk and cream in a heavy 3-quart saucepan over medium heat. Heat the mixture to just below the boiling point, 10 to 12 minutes. Stir the cloves and nutmeg into the mixture, remove the pan from the heat, cover, and let the mixture infuse 30 minutes.

In the bowl of a stand mixer or in a medium bowl, using the wire-whip attachment or a hand-held mixer, whip the egg yolks and sugar together until they are pale yellow and hold a slowly dissolving ribbon when the beater is lifted, about 5 minutes.

Reheat the milk mixture to just below the boiling point. Reduce the mixer speed to low and slowly pour 1 cup of the hot liquid into the egg and sugar mixture. Stir to blend well, then add the egg mixture to the saucepan. Reduce the heat to low and cook, stirring the mixture constantly with a wooden spoon, until the mixture reaches 185F (85C) on a candy thermometer, about 5 minutes. At this point the mixture is thickened and when a line is drawn through the custard on the back of the spoon, it leaves a clearly defined path.

Remove the saucepan from the heat and pour the mixture into a 2-quart bowl. Cover the mixture tightly with plastic wrap, cool, then chill in the refrigerator for several hours or overnight. Process the mixture in an ice cream maker according to the manufacturer's instructions.

Store the ice cream in a covered container in the freezer up to 1 month. If it is frozen solid, soften it in the refrigerator for a few hours before serving.

Apple Raisin Custard Tart

This unusual pastry is a classic Eastern European tart. The apples for the filling are grated, creating a unique texture. Tart apples such as Granny Smiths or Pippins are the type traditionally used.

Makes 1 (9½-inch) tart, 12 servings.

◆ ◆ ◆

1 recipe Pastry Dough (page 102), omitting cloves and nutmeg

¼ cup raw hazelnuts, toasted (see Note, page 71)

4 to 5 tart green apples

1 cup plus 1 tablespoon heavy whipping cream

1 large egg at room temperature

3 tablespoons sugar

1 tablespoon plus 2 teaspoons all-purpose flour

1½ teaspoons freshly ground cloves

¼ teaspoon freshly grated nutmeg

⅓ cup raisins

Make and chill dough as directed on page 102.

Roll out the pastry on a lightly floured work surface to an 11-inch circle about ⅛ inch thick. Gently drape the pastry around the rolling pin and unroll into a deep 9½-inch fluted tart pan with a removable bottom. Carefully lift up the sides of the pastry and fit it into the bottom and against the sides of the tart pan. Trim off any excess pastry at the top of the pan. Chill the pastry shell while preparing the filling.

Place the hazelnuts in the work bowl of a food processor fitted with a steel blade and pulse until they are finely ground, 30 to 60 seconds.

Finely grate the apples and place them in a medium bowl. In another medium bowl combine the cream, egg, 2 tablespoons of the sugar, flour, cloves, nutmeg, and raisins. Blend until smooth, then mix with the grated apples, coating them thoroughly.

Place the tart pan on a jelly-roll pan. Sprinkle the ground hazelnuts evenly over the bottom of the pastry shell, then pour in the filling.

Bake the tart 40 to 45 minutes, until the filling is puffed, golden, and set. Remove from the oven and immediately sprinkle the remaining tablespoon of sugar on top. Cool slightly on a rack. The tart is best eaten while warm. The tart will keep up to 3 days in the refrigerator, wrapped with foil.

Basler Leckerli

Leckerli are classic Swiss spice and honey cookies. They are traditionally baked during the Christmas holiday season. The most famous Leckerli are from Basel. They are very different from the variety made in Zurich, which are not spicy. Leckerli can be shaped with a special leckerli or springerle mold or cut into traditional bar shapes. Leckerli become crisp as they cool. They are ideal to bake ahead, because they keep for up to four months in an airtight container at room temperature.

Makes about 60 (2 × 1-inch) cookies.

◆ ◆ ◆

4½ cups all-purpose flour
1 teaspoon baking soda
½ teaspoon baking powder
1¼ cups honey
1½ cups sugar
1 tablespoon ground cinnamon
2 teaspoons ground cloves
½ teaspoon freshly grated nutmeg
½ teaspoon ground ginger
¼ teaspoon salt
Zest of 1 large lemon, finely minced
1 cup finely chopped candied orange peel
½ cup finely ground almonds (see Note, page 31)

1 cup coarsely chopped unblanched almonds
⅓ cup kirsch
1 tablespoon unsalted butter, at room temperature, for pans

Glaze

1 cup powdered sugar, sifted
2 tablespoons honey
2 tablespoons kirsch, fresh lemon juice, or water

Sift together the flour, baking soda, and baking powder; set aside.

In a heavy-bottomed 2-quart saucepan, combine the honey, sugar, and spices and warm over low heat, stirring frequently with a wooden spoon, until the sugar is dissolved, about 5 minutes.

Remove the saucepan from the heat and stir in the salt, lemon zest, candied orange peel, ground almonds, chopped almonds, and kirsch. Transfer the mixture to the bowl of a stand mixer or a medium bowl. Using the flat-beater attachment or a hand-held mixer, add the flour mixture in 3 or 4 stages, blending well after each addition. Stop occasionally and scrape down the sides of the bowl with a rubber spatula.

Position a rack in the center of the oven. Preheat oven to 350F (175C). Line 2 baking sheets with parchment paper. Use the tablespoon of butter to generously butter each sheet of parchment paper.

Divide the dough into 2 equal pieces. Chill 1 piece of dough while working with the other piece. Roll out the dough between lightly floured sheets of waxed paper to a large rectangle about 12 × 10 inches and ¼ inch thick. Remove top sheet of waxed paper and invert dough on a lined baking sheet. Remove waxed paper. Repeat with the remaining half of the dough. Bake the dough 15 minutes. Switch the baking sheets and bake another 15 minutes.

While the dough is baking, prepare the glaze. Combine the powdered sugar, honey, and kirsch in a small heavy-bottomed saucepan over medium heat. Cook, stirring until the sugar dissolves, then bring the mixture to a boil and cook 3 to 4 minutes. Cool slightly to thicken the glaze. If it is too thick, warm it briefly before use.

Remove the baking sheets from the oven. Brush the dough with the glaze and, while it is warm, use a serrated knife to score it into 2 × 1-inch rectangles. Place the baking sheets on racks and let the cookies cool completely. When cool, cut through the scored lines and separate the cookies into rectangles. Store the cookies up to 4 months at room temperature in an airtight container.

Coriander

◆ ◆ ◆ ◆ ◆ ◆ ◆ ◆ ◆ ◆ ◆

Manna was like
coriander seed, white.

—*Old Testament*, Exodus 16:31

Coriander is one of the world's most popular spices and one of the oldest. It has been recorded in Sanskrit texts as long ago as 5000 B.C. and it was one of the plants that grew in the ancient hanging gardens of Babylon. The Israelites were miraculously given coriander seeds during their flight from Egypt, thus it is one of the foods traditionally eaten at Passover as a remembrance. Coriander was used in Egyptian tombs and its use in burials was mentioned in the Papyrus of Thebes about 1550 B.C.

Coriander traveled throughout the Mediterranean in the old spice caravans. It was used by the ancient Greeks and was mentioned in the writings of Hippocrates, the father of medicine, who used it as a drug. It was the Romans who took coriander on their conquests and spread its use throughout Europe. The medieval Europeans found many uses for coriander, both culinary and medicinal. Coriander was widely grown in the English regions of Essex and East Anglia before it traveled to the New World. Coriander is known to have been grown in Massachusetts earlier than 1670.

Today coriander is widely used in Indian cooking as a part of curry mixtures. It is also widely used in Middle Eastern cooking to flavor meats, stews, and sausages. In Scandinavian and Eastern European countries, coriander is used to flavor gin, bread, cakes, cookies, confections, cheeses, and pickling mixtures. In the United States, coriander is used in many dessert recipes. The essential oil extracted from coriander seed is used in perfumes and incense.

Coriander and cilantro come from the same plant. Coriander is the dried seed, cilantro the fresh leaves. Although they come from the same plant, they do not have similar smells or tastes and are used in different cuisines. Cilantro is heavily used in Latin American and Chinese cooking, while coriander is widely used in the Middle East.

Lore and Myths

◆　◆　◆

The ancient Chinese believed that if coriander seeds were eaten during a spiritual trance, immortality would be achieved. Coriander is thought to have medicinal value as a stimulant and a digestive aid. It is also thought to be an aphrodisiac. In the eighteenth century, coriander comfits, seeds coated with sugar, were very popular.

Characteristics

◆　◆　◆

Coriander is the dried seed, actually the fruit, of an annual plant that is a member of the carrot family. Its botanical name is *Coriandrum sativum*. The plant has thin, feathery upper leaves; broad, flat, light green lower leaves; and clusters of small pink or white flowers. It grows to a height of about 2½ feet.

The seeds are small, measuring from ⅛ to ¼ inch in diameter. They are round or oval, with ribs on their outer surfaces. They are a light yellow-brown color that darkens when they are roasted.

Where and How It's Grown

♦ ♦ ♦

Coriander is native to the Mediterranean region of southern Europe and northern Africa. Currently it is grown in countries throughout the Northern Hemisphere. The biggest producers are Morocco, India, Mexico, Iran, and the United States. Indian coriander is reputed to have a flavor sweeter than that of Moroccan.

Coriander seeds are picked when ripe. The seeds must be harvested early in the day before the sun dries the seed pods. Otherwise the pods will split open and scatter the seeds. The seeds are dried, then sieved to remove extraneous material.

The essential oil is extracted from the seeds and is used to impart flavor to chocolate, liqueurs, and medicines.

How It Tastes and Smells

♦ ♦ ♦

Coriander has a mildly sweet, slightly tangy taste with a citrussy undertone of orange peel. The flavor resembles a mixture of anise and cumin. It has a pungent, slightly peppery, aroma.

Use and Preparation

♦ ♦ ♦

In desserts, coriander is used ground. It is best to buy whole coriander seeds and grind them in a spice grinder or with a mortar and pestle for each use because coriander goes stale quickly.

Tips for Choosing and Storage

♦ ♦ ♦

Buy whole coriander seeds or ground coriander from a source with a high turnover to be sure of freshness. Whole coriander seeds should be stored in tightly sealed glass jars in a cool, dark, dry place for up to 1 year. Store ground coriander the same way for up to 3 months.

Spiced Almonds

Coriander blended with cinnamon and cloves imparts a warm, robust flavor to these crunchy almonds. Keep them in an airtight container at room temperature, since any exposure to humidity can make them soft.

Makes 3 cups.

◆ ◆ ◆

¼ cup granulated sugar

1½ teaspoons ground coriander

1½ teaspoons ground cinnamon

½ teaspoon ground cloves

1 large egg white at room temperature

Zest of ½ large orange, finely minced

2 cups whole unblanched almonds

Position a rack in the center of the oven. Preheat oven to 275F (135C). Line a jelly-roll pan with foil and spray with a nonstick cooking spray.

Combine the sugar and spices in a small bowl and blend well. Beat the egg white in a 2-quart bowl until it is frothy. Add the spice mixture and orange zest and blend thoroughly. Fold the almonds into the egg white mixture, coating them completely.

Turn the nuts out onto the jelly-roll pan, separating them as much as possible. Toast 40 minutes, stirring the nuts every 10 minutes. Remove the pan from the oven, loosen the nuts, and cool in the pan on a rack.

Serve the almonds at room temperature. Store them up to 3 weeks at room temperature, between layers of waxed paper in an airtight container.

Cantaloupe and Coriander Sorbet

Coriander's lemony taste accents the fresh melon flavor in this refreshing sorbet. The taste and texture always transport me to thoughts of summer. This sorbet is delicious on its own or paired with other sorbets and cookies.

Makes about 3½ cups.

◆　◆　◆

1¾ cups sugar

¾ cup water

1 large ripe cantaloupe

1 tablespoon fresh lemon juice

1 tablespoon ground coriander

Combine the sugar and water in a heavy saucepan over medium heat and bring to a boil. Cool.

Cut the cantaloupe in half and remove the seeds. Remove the skin and rind and cut the flesh into thick chunks. Place the melon chunks in the work bowl of a food processor fitted with a steel blade. Add the sugar syrup, lemon juice, and coriander and pulse the mixture until it is a liquid.

Pour the mixture into a bowl, cover tightly with plastic wrap, and refrigerate until cold, several hours or overnight. Process the sorbet in an ice cream maker according to the manufacturer's instructions.

Store the sorbet up to 1 month in a covered container in the freezer. If it is frozen solid, soften it in the refrigerator for a few hours before serving.

Pear and Polenta Tart

This unusual tart has Italian roots. *Polenta* is the Italian word for finely ground cornmeal, which is used often in Italian baking. Here it contributes its crunchy texture and sweet taste to the pastry dough that encloses ripe, juicy pears.

Makes 1 (12 X 8-inch) tart, 12 to 16 servings.

◆ ◆ ◆

Poached Pears

1 cup dry white wine

2 cups water

2 teaspoons fresh lemon juice

¾ cup sugar

2 teaspoons ground coriander

2 whole cloves

4 large ripe Anjou or Bartlett pears

Pastry and Assembly

2¼ cups all-purpose flour

¾ cup fine yellow cornmeal

¼ teaspoon salt

⅔ cup plus 1 tablespoon sugar

2 teaspoons ground coriander

2 sticks (16 tablespoons) unsalted
     butter, chilled, cut into small pieces

3 large egg yolks at room temperature

3 tablespoons water

Poached Pears

Combine the wine, water, lemon juice, and sugar in a heavy-bottomed 3-quart saucepan over medium-high heat. Bring to a boil, add the coriander and cloves, and simmer, partially covered, 5 minutes.

Peel, halve, and core the pears, then add them to the poaching liquid. Poach them gently about 20 minutes, until tender. Remove from the heat, transfer the pears and their liquid to a glass bowl, and cool to room temperature. (The pears can be poached and stored in their liquid in the refrigerator up to 3 days before use.)

Pastry

Position a rack in the center of the oven. Preheat oven to 350F (175C).

Place the flour, cornmeal, salt, ⅔ cup sugar, and coriander in the work bowl of a food processor fitted with a steel blade. Pulse a few times to blend. Add the butter and pulse the mixture until the butter is cut into tiny pieces, about 1 minute.

Beat the egg yolks lightly with the water. With the machine on, pour the liquid through the feed tube and process until the mixture wraps itself around the blade, about 1 minute.

Divide the dough into 2 pieces. Between sheets of waxed paper roll out 1 piece of the pastry dough to a large rectangle about 15 × 10 inches and ⅛ inch thick. Peel off 1 piece of the waxed paper. Using the corners of the remaining piece of waxed paper lift the pastry dough and fit it into a 12 × 8-inch fluted tart pan with removable bottom. Peel off the waxed paper. Trim off the excess pastry dough at the top of the pan and patch any holes in the pastry shell.

To assemble

Strain the pears and pat dry with paper towels. Thinly slice each pear half crosswise, then transfer the slices to the tart pan and place on the pastry dough, center down, fanning out slightly. Place half of the pears along one length of the tart pan and half along the opposite length. Alternate the direction of the pears, tops facing one way, bottoms the other, so they fill out the space. Use a damp pastry brush to dampen the rim of the pastry shell.

Between sheets of waxed paper, roll out the remaining half of the pastry dough to a large rectangle. Peel off 1 sheet of the waxed paper. Using the waxed paper, lift the pastry dough and place it over the top of the pears. Fit the dough to the pan, trim off any excess, and press it to seal with the bottom layer of pastry.

Place the tart on a jelly-roll pan, sprinkle the top with the 1 tablespoon sugar, and pierce a few slits in the top. Bake 35 to 40 minutes, until lightly browned.

Cool in pan on a rack. Remove the sides of the tart pan and cut the tart into squares to serve. The tart will keep up to 3 days in the refrigerator, tightly wrapped with foil.

Ginger

*I must have saffron, to colour the warden pies;
mace,——dates,——none, that's out of my note; nutmegs,
seven; a race or two of ginger.*

—Clown, *The Winter's Tale*,
William Shakespeare

Ginger's Latin name, *Zingiber officinale,* is derived from a Sanskrit word meaning "horn-shaped," possibly referring to the shape of the rhizome (underground stem). Ginger is a spice that has been in use for thousands of years. It is thought to have originated in the tropical climate of southern China or in the Pacific islands near China's coast, although its exact origins are unknown.

In the Mediterranean region, the Greeks and Romans were some of the first to use ginger, which was brought there by Arab traders. About 2000 B.C., a baker on the isle of Rhodes made what is thought to be the first gingerbread. From there, ginger traveled to Egypt, where the Romans encountered it and enthusiastically embraced it. Ginger was used so extensively throughout the Roman Empire that a tax was levied on it.

Ginger was one of the first spices to reach southeastern Europe on the ancient spice route. The Crusaders increased its popularity so greatly that during the Middle Ages, when Venice monopolized the spice trade, ginger was one of the most sought after and most expensive spices. Marco Polo wrote about ginger during his travels. Because of the great demand, the Spanish opened markets with Jamaica and developed a thriving trade in Jamaican ginger with continental Europe in the fifteenth century.

Lore and Myths

◆ ◆ ◆

Ginger has long been thought to be an aphrodisiac. It is known for its warming qualities and ability to increase blood circulation, and is widely believed to ease travel sickness. The word *ginger* has even spiced up the English language. *Ginger* is the term used to refer to red-haired people and implies they have a hot temperament.

Characteristics

◆ ◆ ◆

Ginger is a herbaceous, perennial plant with reedlike stems reaching up to 3 feet tall. The plant has two perpendicular rows of shiny, slender leaves with small yellow flowers tipped with purple. Ginger has a system of creeping rhizomes and propagates by division. It is these rhizomes that are the spice.

Where and How It's Grown

◆ ◆ ◆

Native to Southeast Asia, today ginger is grown in many countries with tropical climates, including Australia, Brazil, China, Costa Rica, Jamaica, Japan, Hawaii, India, and Sierra Leone. The biggest producers are China and India. Jamaican ginger is reputed to be the most flavorful, but it has not been imported into the United States for several years because it is very labor-intensive to produce, making it very expensive. Australian ginger is very high quality and is rapidly taking a large share of the market.

The rhizomes are harvested anytime after 5 to 6 months. To produce fresh ginger, also called green ginger, the rhizomes are washed and sun-dried for a day or two, then stored in controlled conditions for several months. For dried ginger, the rhizomes are washed and sun-dried to evaporate their moisture. There is an outer corklike layer that is often removed before ginger is dried to produce a light-colored ginger. After drying, the rhizomes are ground to a powder. Very young ginger (6 months or less), or stem ginger, the part closest to the stem, has a delicate flavor and is used to make crystallized ginger.

How It Tastes and Smells

• • •

Ginger has a flavor that's all its own. It's slightly sweet, peppery, rich, pungent, and mildly hot. It rounds out and accents many flavors. Ginger has a full-bodied and rich aroma.

Use and Preparation

• • •

For desserts, ginger is primarily ground and crystallized although occasionally it is used fresh. Crystallized ginger is usually cut into small pieces. It is used for both flavoring and decoration. Fresh ginger should be peeled before use with a vegetable peeler or sharp knife. Slice it across the fibers, then mince it finely or grate it.

Tips for Choosing and Storing

• • •

Buy ground ginger in small quantities and use within 4 months. Buy crystallized ginger also in small quantities (1 to 2 cups) and use within 1 year. Fresh ginger should feel firm. The rhizome is off-white to tan-colored, knobby, and branched. The flesh should be pale yellow and slightly fibrous.

Store ground and crystallized ginger in airtight containers in a cool, dark, dry place. Replace ground ginger every 4 to 6 months. Crystallized ginger will last for up to one year. Store fresh ginger tightly wrapped in damp paper towels in a plastic bag in the refrigerator for up to 1 month.

Double-Ginger Shortbread

The sweet-hot, piquant flavor of ginger is added to traditional buttery Scottish shortbread. Ginger is used in two forms, ground and crystallized, giving the cookies extra flavor and texture. The recipe makes a big batch, but these always disappear quickly.

Makes 60 (2½ × 1-inch) cookies.

◆ ◆ ◆

4 sticks unsalted butter, softened

1 cup superfine sugar (see Note, page 21)

½ teaspoon salt

2 teaspoons ground ginger

½ teaspoon freshly grated nutmeg

4 cups all-purpose flour

⅓ cup finely minced crystallized ginger

In the bowl of a stand mixer or in a medium bowl, using the flat-beater attachment or a hand-held mixer, beat the butter until it is light and fluffy, about 2 minutes. Add the sugar and continue beating until thoroughly blended.

Blend the salt and spices into the flour in a medium bowl and add to the butter in 4 stages, stopping and scraping down the sides of the bowl after each addition. After all the flour has been added, blend in the crystallized ginger and continue to mix another 1 or 2 minutes, until the dough is smooth and soft.

Lightly flour a baking sheet or jelly-roll pan. Pat and roll the dough out on the pan to a ⅜-inch thickness. Use a ruler and mark off pieces that are 1 inch wide and 2½ inches long. Pierce each piece in three places on the diagonal with a fork. Cover the dough and chill in the refrigerator at least 1 hour.

Position racks in the upper and lower thirds of the oven. Preheat oven to 325F (165C). Line 2 baking sheets with parchment paper.

Cut the chilled shortbread through the lines and place on the lined baking pans with 1 inch of space between them. Place the baking sheets in the oven and reduce heat to 300F (150C). Bake 25 minutes. Switch baking sheets and bake another 8 to 10 minutes. The shortbread should be light golden on the bottom and sand-colored on top.

Cool on baking sheets on racks. Store the shortbread up to 2 weeks at room temperature, between layers of waxed paper in an airtight container.

Ginger Ice Cream

Crystallized ginger spices up this classic, rich ice cream, which is sure to hit the spot on a hot summer day! It's also great as dessert during the fall and winter months. Try serving it with gingerbread.

Makes 1 quart, 8 servings.

◆ ◆ ◆

2 cups milk

4 large egg yolks at room temperature

1 cup sugar

Pinch of salt

2 cups heavy whipping cream, chilled

1 teaspoon pure vanilla extract

¾ cup finely chopped crystallized ginger

In a heavy-bottomed 3-quart saucepan over medium heat, bring the milk almost to a simmer. In the bowl of a stand mixer or in a medium bowl, using the wire-whip attachment or a hand-held mixer, whip the egg yolks, sugar, and salt together until pale yellow and very thick, about 5 minutes.

Ladle half of the hot milk into a measuring cup with a spout and slowly pour into the egg mixture. Blend together thoroughly, then pour back into the remaining milk in the saucepan. Stir the mixture constantly with a long-handled wooden spoon until it is thick enough to coat the spoon, 5 to 8 minutes. If using a candy thermometer, it should register 185F (85C).

Immediately remove the mixture from the heat and pour into a 3-quart bowl. Stir in the cream and vanilla and blend thoroughly. Cover the mixture loosely with plastic wrap and cool, then chill in the refrigerator at least 2 hours. Process the mixture in an ice cream maker according to manufacturer's instructions. When the mixture is half frozen, stir in the ginger.

Serve scoops of the ice cream immediately or store it in a tightly covered container up to 2 months in the freezer. If it is frozen solid, soften it briefly in the refrigerator before serving.

Gingerbread

Gingerbread is a worldwide favorite sweet, rich and aromatic with the spicy flavors of ginger, cinnamon, cloves, and nutmeg. This version of gingerbread is soft and cakelike, and is especially good with a dollop of whipped cream for garnish.

Makes 16 (2-inch) squares.

◆ ◆ ◆

1 tablespoon unsalted butter for pan

1 tablespoon all-purpose flour for pan

2½ cups all-purpose flour

2 teaspoons baking soda

1 tablespoon ground ginger

1 teaspoon ground cinnamon

½ teaspoon ground cloves

¼ teaspoon freshly grated nutmeg

¼ teaspoon salt

1 stick (8 tablespoons) unsalted butter, softened

¼ cup firmly packed golden brown sugar

¼ cup granulated sugar

2 large eggs at room temperature, lightly beaten

1 cup dark molasses

1 cup boiling water

½ cup heavy whipping cream

Position a rack in the center of the oven. Preheat oven to 350F (175C). Butter an 8-inch-square baking pan with the 1 tablespoon butter, sprinkle with the 1 tablespoon flour, and shake out the excess.

Sift the flour, baking soda, spices, and salt together onto a large piece of waxed paper. Set this mixture aside.

In the bowl of a stand mixer or in a medium bowl, using the flat-beater attachment or a hand-held mixer, beat the butter until it is soft and fluffy, about 2 minutes. Add the brown sugar and granulated sugar and continue to beat until the mixture is well blended, about 2 more minutes, stopping and scraping down the sides of the bowl with a rubber spatula twice.

Blend in the eggs and the molasses, beating well, then add the boiling water. Scrape down the bottom and sides of the bowl. With the mixer on low speed, add the dry ingredients in several small batches, beating to blend well after each addition.

Turn the mixture into the prepared pan and bake 45 minutes, until the top springs back when lightly touched and a cake tester inserted into the center comes out clean. Cool in pan on a rack.

Pour the whipping cream into the bowl of a stand mixer or a medium bowl. Using the wire-whip attachment or a hand-held mixer, whip the cream on medium speed to soft peaks. Cut the gingerbread into squares and serve with a dollop of whipped cream.

The gingerbread will keep 3 days at room temperature, well wrapped in foil.

Gingersnaps

Both ground and crystallized ginger give their full-bodied flavor to these yummy cookies. These are great year-round but seem to taste even better in the fall and winter, when it's cold outside. They keep well, too, so it's easy to have them on hand.

Makes about 60 cookies.

◆　◆　◆

2¼ cups all-purpose flour

1 teaspoon baking soda

2 teaspoons ground ginger

1¼ teaspoons ground cinnamon

½ teaspoon ground cloves

¼ teaspoon salt

2 tablespoons finely minced crystallized ginger

1½ sticks (12 tablespoons) unsalted butter, softened

¾ cup sugar

1 large egg at room temperature

⅓ cup dark molasses

Sift the flour with the baking soda, ground ginger, cinnamon, cloves, and salt into a medium bowl. Add crystallized ginger and toss to blend well; set aside.

Place the butter in the bowl of a stand mixer or in a medium bowl. Using the flat-beater attachment or a hand-held mixer, beat the butter until it is fluffy, about 2 minutes. Add the sugar and beat until thoroughly blended. Add the egg and molasses and blend thoroughly, stopping occasionally and scraping down the sides and bottom of the bowl with a rubber spatula. Add the flour mixture in 3 stages, blending well after each addition. Cover the bowl with plastic wrap and chill the dough in the refrigerator 30 minutes.

Position a rack in the upper third of the oven. Preheat oven to 350F (175C). Line 4 baking sheets with parchment paper.

Remove the bowl of cookie dough from the refrigerator. Dampen your hands with cold water. Pinch off walnut-sized pieces of dough and roll into balls. Place the balls on the baking sheets. Leave 2 inches of space between each ball.

Bake 1 baking sheet of cookies at a time on the upper rack 12 minutes, until firm and the tops are cracked. Use a metal spatula to transfer the cookies to racks to cool completely. The cookies will keep up to 10 days at room temperature in an airtight container.

Pear and Ginger Pie

This recipe first appeared in my column, "The Pastry Chef," for the electronic Gourmet Guide (eGG) on America Online®. Ginger highlights the pears and adds its special warmth to the filling. The crust is a classic French pastry dough made with all butter, which gives it a delicious taste. Use the crust for any pie recipe.

Makes 1 (10-inch) pie, 8 to 10 servings.

◆　◆　◆

Pastry

2¼ cups all-purpose flour

1 tablespoon granulated sugar

½ teaspoon salt

1½ sticks (12 tablespoons) unsalted
    butter, chilled, cut into small pieces

7 tablespoons cold water

Filling

5 to 6 firm ripe pears, such as Comice,
    Anjou, or Bosc

2 tablespoons fresh lemon juice

¼ cup granulated sugar

⅓ cup firmly packed golden brown
    sugar

3 tablespoons all-purpose flour

3 tablespoons finely minced crystallized
    ginger

½ teaspoon ground ginger

¼ teaspoon ground cloves

Pinch ground cardamom

Glaze

1 tablespoon milk

Pastry

Place the flour, sugar, and salt in the bowl of a food processor, an electric mixer, or a medium bowl. Use the steel blade for the food processor, the flat beater for the electric mixer, or a hand-held mixer and pulse or mix for a few seconds. Add the butter and, in the food processor, pulse using on/off turns, or if using the electric mixer or a hand-held mixer, blend until the butter is cut into very tiny pieces, about 1 minute. With the machine on, add the cold water in a steady stream. Continue to process or mix until the dough forms a ball or wraps itself around the blade, about 1 minute.

Cover the dough with plastic wrap and chill in the refrigerator at least 2 hours before using. (The dough will keep 4 days in the refrigerator or it can be frozen for up to 4 months, if very well wrapped. If frozen, defrost it in the refrigerator for 24 hours before using.) If the dough is very cold, let it sit at room temperature until it is pliable, but not soft, before using.

Filling

Peel, halve, and core the pears. Cut the halves into ½-inch-thick slices and place in a large bowl. Sprinkle with the lemon juice and toss to coat the pear slices.

In a small bowl combine the granulated sugar, brown sugar, flour, crystallized ginger, ground ginger, cloves, and cardamom and toss to blend well. Add this mixture to the pears and gently stir to coat the pears.

To assemble

Position a rack in the center of the oven. Preheat oven to 425F (220C). Roll out half of the dough on a lightly floured work surface to a large circle about 12 inches in diameter. Carefully roll the dough around the rolling pin, then gently unroll the dough into a 10-inch pie pan. Gently lift up the edges of the pie dough and fit it into the bottom and against the sides of the pan. Transfer the filling to the pie shell.

Roll out the remaining half of the pie dough on a lightly floured work surface to a large circle, about 13 inches in diameter. Use a pastry brush to dampen the edges of the lower crust. Transfer the top crust to the pie and trim off any large edges. Pinch the edges of both crusts together and shape them into a fluted edge. Use a sharp knife to make several slits in the top crust. Brush with milk.

Place the pie on a jelly-roll pan. Bake 10 minutes. Reduce oven temperature to 375F (190C) and bake another 45 minutes, until the crust is golden and the filling is bubbling. Cool in pan on a rack. The pie will keep 3 days at room temperature, wrapped in foil.

Nutmeg and Mace

• • • • • • • • • •

. . . gingerbread that was so fun and licorice,
and eek common with sugar that is true,
also of nutmeg put in ale.

—Chaucer, *The Canterbury Tales*

Nutmeg, and its sister spice, mace, are unique because they are two distinct spices that come from the same tree, *Mystica fragrans*. Like many spices, nutmeg and mace come from Indonesia. They became known in Europe in about the sixth century A.D., having traveled west slowly with the spice caravans. First they went to Java, then to India, and from there, on to Alexandria in Egypt. From Alexandria they traveled to Venice, where spice merchants spread them throughout Europe. Recognizing the value of nutmeg and mace, the Indians began to cultivate the trees. However, their trees never reached the quality of those from Indonesia, and the resulting inferior spices were not bought by the Europeans. When the Portuguese held a monopoly on Indonesia, they zealously pursued development of the trade in nutmeg and mace.

During the Middle Ages, mace was used heavily by Europeans to flavor both sweet and savory dishes. By the eighteenth century, nutmeg was so popular that it was very fashionable to carry one's own nutmeg and nutmeg grater. In the late eighteenth century, the English gained control of the nutmeg and mace trade and began to cultivate trees on the West Indian island of Grenada.

Today nutmeg and mace are widely used in desserts, pastries, and confections in Europe, Canada, and the United States. They are often blended with other spices such as cinnamon, cloves, and ginger. Nutmeg and mace are also used to flavor savory dishes in the Middle East. The Dutch use nutmeg in many vegetable dishes and the Italians use nutmeg to flavor several filled pastas, pasta sauces, and vegetables.

The essential oil extracted from the fruit is used in perfumes, shampoos, and medicines.

Lore and Myths
◆　◆　◆

Nutmeg has long been valued for its use as a digestive aid. It was often chewed to sweeten breath. Nutmeg has also been used to ward off the plague.

During the Middle Ages, the use of nutmeg as a medicine was guarded carefully, because its essential oil has some hallucinogenic properties.

Characteristics
◆　◆　◆

Mace is the netlike, lacy outer covering, called the aril, that surrounds the nutmeg seed. The fruit that contains both nutmeg and mace resembles a peach and grows on the nutmeg tree, a tropical evergreen that reaches heights of up to 40 feet. The tree has oval, deep green leaves and tiny yellow flowers.

Nutmeg is a grayish-brown, oval-shaped hard seed, about 1 inch long. Its exterior surface looks wrinkled, but in fact, it's smooth to the touch. The inside of the nutmeg seed has dark brown veins. When ground, nutmeg is a dull brown color. Nutmeg is available either whole or ground.

Mace is bright scarlet and turns reddish-orange or yellowish-orange as it dries. It comes in two forms, as blades and ground.

Where and How It's Grown

◆ ◆ ◆

Nutmeg and mace are native to the Moluccas, the Spice Islands of Indonesia. The trees thrive only in tropical maritime climates. Today nutmeg trees are cultivated in Sri Lanka, Malaysia, and Grenada in the West Indies, which exports about 40 percent of the world's supply.

The nutmeg tree does not bear fruit for the first 6 or 7 years of its life, but once begun, it continues for about 60 years. A nutmeg tree will bear about 1,000 nutmegs a year.

The fruit is harvested when it falls from the tree, about six months after it has flowered. The fruit is cracked open and the outer shell removed. The mace is removed and laid flat to dry until it is brittle. Then it is broken into blades. Because mace is handled completely by hand, it is an expensive spice to produce and always costs more than nutmeg.

The nutmeg seeds are dried for several weeks until they rattle in their shells. Then the shells are cracked, the nutmeg seeds are removed, and graded by appearance and quality.

How It Tastes and Smells

◆ ◆ ◆

Nutmeg has a strong, rich, warm, sweet flavor. The taste of mace is similar but more powerful than nutmeg. Both have a warm, rich, pungent smell. Mace and nutmeg can be easily interchanged.

Use and Preparation

◆ ◆ ◆

For desserts, nutmeg is used grated or ground, whereas mace is used ground. To grate or grind nutmeg, use a nutmeg grater or grinder. Mace is usually always bought ground, but the blades can be ground in a spice mill or grinder.

Tips for Choosing and Storing

◆ ◆ ◆

Nutmeg is available both whole and ground. It's best to buy it whole and grate or grind it just before use to ensure freshness. Ground mace holds its flavor longer than other ground spices. Blades of mace are rare and much harder to find than ground mace. Buy both whole and ground forms from a source with a high turnover to ensure freshness.

Store whole nutmeg and mace in glass jars in a cool, dark, dry place. Whole nutmeg will last for years. Grated nutmeg loses its flavor rapidly. Ground mace will stay flavorful for several months.

Honey Mace Ice Cream

This ice cream truly melts in your mouth. It has a velvety texture and a subtle spicy flavor. It may sound unusual, but I think it will become one of your favorite ice cream flavors.

Makes 1 pint, 4 servings.

◆　◆　◆

1¼ cups milk

½ cup honey

2 teaspoons freshly grated nutmeg

¼ teaspoon (heaping) ground mace

3 large egg yolks at room temperature

½ cup heavy whipping cream

Bring the milk to a boil in a heavy 2-quart saucepan. Add the honey, stir to blend, and reduce the heat to low. Blend in the nutmeg and mace. Remove from heat, cover the mixture, and infuse 10 minutes.

In the bowl of a stand mixer or in a medium bowl, using the wire-whip attachment or a hand-held mixer, whip the egg yolks until they are pale yellow and hold a slowly dissolving ribbon when the beater is lifted, about 8 minutes.

Reheat the milk mixture to just below the boiling point. Reduce the mixer speed to low and slowly pour 1 cup of the hot liquid into the eggs. Stir to blend well, then add the mixture to the milk in the saucepan. Reduce the heat to low and cook, stirring constantly with a wooden spoon, until the mixture reaches 185F (85C) on a candy thermometer, 5 to 8 minutes. At this point the mixture will be thickened and when a line is drawn through the custard on the back of the spoon, it leaves a clearly defined path.

Remove the saucepan from the heat and pour the mixture into a 2-quart bowl. Cover the mixture tightly with plastic wrap, cool, then chill in the refrigerator for several hours or overnight.

In the bowl of a stand mixer or in a medium bowl, using the wire-whip attachment or a hand-held mixer, whip the cream to soft peaks. Fold the whipped cream into the custard, blending thoroughly. Immediately process the mixture in an ice cream mixer according to the manufacturer's instructions.

Store the ice cream up to 1 month in a covered container in the freezer. If it is frozen solid, soften it in the refrigerator for a few hours before serving.

Mace Shortcakes with Lemon Curd and Fresh Berries

Nothing says summer quite like shortcake with fresh berries. In this version, mace adds its lively flavor to the biscuits, which are a superb foil for the tart lemon curd and sweet berries.

Makes 8 (3-inch) biscuits, 8 servings.

◆　◆　◆

Lemon Curd (page 136)

Shortcakes

1 cup all-purpose flour
2 teaspoons baking powder
¾ teaspoon ground mace
¼ teaspoon freshly grated nutmeg
¼ teaspoon salt
4 tablespoons (½ stick) unsalted butter, chilled, cut into small pieces

⅓ cup milk
1 teaspoon sugar

Assembly

½ cup heavy whipping cream
¼ teaspoon ground mace
2 cups fresh berries (strawberries, raspberries, blackberries, or blueberries), rinsed, hulled, and sliced (if necessary)

Lemon Curd

Prepare Lemon Curd as directed on page 136. Cover with plastic wrap and cool to room temperature. Refrigerate the lemon curd for at least 2 hours before using.

Shortcakes

Position a rack in the center of the oven. Preheat oven to 425F (220C). Line a baking sheet with parchment paper.

In the work bowl of a food processor fitted with a steel blade, combine the flour, baking powder, mace, nutmeg, and salt. Pulse briefly to mix. Add the butter and pulse until the butter is cut into very tiny pieces, about 1 minute. With the machine on, pour the milk through the feed tube and process just until the mixture is combined.

Turn the dough out onto a lightly floured surface and roll out to a ½-inch thickness. Using a 3-inch-round cutter, cut out circles. Transfer the circles to the baking sheet, leaving 1 inch of space between them. Gather up the scraps of dough, re-roll, and cut out. Sprinkle the tops of the circles with the sugar.

Bake until golden brown, about 15 minutes. Remove from the oven and cool the shortcakes on the baking sheet on a rack.

To assemble

Pour the whipping cream into the bowl of a stand mixer or a medium bowl. Using the wire-whip attachment or a hand-held mixer, whip the cream on medium speed until it is frothy. Add the mace and continue to whip the cream until it holds soft peaks, 2 to 3 minutes.

Split the shortcakes in half horizontally. Place the bottom halves on individual plates, top with 2 to 3 tablespoons of lemon curd, then 2 to 3 tablespoons of fresh berries. Place the top half of the shortcake on the berries and garnish with a dollop of whipped cream. Serve immediately.

Lemon-Mace Roll

A tart, creamy lemon filling accented with mace is the highlight of this cake. It's easy to prepare ahead in stages and makes several servings, so it's great for a family gathering, any festive occasion, or party.

Makes 1 (15-inch) rolled cake, 14 servings.

◆　◆　◆

Lemon Curd

2 large lemons
5 large egg yolks at room temperature
½ cup granulated sugar
4 tablespoons (½ stick) unsalted butter, melted

Cake

1 tablespoon unsalted butter for parchment paper
6 large eggs at room temperature
¾ cup superfine sugar (see Note, page 21)
Zest of 1 large lemon, finely minced
1½ teaspoons lemon extract

1 cup plus 2 tablespoons sifted cake flour
1½ teaspoons baking powder
¼ teaspoon salt
1 teaspoon ground mace
½ teaspoon finely ground cloves
¼ teaspoon ground ginger
Powdered sugar

Filling and assembling

2 cups heavy whipping cream
2 tablespoons superfine sugar
½ teaspoon ground mace
¼ teaspoon finely ground cloves
¼ teaspoon ground ginger

Lemon Curd

Zest the lemons and mince the zest very finely. Squeeze the juice from the lemons and strain it. In the top of a double boiler over medium heat, combine the egg yolks and sugar. Stir together to dissolve the sugar. Add the lemon juice and zest, then add the melted butter. Stir the mixture constantly over hot water until it thickens, 10 to 15 minutes. Pour the mixture into a bowl and cover. Cool to room temperature, then refrigerate until well chilled, at least 3 hours. (Lemon curd will keep in a well-covered container in the refrigerator 1 month.)

Cake

Position a rack in the center of the oven. Preheat oven to 375F (190C). Line a jelly-roll pan with a sheet of parchment paper and butter the paper evenly with the 1 tablespoon butter. Set the prepared pan aside.

In the bowl of a stand mixer or in a large bowl, using the wire-whip attachment or a hand-held mixer, whip the eggs on medium-high speed until they are frothy. Sprinkle with the sugar and continue to whip until the mixture is very thick, pale yellow, and holds a slowly dissolving ribbon as the beater is lifted, about 5 minutes. Blend in the lemon zest and lemon extract.

In a medium bowl, combine the flour, baking powder, salt, mace, cloves, and ginger. Fold this mixture into the eggs in 3 stages, blending thoroughly after each addition.

Turn the mixture into the prepared pan and use an offset spatula to spread it smoothly and evenly on the parchment paper. Bake the cake 15 to 18 minutes, until it's evenly colored and the top springs back when touched.

Remove the cake from the oven and use a sharp knife to loosen the edges. Lay a kitchen towel on a smooth surface, cover it with a sheet of parchment paper, and dust the parchment paper lightly with powdered sugar. Quickly turn the cake out onto the sugared parchment paper and gently peel the parchment paper off the back of the cake. Immediately roll up the cake and parchment paper tightly in the towel, starting from 1 long side. Let the cake cool completely, rolled in the towel. The cake can be prepared up to 2 days in advance. Wrap it tightly in plastic wrap and refrigerate until ready to use.

Filling and assembling

Whip the cream in a chilled bowl with a chilled beater until it holds soft peaks. Add the superfine sugar, mace, cloves, and ginger. Continue to whip the cream until it holds firm, but not stiff, peaks. Fold one-third of the whipped cream into the lemon curd. Reserve the remaining cream in the refrigerator for finishing.

Unroll the cake and remove the towel. Trim off any rough ends or edges. Use an offset spatula to evenly spread the lemon cream over the cake. Roll up the cake, using the parchment paper as a guide. To make a tight roll, pull part of the parchment paper over the top of the cake, leaving a piece to hold from underneath. Wedge a ruler against the cake and push away from yourself while pulling the bottom piece of parchment paper toward yourself. Carefully place the rolled cake on a rectangular serving plate, seam side down, and discard the parchment paper.

Fit a 14-inch pastry bag with a large closed-star tip (number 3 or 4) and partially fill with the remaining whipped cream. Pipe parallel rows of cream from one end of the cake to the other, starting from the bottom and moving toward the top. Turn the serving plate around and repeat piping the cream on the other side of the cake.

Refrigerate the cake until ready to serve or up to 3 hours. Cut the cake crosswise into serving pieces.

Granny Smith Apple Turnovers

I chose to use mace as the accent for these pastries, rather than cinnamon, which is traditionally used. My tasting panel enthusiastically concurred that it was a good choice. Pearl sugar, also called coarse or decorating sugar, is white sugar that has been processed into small, round balls resembling pearls, about 4 to 6 times larger than grains of granulated sugar. It is not used as a sweetener but as a garnish for sweets. It's sprinkled on the turnovers before they are baked to make a crisp topping. Pearl sugar is available in the baking sections of some supermarkets and in cookware shops. If you have trouble locating it, it's fine to substitute granulated sugar.

Makes 18 servings.

◆　◆　◆

1½ pounds (4 to 5) Granny Smith
　apples
3 tablespoons unsalted butter
⅓ cup superfine sugar (see Note, page
　21)
¾ teaspoon ground mace

½ teaspoon finely ground cloves
½ teaspoon cassia cinnamon
2 sheets frozen puff pastry (1 box),
　thawed
1 large egg at room temperature
2 tablespoons pearl sugar

Peel, quarter, and core apples, then cut them into 1-inch cubes. Melt the butter in a large skillet over medium heat. Add the apples, sprinkle with the sugar and spices, and stir until apples are thoroughly coated. Cook the apples, stirring gently, until they are soft, but not limp, 5 to 8 minutes. Drain the apples and cool slightly before using.

Position a rack in the center of the oven. Preheat oven to 425F (220C). Line 2 baking sheets with parchment paper.

Roll each sheet of puff pastry out on a lightly floured work surface to a 14-inch square. Cut each square into 3 equal lengthwise strips, then cut each strip into 3 equal squares to make 18 (4½-inch) squares. Brush any excess flour off of the squares.

Lightly beat the egg and brush 2 edges of adjoining sides of each square with egg. Place a heaping tablespoon of filling in the center of each square and fold the dough over the filling to form a triangle, making sure the edges are even. Gently press down on the edges to seal, then use a fork to form a pattern in the edges. Transfer the turnovers to the lined baking sheets, leaving about 1 inch of space between them. Brush the top of each turnover twice with the beaten egg, then sprinkle with pearl sugar.

Bake the turnovers 8 minutes. Switch the baking sheets and bake another 7 minutes. Reduce the oven temperature to 375F (190C). Switch the baking sheets again and bake the turnovers another 10 to 15 minutes, until golden brown. Transfer to a rack to cool.

The turnovers are best served warm. Once cool, store them in the refrigerator, tightly covered with plastic wrap. They can be reheated in a 300F (150C) oven just before serving.

Nutmeg Madeleines

These traditional, light, seashell-shaped little cakes were immortalized in the writings of French novelist Marcel Proust. They are baked in oval-shaped molds that have a ribbed, scallop-shell form, which gives them their characteristic appearance. This version of madeleines is enlivened with a generous helping of freshly grated nutmeg. Although the origins of madeleines are cloudy, they are thought to have originated in the town of Commercy, in the region of Lorraine, France, in the eighteenth century. They are named after Madeleine, the girl who brought them to the court and the attention of the Duke of Lorraine, who was the father-in-law of Louis XV.

Makes 36 madeleines.

◆　◆　◆

2 tablespoons unsalted butter, melted and cooled, for pans

2 tablespoons cake flour for pans

1½ (scant) cups sifted cake flour

½ teaspoon baking powder

Pinch of ground cloves

¼ teaspoon salt

1½ teaspoons freshly grated nutmeg

3 large eggs at room temperature

⅔ cup sugar

2 teaspoons lemon zest, finely minced

1½ sticks (12 tablespoons) unsalted butter, melted and cooled

Position a rack in the center of the oven. Preheat oven to 350F (175C). Lightly brush the inside of 3 (12-impression) madeleine pans with the 2 tablespoons butter. Dust them with the 2 tablespoons flour and tap out the excess.

Sift together the flour, baking powder, cloves, and salt into a medium bowl, then toss this mixture with the nutmeg.

Place the eggs in the bowl of a stand mixer or a medium bowl. Using the wire-whip attachment or a hand-held mixer, whip eggs until frothy. Add the sugar and beat the mixture at medium-high speed until it is very pale yellow and holds a slowly dissolving ribbon when the beater is lifted, about 5 minutes. Add the lemon zest and blend well.

Fold the flour mixture into the batter in 3 stages, then fold in the melted butter in 3 stages. Spoon the batter into the prepared pans, filling each impression only three-quarters full. Place the madeleine pans on baking sheets and bake 6 minutes. Switch the baking sheets and bake another 6 minutes, until the madeleines are puffed, lightly browned, and spring back when lightly touched on top.

Remove the pans from the oven and immediately turn them upside down. Shake gently to release the madeleines. Cool madeleines on racks. The madeleines will keep up to 4 days at room temperature in an airtight container.

Fresh Fig Tart

A creamy almond filling, enhanced with freshly grated nutmeg, encloses fresh figs in this elegant tart. Fresh figs have a short season, from the end of August into early September. They are always best when just picked, before they have a chance to dry out. If you have your own fig tree or a neighbor has one, you're in luck. If not, try to buy them from a roadside stand or a farmer's market.

Makes 1 (9½-inch) tart, 8 to 10 servings.

◆　◆　◆

Pastry (page 28) with ¼ teaspoon freshly grated nutmeg added

Filling

½ cup almond paste
⅓ cup granulated sugar
2 tablespoons unsalted butter, softened

¾ teaspoon freshly grated nutmeg
1 teaspoon almond extract
1 teaspoon orange liqueur
1 teaspoon orange zest, finely minced
2 large eggs at room temperature, lightly beaten
6 to 8 large ripe Black Mission figs

Pastry

Prepare dough as directed on page 28.

Position a rack in the center of the oven. Preheat oven to 350F (175C). Roll out dough on a lightly floured work surface to an 11-inch circle about ⅛ inch thick. Gently drape the pastry around the rolling pin and unroll into a 9½-inch fluted tart pan with a removable bottom. Carefully lift up the sides of the pastry and fit it into the bottom and against the sides of the tart pan. Trim off the excess pastry at the top of the pan. Chill the pastry shell while preparing the filling.

Filling

Combine the almond paste and sugar in the bowl of a stand mixer or in a medium bowl. Using the flat-beater attachment or a hand-held mixer, blend together thoroughly.

Add the butter and nutmeg and blend until smooth, 1 to 2 minutes. Mix the almond extract, orange liqueur, and orange zest with the eggs and add to the almond paste mixture. Beat until smooth.

Pour the filling into the pastry shell. Cut off the stems and carefully peel the figs. Slice each fig lengthwise into quarters. Place the fig quarters close together in the filling with the top ends toward the outside of the tart and the center of the figs facing up. Fill in the center of the tart with a slice or two of fig.

Bake the tart 40 to 45 minutes, until the filling is puffed, golden, and set. Cool in pan on a rack. The tart is best eaten while warm, but will last for up to 3 days at room temperature, tightly wrapped with foil.

Tuiles

Tuile is the French word for "tile." These classic thin, crisp, curved almond cookies take their name from their arched shapes, which resemble the red roof tiles used throughout the south of France. The cookies are formed by placing them over a rolling pin or into a curved mold while still warm. Other nuts can replace the almonds that are traditionally used. *Tuiles* are delicious on their own, as part of an assortment of cookies, or as an accompaniment to ice cream, sorbet, or mousse.

Makes about 24 cookies.

◆　　◆　　◆

1 tablespoon unsalted butter, softened, for pans

3½ tablespoons unsalted butter, softened

½ cup superfine sugar (see Note, page 21)

2 large egg whites at room temperature

½ teaspoon pure vanilla extract

⅓ cup all-purpose flour

1½ teaspoons freshly grated nutmeg

¼ teaspoon ground ginger

¼ teaspoon ground cloves

Pinch of salt

⅓ cup finely ground almonds (see Note, page 31)

⅓ to ½ cup raw sliced almonds

Line 2 baking sheets with parchment paper or foil. Use the 1 tablespoon butter to butter the parchment or foil. Position a rack in the center of the oven. Preheat oven to 425F (220C).

In the bowl of a stand mixer or a medium bowl, using the flat-beater attachment or a hand-held mixer, beat the butter until light and fluffy, about 2 minutes. Add the sugar and beat together until well blended, stopping and scraping down the sides of the bowl occasionally with a rubber spatula. Add the egg whites and blend until well combined, about 1 minute. Blend in the vanilla.

Combine the flour with the spices and salt and toss to blend. Add the flour mixture in 3 to 4 stages, blending well after each addition. Add the ground almonds and blend well.

Drop teaspoonfuls of the batter onto the prepared baking sheets, leaving 3 inches of space between them. Use the back of a spoon dipped in cold water to flatten the drops into circles about 2 to 3 inches in diameter. Sprinkle the sliced almonds on top of the circles.

Bake 1 sheet of the cookies at a time 6 to 8 minutes, until the outer edges are golden brown and the centers are set. Remove the baking sheet from the oven. Using a small offset spatula, work very quickly to lift the cookies off the baking pan. Drape the cookies over a rolling pin or place them in a *tuile* cookie mold and leave them to cool in their curved shape. If the cookies become difficult to remove from the baking pan, return the pan to the oven 30 to 45 seconds to warm. Bake the second pan of cookies and repeat the process of removing them from the pan and draping them over a rolling pin or placing them into the molds to form their curved shape.

The cookies will keep 5 to 6 days at room temperature in an airtight container.

Spicy Hazelnut Cookies

It is very difficult to eat only one or two of these delicate cookies. They seem to have a way of jumping into your mouth. But why try to resist something so scrumptious?

Makes about 60 cookies.

◆　　◆　　◆

1 cup raw hazelnuts, toasted (see Note, page 71)

1 tablespoon granulated sugar for pan

2 sticks (16 tablespoons) unsalted butter, softened

1 cup plus 2 tablespoons powdered sugar, sifted

1¾ teaspoons freshly grated nutmeg

¼ teaspoon ground cinnamon

¼ teaspoon ground cloves

½ teaspoon pure vanilla extract

Pinch of salt

2 cups plus 2 tablespoons all-purpose flour

1 large egg white at room temperature

8 ounces semisweet or bittersweet chocolate (optional), finely chopped

With a chef's knife, chop the hazelnuts roughly.

Sprinkle the tablespoon of granulated sugar inside a 10 × 7-inch glass baking pan. Place the softened butter in the bowl of a stand mixer or a medium bowl. Using the flat-beater attachment or a hand-held mixer, beat the butter until very soft and fluffy, about 2 minutes. Add the powdered sugar and beat until fluffy, about 3 minutes. Add the spices and vanilla and blend well, stopping and scraping down the sides of the bowl with a rubber spatula as needed.

Blend the salt into the flour and add the flour in 4 stages, mixing well after each addition. Add the egg white and blend in thoroughly. Add the hazelnuts and mix to combine.

Transfer the dough to the baking pan and with floured fingertips, form it into a rectangle to fit the width of the pan, 1 inch deep and about 8 inches long. Cover the dough tightly with plastic wrap and chill in the refrigerator overnight. (The dough may be frozen at this point if very well wrapped.)

Position racks in the upper and lower thirds of the oven. Preheat oven to 350F (175C). Line 3 baking sheets with parchment paper.

Cut the chilled dough into strips about 1¼ inches wide, then cut each strip into blocks about ½ inch wide. Place the blocks on the baking sheets with about 1 inch of space between them. Bake 8 minutes. Switch the baking pans and bake another 6 to 8 minutes, until light golden brown. Cool on baking sheets on racks.

To prepare the chocolate, if using, melt two-thirds of the chocolate in the top of a double boiler over hot, not simmering water, stirring frequently with a rubber spatula until smooth. Remove the double boiler from the heat, then remove the top pan of the double boiler and wipe it completely dry. Stir in the remaining chocolate in 3 batches, making sure that each batch is completely melted before adding the next. When all the chocolate has been added, the chocolate will be at the correct temperature. To test for this, place a dab of chocolate under your lower lip. It should feel comfortable, not hot and not cool.

Line 2 baking sheets with waxed paper. Dip each cookie into the chocolate on a diagonal about halfway to the center. Place the dipped cookies on the lined baking sheets, then place the baking sheets in the refrigerator 20 minutes to set the chocolate. Store the cookies 3 to 4 days at room temperature in an airtight container between layers of waxed paper.

Peek-a-Boo Tart

The French name for this tart is *jalousie*, which translates to mean "Venetian blinds," through which you can peek. This treat looks and tastes like it took all day to prepare, but the truth is it's a snap. The secret is to use store-bought puff pastry, which you can keep on hand in the freezer. The filling is a rich, classic frangipane (almond cream) accented with nutmeg.

Makes 1 (14 × 6-inch) tart, 9 to 10 servings.

◆　◆　◆

1 sheet frozen puff pastry, thawed

Filling

½ cup almond paste

⅓ cup sugar

2 tablespoons unsalted butter, softened

1 teaspoon freshly grated nutmeg

⅛ teaspoon freshly ground cloves

1 teaspoon freshly squeezed lemon juice

1 teaspoon lemon zest, finely minced

2 large eggs at room temperature,
　lightly beaten

Egg Wash

1 large egg at room temperature

1 teaspoon water

Glaze

2 tablespoons apricot preserves

2 teaspoons orange liqueur or water

Roll out the pastry on a lightly floured work surface to a large rectangle 15 × 13 inches. Cut the pastry lengthwise into 2 rectangles, one measuring 7 inches wide and the other measuring 6 inches wide. Line a baking sheet with parchment paper and place the wider rectangle on it. Place both pastry rectangles in the refrigerator while preparing the filling.

Filling

Combine the almond paste and sugar in the bowl of a stand mixer or a medium bowl. Using the flat-beater attachment or a hand-held mixer, blend together thoroughly. Add the butter and blend until smooth, 1 to 2 minutes. Stir in the nutmeg and cloves and blend. Mix the lemon juice and zest with the lightly beaten eggs and add to the almond paste mixture. Blend until smooth.

Remove the pastry rectangles from the refrigerator. Spread the filling down the center of the pastry on the baking sheet, leaving a ½-inch border all around. Dampen the pastry border with water and turn it in, making a rim around the filling.

Fold the second pastry rectangle in half lengthwise. Measure the opening of the filled half of the pastry and mark the second pastry as a guide. Working from the fold, cut 1¼-inch-long slits in the folded dough, spacing the cuts ½ inch apart. Lightly brush the edges of the filled pastry with water. Unfold the folded pastry over the filled pastry, centering it. Use a fork to press the edges together and create a design. Chill the pastry in the refrigerator 30 minutes. Position a rack in the center of the oven. Preheat oven to 375F (190C).

Egg Wash

Combine the egg and water in a small bowl and beat lightly with a fork to blend. Brush the top of the pastry twice with the egg wash.

Bake the pastry 30 minutes, until puffed and golden brown. Cool on baking sheet on a rack.

Glaze

Combine the apricot preserves and liqueur in a small saucepan. Bring to a boil over medium heat and boil 2 or 3 minutes. Strain the mixture through a sieve, pushing through as much of the fruit pulp as possible. Brush the top of the warm tart with the apricot glaze.

The tart is best served while warm. It will keep 3 days at room temperature, wrapped in foil. The pastry can be warmed in a 325F (165C) oven 15 minutes before serving.

Triple Berry Bundles

Make these in late summer when berries are at their sweetest and the largest selection is available. You can certainly use only one type of berry, but I like to mix them to get the different colors as well as flavors. These pretty pastries bring rave reviews whenever I serve them. They look so regal sitting on a plate surrounded by a pool of berry sauce. These appear to be a lot harder to prepare than they really are. My secret ingredient is store-bought puff pastry, which I always have on hand in the freezer.

Makes 12 bundles.

◆   ◆   ◆

2 cups mixed fresh berries (raspberries,
    blueberries, and blackberries)
¼ cup granulated sugar
1 teaspoon freshly grated nutmeg
Pinch of ground cloves
Pinch of ground cinnamon
3 sheets frozen puff pastry (1½ boxes),
    thawed
Powdered sugar for garnish

Sauce

1 cup fresh berries
1 tablespoon granulated sugar
1 teaspoon lemon zest, finely minced
1 teaspoon fresh lemon juice
2 teaspoons orange liqueur

Position racks in the upper and lower thirds of the oven. Preheat oven to 400F (205C). Line 2 baking sheets with parchment paper.

Place the berries in a medium bowl. Add the granulated sugar, nutmeg, cloves, and cinnamon and toss to blend well.

Roll out each sheet of puff pastry on a lightly floured work surface to a 12-inch square. Cut the square in half lengthwise and again in half horizontally, creating 4 smaller squares. Place about 2 tablespoons berry mixture in the center of each square. Bring the points of each square together in the center above the filling. Squeeze the pastry together just above the filling, then spread out the top edges. Place the bundles on the lined baking sheets with about 3 inches of space between them.

Bake 15 minutes, until golden brown. Cool bundles slightly on a rack. The bundles are best served while slightly warm.

Sauce

Pulse the berries in the work bowl of a food processor fitted with a steel blade until they are liquid, about 1 minute. Strain to remove the seeds. Transfer the berry puree to a small bowl and add the sugar, lemon zest, lemon juice, and orange liqueur. Blend together well.

To serve

Place a small pool of sauce on one side of the serving plate. Place the bundle near the sauce and dust the top with powdered sugar.

The bundles can be prepared up to 1 day in advance and kept at room temperature, tightly covered with foil. Warm them in a 325F (165C) oven 10 minutes before serving. The sauce can be prepared up to 4 days in advance and kept in a tightly covered container in the refrigerator.

Mixed Spice Cake

This moist cake has a delicate crumb. To dress it up I like to make it in a kugelhopf or Bundt pan with deeply grooved sections. The only decoration it needs is a light dusting of powdered sugar, making it festive enough to be served after the most sophisticated meal.

Makes 1 (9-inch) tube cake, 12 to 14 servings.

◆　　◆　　◆

2 teaspoons unsalted butter, melted and cooled, for pan

2 teaspoons all-purpose flour for pan

2 cups sifted cake flour

1 teaspoon baking powder

1 teaspoon ground cinnamon

1 teaspoon freshly grated nutmeg

½ teaspoon ground ginger

¼ teaspoon ground cloves

¼ teaspoon salt

2 sticks (16 tablespoons) unsalted butter, softened

1⅔ cups granulated sugar

5 large eggs at room temperature

1½ teaspoons pure vanilla extract

2 tablespoons powdered sugar

Position a rack in the center of the oven. Preheat oven to 325F (165C). Brush the insides of a 9-inch-round tube or kugelhopf pan with the 2 teaspoons butter, then lightly dust with the 2 teaspoons flour, and shake out the excess.

Sift together the cake flour, baking powder, spices, and salt into a medium bowl; set aside.

In the bowl of a stand mixer or a medium bowl, using the flat-beater attachment or a hand-held mixer, beat the butter until light and fluffy, about 2 minutes. Gradually add the sugar and beat the mixture until thoroughly blended. Add the eggs, one at a time, beating well after each addition. Stop and scrape down the sides and bottom of the bowl with a rubber spatula frequently. Add the vanilla and blend well. Blend in the dry ingredients in 3 stages, mixing well after each addition.

Spoon the batter into the prepared pan and bake 55 to 60 minutes, until a wooden pick inserted near the center comes out clean. Cool in pan on a rack 15 minutes. Then invert the pan onto the rack and leave a few minutes for the cake to drop out of the pan. Remove the pan and let the cake cool completely.

Dust the top of the cake with powdered sugar before serving. The cake will keep 3 days at room temperature, well wrapped in plastic wrap.

Black and White Pepper

. . . .

Here's the challenge; read it:
I warrant there's vinegar and pepper in't.

—William Shakespeare, *Twelfth Night*

He who has plenty of pepper may season
his food as he likes.

—Erasmus, *Adagia*

Once worth its weight in gold, pepper is also called the king of spices. It is the most ubiquitous spice in the Western world, found on practically every table. Pepper has been highly valued by many cultures and has been used for thousands of years. There are Sanskrit writings about pepper that date as far back as the fourth century B.C. In fact, the name "pepper" derives from the Sanskrit word *pippali*, meaning "berry," which became *piper* in Latin. Variations of this word are found in most languages.

The ancient Greeks and Romans used such large quantities of pepper that they made the Arab spice traders rich. When the Visigoths sacked Rome in A.D. 408, among other payments, Alaric demanded and received 3,000 pounds of pepper. Marco Polo wrote about the pepper plantations he visited during his travels to the west coast of India.

Of all spices, pepper had the most significant influence on world history. During the Middle Ages, pepper was so valuable that it was used to pay taxes, rents, and dowries. It was the search for pepper that spurred Vasco da Gama and other Europeans to look for sea routes to the east. The Dutch and the Venetians battled for control of the pepper trade. It was Pierre Poivre ("pepper" in French) who broke the pepper monopoly by planting trees on the island of Bourbon, today known as Reunion.

Today pepper is easily found in markets everywhere and it is inexpensive. It is a kitchen staple in Western countries and is used to some degree in most cuisines. Pepper is used primarily for savory dishes but is often used as an ingredient in desserts.

Lore and Myths
◆ ◆ ◆

Pepper was thought to be a digestive aid. It was also used as a stimulant, a diuretic, and an aphrodisiac. It has been used as a preservative for meats for hundreds of years.

Characteristics
◆ ◆ ◆

Pepper is the berry of the *Piper nigrum* plant, a tropical perennial climbing vine that has dark-green, broad, oval leaves and clusters of tiny white flowers. The round, pea-sized, wrinkled berries grow in spikes of twenty to thirty. Black and white peppercorns come from the same plant. The black peppercorn is less ripe than the white. Black peppercorns have a shriveled outer surface, while white peppercorns are smooth.

Besides whole peppercorns, pepper is also available ground in various textures, from roughly cracked to fine. The grinds are defined by the size of the mesh on the screen used to sift them.

Where and How It's Grown
• • •

Pepper is native to Malabar, on the west coast of India, and India is still the world's biggest producer. Pepper grows only in tropical climates within 20 degrees of the Equator. Besides India, today pepper is grown in Indonesia, Malaysia, Vietnam, Sri Lanka, and Brazil.

There are at least thirteen distinct types of black peppercorns, named for their place of origin or the port from which they are shipped. Tellicherry and Malabar come from India, Lampong from Indonesia, and Sarawak from Malaysia.

The vines of pepper plants are trained to grow up stakes or the trunks of shade trees on coffee plantations. They start to produce berries at about 7 or 8 years of age and continue for up to 20 years. The berries of the pepper plant are green when immature and begin to turn red when ripe. The pepper berries are harvested twice a year, in spring and fall.

Black peppercorns are processed from the immature berries that are picked and fermented for a few days before they are sun-dried. As they dry, their outer skin shrivels and they turn black. White peppercorns are processed from ripe berries that are soaked in water to remove their outer skin, then sun-dried until they turn creamy white. Muntok, an island near Sumatra, produces the finest white pepper and the only white pepper to be named by its origin.

Pink peppercorns are not true pepper. They are the fruit of *Schinus terebinthifolius*, a South American tree. They are usually combined in a mixture with black and white peppercorns.

Peppercorns are graded according to size. Generally the larger the berry, the more flavorful.

How It Tastes and Smells
• • •

Pepper itself is used to describe the flavor of many spices and dishes. It has a strong, penetrating, pungent flavor and aroma. The flavor and aroma come from its essential oil and *piperin*, an alkaloid crystalline substance. White pepper is less pungent and has a finer, less harsh flavor than black pepper.

Of the various types of black pepper, Tellicherry from India, considered the most superior, has a complex flavor, rich and bold with a sweet, fruity, spicy aroma. These peppercorns are allowed to ripen completely before they are harvested, making them larger, sweeter, and more flavorful. Malabar pepper is produced on a larger scale than Tellicherry. It has a hotter, more biting, zesty flavor with a spicy, woody aroma. Lampong pepper, which comes from Indonesia, is produced on a very large scale. It has a softer, less complex, more woody flavor than Malabar. Sarawak, from Malaysia, is used primarily in Britain. It is smaller and lighter in color than the other peppers. Its aroma is not as pungent, nor its flavor as biting.

Use and Preparation
◆ ◆ ◆

In desserts, pepper is used ground or cracked. White pepper is used when the dark specks of black pepper are undesirable, such as in soufflés and some sauces, and when a softer pepper flavor is preferred.

Tips for Choosing and Storing
◆ ◆ ◆

Buy whole peppercorns and ground pepper from a source with a high turnover to ensure freshness.

Because pepper loses its flavor so quickly once it is ground, grind whole peppercorns in a pepper mill as needed. Pepper can also be crushed with a rolling pin. Place whole peppercorns in a plastic bag and run the rolling pin over them until they are the desired consistency.

Store whole peppercorns in an airtight glass jar or a pepper mill in a cool, dark, dry place. Whole peppercorns will last for years. Store ground pepper the same as whole peppercorns for up to 3 months. Ground pepper loses its flavor rapidly.

Pfeffernüesse

These classic German Christmas cookies translate as "pepper nuts." Although several spices are used in the recipe, it's the use of pepper that they are known for.

Makes about 84 (1-inch) cookies.

◆　　◆　　◆

¾ cup honey

½ cup dark molasses

4 tablespoons (½ stick) unsalted butter,
    softened

¼ cup firmly packed golden brown
    sugar

4 cups all-purpose flour

1 teaspoon baking powder

1 teaspoon baking soda

1 teaspoon ground allspice

1 teaspoon freshly grated nutmeg

¾ teaspoon ground cardamom

½ teaspoon freshly grated black pepper

¼ teaspoon anise seeds, crushed

½ teaspoon salt

Powdered sugar

Place the honey, molasses, and butter in a 1-quart saucepan. Warm over medium heat until the butter is melted. Transfer the mixture to the bowl of a stand mixer or a medium bowl. Using the flat-beater attachment or a hand-held mixer, blend in the brown sugar.

Sift together the flour, baking powder, baking soda, and allspice. Blend in the remaining spices and salt. With the mixer on low speed, sprinkle the dry ingredients into the liquid, then blend together thoroughly. Cover the bowl tightly with plastic wrap and chill in the refrigerator 30 minutes.

Position racks in the upper and lower thirds of the oven. Preheat oven to 350F (175C). Line 3 baking sheets with parchment paper.

Pinch off walnut-size pieces of the dough and roll into 1-inch balls with your hands. Place the balls on the baking sheets. Refrigerate 1 sheet of the cookies while the others are baking. Bake cookies 8 minutes. Switch baking sheets and bake another 5 to 7 minutes, until firm. Cool on baking sheets on racks.

Dust the cookies lightly with powdered sugar. Store up to 5 days at room temperature in an airtight container.

Black Pepper Biscotti

Pepper gives the surprise bite in these unusual biscotti. Be sure to use freshly cracked pepper for the most pungent flavor. An easy way to crack peppercorns is to place them in a plastic bag and use a rolling pin to crush them. As with other types of biscotti, these keep very well.

Makes 42 biscotti.

◆   ◆   ◆

2¼ cups all-purpose flour

1½ teaspoons baking powder

¼ teaspoon salt

2 teaspoons coarsely cracked or ground
    black pepper

1 stick (8 tablespoons) unsalted butter,
    softened

¾ cup sugar

Zest of 1 medium lemon, finely minced

2 teaspoons pure vanilla extract

2 large eggs at room temperature,
    lightly beaten

Position a rack in the center of the oven. Preheat oven to 325F (165C). Line a baking sheet with parchment paper.

Place the flour, baking powder, salt, and pepper in a medium bowl and stir together to blend well.

In the bowl of a stand mixer or a medium bowl, using the flat-beater attachment or a hand-held mixer, beat the butter until light and fluffy. Add the sugar and beat until thoroughly blended, then blend in the lemon zest. Stir the vanilla into the eggs, then add and mix well. Add the dry ingredients in 4 stages and mix until well blended, about 1 minute.

Dust your hands and a work surface with flour. Divide the dough into 3 equal pieces. Roll each piece of dough into a log about 2 inches wide and 10 to 12 inches long. Transfer each log to the baking sheet, leaving space between them.

Bake the biscotti 25 minutes, until lightly browned and set. Cool on baking sheet on a rack 5 minutes. Slice each log on the diagonal into ½-inch-thick slices. Then place the slices on their sides on the baking sheet. Return the baking sheet to the oven for 10 to 15 minutes, until the biscotti are firm. Cool on baking sheet on a rack.

Store the biscotti up to 3 weeks at room temperature in an airtight container.

Baked Figs with Black Pepper

Although it seems like an unusual combination, fresh figs, honey, and black pepper are traditionally found in the Middle East. I created this dessert to highlight these three elements.

Makes 4 servings.

◆ ◆ ◆

8 large ripe fresh figs

½ tablespoon unsalted butter

¼ cup superfine sugar (see Note, page 21)

⅔ cup heavy whipping cream

1 heaping tablespoon honey

¾ teaspoon freshly ground black pepper, preferably Tellicherry

Position a rack in the center of the oven. Preheat oven to 375F (190C). Rinse the figs, pat them dry on paper towels and cut off their stems. Slice the figs in half lengthwise and place in a 2-quart baking dish.

Melt the butter in a 1-quart saucepan over low heat. Add the sugar, increase heat to medium, and cook, stirring, until the sugar melts and turns a light caramel color, 3 to 4 minutes. At the same time warm the cream over medium heat in a separate small saucepan. Pour the warm cream into the sugar mixture, stirring constantly with a long-handled wooden spoon. Be careful, as the cream may bubble and foam. Keep stirring the mixture to remove any lumps that may have formed, then blend in the honey.

Pour the mixture over the figs, then scatter ½ teaspoon pepper over them. Bake the figs 15 minutes, until they are soft when pierced with a knife. Cool briefly on a rack.

For each serving place 4 fig halves on a plate and spoon some of the sauce over them. Sprinkle the remaining ¼ teaspoon of pepper over the figs.

Panforte di Siena

This classic Italian sweet, a cross between a cake and a candy, is a very dense, rich confection loaded with nuts, dried fruit, and spices. Panforte has become a traditional Italian Christmas confection. Its origins are cloudy, but it seems to date back to the very early Middle Ages, when the first references to it are found in Siena. It showcases the many spices that were available at that time in history, particularly white pepper, its most unusual ingredient. Panforte keeps very well, which may be the reason that the Crusaders took it with them on their voyages.

Makes 1 (9¹/₂-inch) cake, 16 to 18 servings.

◆   ◆   ◆

1 cup raw hazelnuts

1 cup unblanched whole almonds

1 tablespoon unsalted butter for pan

1½ cups finely chopped candied orange peel

½ cup finely chopped candied lemon peel or candied citron

½ cup all-purpose flour

3 tablespoons unsweetened Dutch-processed cocoa powder

Zest of 1 small lemon, finely minced

1 teaspoon ground cinnamon

¼ teaspoon ground cloves

¼ teaspoon ground coriander

¼ teaspoon freshly ground nutmeg

Large pinch of freshly ground white pepper

¾ cup granulated sugar

¾ cup honey

2 tablespoons unsalted butter

Powdered sugar

Position a rack in the center of the oven. Preheat oven to 350F (175C). Place the hazelnuts on a jelly-roll pan and toast in the oven 15 to 18 minutes, until the skins split and the nuts turn light golden brown. Remove the pan from the oven and cool on a rack 10 minutes, then rub the nuts between your hands or in a towel to help remove the skins.

Place the almonds on a jelly-roll pan and toast in the oven 10 to 12 minutes, shaking the pan every 4 minutes. Cool almonds in the pan on a rack. Reduce oven temperature to 300F (150C).

Cut a sheet of rice paper (see Note, below) to fit the bottom of a 9½-inch-round springform pan. Use some of the 1 tablespoon butter to butter the bottom and halfway up the sides of the pan, then place the rice paper round in the bottom of the pan and butter it. Set the pan aside.

In a 2-quart bowl, combine the candied peels, flour, cocoa, lemon zest, and spices. In the work bowl of a food processor fitted with a steel blade, combine the hazelnuts and almonds. Pulse to chop the nuts coarsely, about 45 seconds, or use a chef's knife to chop the nuts. Add the chopped nuts to the flour mixture and toss everything together to blend well.

In a heavy 1-quart saucepan, combine the sugar, honey, and butter. Bring the mixture to a boil, then brush down the sides of the pan with a pastry brush dipped in water. Cook the mixture until it registers 246F (120C) on a candy thermometer, about 12 minutes.

Immediately pour the cooked sugar syrup into the flour mixture. Working rapidly, stir the sugar syrup into the mixture until thoroughly blended. Quickly turn the mixture into the prepared pan. With damp hands, press the top of the cake out to the edges of the pan, and smooth and even the top.

Bake the panforte 30 minutes. It will not look set, but will firm up as it cools. Remove the pan from the oven and cool completely on a rack. Use a thin-bladed small knife to loosen the panforte from the sides of the pan. Release the sides of the springform pan and remove them. Dust the top of the panforte heavily with powdered sugar. Use a sharp knife to cut the panforte into very thin slices.

The panforte will keep up to 1 month at room temperature in an airtight container.

Note

Rice paper, an edible, translucent paper, is often used to line baking sheets when baking delicate cookies. The rice paper will stick to the bottom of the cookies as they are baked. Rice paper is available from Asian markets.

White Pepper Ice Cream

You may wrinkle your nose at the thought of pepper in ice cream, but don't be too hasty. This ice cream has a lush, creamy texture and a rich, deep flavor. The pepper gives it a subtle bite that makes you take another taste, and another.

Makes about 3 cups, 6 servings.

◆　◆　◆

1½ cups heavy whipping cream　　1 tablespoon white peppercorns
1 cup milk　　　　　　　　　　　5 large egg yolks at room temperature
1 vanilla bean　　　　　　　　　½ cup sugar

Combine the cream and milk in a heavy 3-quart saucepan. Split the vanilla bean lengthwise and scrape the seeds from the pods. Place both the seeds and pod in the liquid. Crush the peppercorns coarsely either by using a mortar and pestle or placing them in a plastic bag and using a rolling pin. Place them in the liquid and bring the mixture to a boil over medium heat. Remove from heat, cover the mixture, and let it infuse 20 minutes.

In the bowl of a stand mixer or a medium bowl, using the wire-whip attachment or a hand-held mixer, whip the egg yolks and sugar together until they are pale yellow and hold a slowly dissolving ribbon when the beater is lifted, about 5 minutes.

Reheat the cream mixture to just below the boiling point. Reduce the mixer speed to low and slowly pour 1 cup of the hot cream mixture into the egg and sugar mixture. Stir to blend well, then return the mixture to the cream mixture in the saucepan. Reduce the heat to low and stir the mixture constantly with a wooden spoon until the mixture reaches 185F (85C) on a candy thermometer, 5 to 8 minutes. At this point the mixture will be thickened and when a line is drawn through the custard on the back of the spoon it leaves a clearly defined path.

Strain the mixture into a 2-quart bowl. Cover the mixture tightly with plastic wrap, cool to room temperature, then chill in the refrigerator several hours or overnight. Process the mixture in an ice cream maker according to the manufacturer's instructions.

Store the ice cream in a covered container in the freezer for up to 1 month. If it is frozen solid, soften it in the refrigerator for a few hours before serving.

Poppy Seeds

Visions for those too tired to sleep
These seeds case a film over eyes which weep.

—Amy Lowell, "Sword Blades and Poppy Seed"

One of the most ancient plants, the poppy has been grown for thousands of years, both for its seeds and for the narcotic aspects of opium. The ancient Egyptians valued opium for its medicinal properties. It wasn't until the nineteenth century that opium's use as a narcotic was exploited. The ancient Greeks and Romans also used poppy seeds in their cuisines and for medicines. Poppy seeds have long been a staple in India, where they were introduced by Mohammed's missionaries in the seventh century. The Middle East, too, has warmly embraced poppy seeds where they have found their way into many cuisines.

Today poppy seeds are used in both sweet and savory dishes, especially in breads, cakes, and cookies in many eastern and northern European countries, in India, and in many countries of the Middle East. They are easy to find in many markets but are not inexpensive. In India the white seeds are crushed to form a paste, which is most often used as a thickener. The brown Turkish seeds are ground to a paste and used in many dishes, especially in halvah, a traditional confection.

Poppy seeds are the filling in Hamantaschen, a traditional Jewish pastry made during the festival of Purim, which commemorates the defeat of the wicked Haman, who plotted the death of the Persian Jews.

Lore and Myths
◆ ◆ ◆

Poppy seeds were thought to have magical properties. If they were placed in your shoes, you would become invisible, especially to your creditors. They were also thought to have sleep-inducing capabilities, and it was believed that the juice would help eliminate warts. It was also used to treat malaria, dysentery, and cholera.

Throughout history the red poppy flower has been the symbol of fallen warriors. It is an emblem used to commemorate Armistice Day in the United States.

Characteristics
◆ ◆ ◆

Poppy seeds are the dried mature seeds of *Papaver somniferum*, an annual plant that reaches a height of 3 feet. They come in three colors: slate blue-gray, which is most common to Europe; ivory, found in India; and brown, found usually in Turkey. The seeds are kidney shaped and very tiny, measuring only about $\frac{1}{25}$ inch in length. Their outer surface has slightly raised ridges that are difficult to see with the naked eye. It takes about 900,000 poppy seeds to make 1 pound.

Where and How It's Grown
◆ ◆ ◆

The poppy is native to China, Asia, and the eastern Mediterranean. Today it is grown in Canada, China, France, Iran, India, Turkey, and Holland, which is reputed to grow the finest quality.

Poppy seeds grow in oval seed heads on the plants, which have tall, branched stems with central ribs and flowers that range in color from creamy white to lavender. Opium is produced by slitting the seed heads before they are ripe, allowing the liquid surrounding the seeds to seep out. The seeds themselves do not contain any narcotic qualities. When ripe, the seed heads are ribbed on the outside and topped with a stigma. On the inside are several separate areas that hold the tiny seeds. The ripe seeds are harvested by cutting down the plants, removing the capsules, and drying them before they burst open and scatter the seeds.

How It Tastes and Smells

◆ ◆ ◆

Poppy seeds have a sweet nutty flavor, a crunchy texture, and a mild nutty aroma. Poppy seed oil has a slight almond flavor.

Use and Preparation

◆ ◆ ◆

In desserts, poppy seeds are used both whole and ground. A light, delicate oil that is pressed from the seeds is used in cooking and for salads.

The whole seeds can be crushed in a spice or coffee grinder or with a mortar and pestle. A special tool called a poppy seed mill is also used. The nutty flavor of the seeds can be enhanced by lightly toasting before use.

Tips for Choosing and Storing

◆ ◆ ◆

Buy poppy seeds from a source with a high turnover to ensure freshness. Poppy seed paste is sometimes available in cans in supermarkets. Be sure to check the can for the expiration date.

Because of the high natural oil content of poppy seeds, it is best to store them in an airtight container in the refrigerator during the summer. During other seasons, store them in an airtight glass jar in a cool, dark, dry place. If stored properly, they will last up to 3 years.

Lemon–Poppy Seed Pound Cake

Lemon is the perfect counterpoint to poppy seeds. It adds just the right touch of tartness. Here the two ingredients are combined to make a rich, moist pound cake. It's perfect on its own for afternoon coffee or tea or divine when accompanied by a dollop of whipped cream, a scoop of your favorite ice cream, or a fresh fruit sauce, such as raspberry.

Makes 1 (9-inch) loaf, 12 servings.

◆　◆　◆

1 tablespoon unsalted butter for pan
1 tablespoon cake flour for pan
2 cups plus 3 tablespoons sifted cake flour
1 teaspoon baking powder
¼ teaspoon salt
2 sticks (16 tablespoons) unsalted butter, softened
1½ cups superfine sugar (see Note, page 21)

4 large eggs at room temperature
3 tablespoons milk
Zest of 1 large lemon, finely minced
2 teaspoons fresh lemon juice
1 tablespoon lemon extract
3 tablespoons poppy seeds
Powdered sugar

Position a rack in the center of the oven. Preheat oven to 325F (165C). With the 1 tablespoon of butter, generously butter the inside of a 9 × 5-inch loaf pan. Dust the inside of the pan with the 1 tablespoon cake flour, then tap out the excess. Set the pan aside.

Sift together the cake flour, baking powder, and salt; set aside.

In the bowl of a stand mixer or a medium bowl, using a flat-beater attachment or a hand-held beater, beat the butter until it is fluffy, about 2 minutes. Gradually add the sugar and continue beating until thoroughly blended, about 2 more minutes, stopping and scraping down the sides of the bowl with a rubber spatula occasionally.

Add the eggs, one at a time, beating well to blend after each addition. Combine the milk with the lemon zest, lemon juice, and lemon extract. Add to the batter and blend well.

With the mixer on low speed, slowly add the dry ingredients to the batter, stopping and scraping down the sides of the bowl with a rubber spatula occasionally as the batter is mixing. Add the poppy seeds and blend well. When the batter is thoroughly mixed, transfer it to the prepared loaf pan. Use the rubber spatula to smooth the top.

Bake the cake 1 hour and 12 minutes, until the top is risen, the cake is golden brown, and a wooden pick inserted into the center has a few crumbs clinging to it.

Cool the cake in the pan on a rack 15 minutes. Run a thin-bladed knife around the inside rim of the loaf pan to loosen the cake. Turn the cake out of the pan, then turn it right side up. Cool cake completely on the rack. Dust the top of the cake generously with powdered sugar before serving.

The cake will keep 4 days at room temperature, well wrapped in foil, or it can be frozen. If frozen, defrost it in the refrigerator 24 hours before serving.

Poppy Seed Cake

It's best to wait for a few hours after baking to eat this yummy cake, loaded with poppy seeds, because as it rests, its intriguing flavor develops. The only decoration the cake needs is a light dusting of powdered sugar, but a spectacular accompaniment is a scoop of Vanilla Bean Ice Cream (page 208).

Makes 1 (9-inch) tube cake, 12 to 14 servings.

◆　◆　◆

2 teaspoons unsalted butter, melted and cooled, for pan

2 teaspoons all-purpose flour for pan

1 cup poppy seeds

⅓ cup honey

¼ cup water

2 sticks (16 tablespoons) unsalted butter, softened

1½ cups granulated sugar

4 large eggs at room temperature, separated

1 teaspoon pure vanilla extract

1 cup sour cream

2½ cups all-purpose flour

1 teaspoon baking soda

½ teaspoon salt

¼ teaspoon cream of tartar

2 tablespoons powdered sugar

Position a rack in the center of the oven. Preheat oven to 350F (175C). Brush the insides of a 9-inch-round tube or kugelhopf pan with the 2 teaspoons butter, then lightly dust with the 2 teaspoons flour, and shake out the excess.

Combine the poppy seeds, honey, and water in a heavy-bottomed 1-quart saucepan over low heat and cook, stirring frequently with a wooden spoon, until the poppy seeds absorb the liquid, about 5 minutes.

In the bowl of a stand mixer or in a medium bowl, using the flat-beater attachment or a hand-held mixer, beat the butter until light and fluffy, about 2 minutes. Add the granulated sugar and beat until thoroughly blended. Add the poppy seed mixture and stir to blend.

Add the egg yolks, one at a time, to the poppy seed mixture, blending well after each addition. Add the vanilla and sour cream and blend the mixture well.

Sift together the flour, baking soda, and salt. Add the dry ingredients to the poppy seed mixture in 3 or 4 stages, blending well after each addition.

In a greasefree medium bowl, using the wire-whip attachment or a hand-held mixer, whip the egg whites with the cream of tartar on medium-high speed until they hold stiff, but not dry, peaks. Stir one-quarter of the whites into the poppy seed mixture, then fold in the remaining whites in 3 stages.

Spoon the batter into the pan and use a rubber spatula to smooth and even the top. Bake 1 hour and 5 minutes, until a wooden pick inserted near the center comes out clean. Cool cake in pan on a rack 15 minutes. Then invert the pan onto the rack, remove the pan, and let the cake cool completely.

Dust the top of the cake with powdered sugar before serving. The cake will keep 4 days at room temperature, well wrapped in plastic wrap.

Poppy Seed Scones

Poppy seeds give an unusual texture to these scones. Serve them warm with afternoon tea or coffee accompanied by a variety of jams or by softly whipped cream flavored with finely minced lemon zest.

Makes 8 (3½-inch) wedges or 12 (2½-inch) rounds.

◆　◆　◆

1¾ (scant) cups sifted cake flour

4 tablespoons sugar

¾ teaspoon baking powder

¼ teaspoon baking soda

Pinch of salt

1 tablespoon poppy seeds

Zest of 1 large lemon

Zest of ½ large orange

4 tablespoons (½ stick) unsalted butter, cut into small pieces, softened

1 tablespoon fresh lemon juice

1 tablespoon fresh orange juice

⅓ cup buttermilk

1 large egg at room temperature

Position a rack in the center of the oven. Preheat oven to 425F (220C). Line a baking sheet with parchment paper.

Place the flour, 3 tablespoons of the sugar, baking powder, baking soda, salt, poppy seeds, lemon and orange zests in the work bowl of a food processor fitted with a steel blade. Pulse for a few seconds to blend the mixture. Add the butter and pulse until the butter is cut into tiny pieces, about 1 minute.

Combine the lemon juice, orange juice, and buttermilk in a liquid measuring cup. With the machine on, pour the liquid through the feed tube. Process just until the dough holds together, about 20 seconds. It should be slightly lumpy.

Turn the dough out onto a lightly floured work surface and knead until it is smooth, about 30 seconds. Roll the dough out to an 8-inch circle or a rectangle about ½ inch thick. Cut the dough circle into 8 wedges with a sharp knife, or use a 2½-inch-round cutter to cut circles from the dough rectangle.

Transfer the scones to the lined baking sheet, leaving 1 inch of space between them. Lightly beat the egg with a fork, then brush the tops of the scones 2 times with the beaten egg. Sprinkle the scones with the remaining 1 tablespoon of sugar.

Bake the scones 10 minutes, until the tops are lightly browned. Cool scones slightly on a rack.

Serve the scones warm or at room temperature. They can be reheated before serving in a 350F (175C) oven. Store the scones up to 4 days at room temperature, tightly covered with foil.

Poppy Seed Turnovers

These crispy turnovers are like individual strudels with a classic poppy seed filling enclosed in layers of buttery, rich phyllo dough.

Makes 12 turnovers.

◆ ◆ ◆

½ cup whole unblanched almonds

½ cup poppy seeds

¼ cup water

3 tablespoons honey

Zest of ½ large lemon, finely minced or grated

4 tablespoons (½ stick) unsalted butter, melted

½ pound (½ box) frozen phyllo pastry dough, thawed

Powdered sugar

Position a rack in the center of the oven. Preheat oven to 325F (165C). Place the almonds in a shallow baking pan and toast 5 to 8 minutes, stirring after 4 minutes, until light golden brown. Cool on a rack, then chop coarsely. Increase oven temperature to 375F (190C). Line a baking sheet with parchment paper and set aside.

In a heavy 1-quart saucepan, combine the poppy seeds, water, and honey over medium-high heat. Bring to a boil and cook 5 minutes. Cool slightly, then blend in the lemon zest and almonds.

Unroll the phyllo pastry dough and cut lengthwise in half. Roll up one-half of the dough, rewrap, and refreeze. Cut the remaining phyllo dough lengthwise in half again. Stack the phyllo and cover with a damp cloth.

Remove a stack of 4 sheets of phyllo dough. Brush the top sheet of the phyllo dough with melted butter. Place 1 tablespoon of the poppy seed mixture in the lower left hand corner. Fold the left hand corner (of all 4 sheets) up to the right side of the dough, forming a triangle. Brush the dough with butter and continue to fold it in a triangle shape, alternating folding to the left side, up, then to the right side. At the end of the phyllo dough rectangle, brush the entire triangle with butter and place on the baking sheet. Repeat with remaining dough and filling.

Bake the triangles 18 to 20 minutes, until golden brown. Cool on baking sheet on a rack. Dust the tops of the turnovers generously with powdered sugar before serving. The turnovers will keep up to 3 days at room temperature, tightly covered with foil. They can be warmed in a 300F (150C) oven 10 minutes before serving.

Poppy Seed and Dried Cherry Tart

The tartness of dried cherries enhances the poppy seeds in this unique tart. Serve this with a dollop of whipped cream or a scoop of Vanilla Bean Ice Cream (page 208).

Makes 1 (12 × 8-inch) tart, 12 servings.

◆ ◆ ◆

Pastry (page 102)

Filling

3 large eggs at room temperature,
 separated

⅔ cup superfine sugar (see Note, page
 21)

⅓ cup dried Montmorency cherries,
 coarsely chopped

Zest of 1 large lemon, finely minced

⅔ cup poppy seeds

Pinch of salt

1 teaspoon lemon extract

¼ teaspoon cream of tartar

Garnish

Powdered sugar

Pastry

Prepare and chill dough as directed on page 102.

If the pastry dough is very cold, let it sit at room temperature until it is pliable, but not soft, then knead it briefly before using. Roll out the pastry dough on a lightly floured work surface to a large rectangle about 15 × 10 inches. Gently drape the pastry around the rolling pin and unroll into a 12 × 8½-inch fluted tart pan with a removable bottom. Carefully lift up the sides of the pastry and fit it into the bottom and against the sides of the tart pan. Trim off the excess pastry at the top of the pan.

Position a rack in the center of the oven. Preheat oven to 375F (190C). Line the pastry shell with a large piece of foil and weight with pie weights. Bake 15 minutes, remove the foil and weights and bake another 8 minutes. Remove from the oven and cool slightly.

Filling

Place the egg yolks in the bowl of a stand mixer or a medium bowl. Using the wire-whip attachment or a hand-held mixer, beat egg yolks lightly. Add the sugar and beat until the mixture is very thick and holds a slowly dissolving ribbon as the beater is lifted, about 5 minutes. Add the dried cherries, lemon zest, poppy seeds, salt, and lemon extract and blend thoroughly.

In a greasefree bowl with a clean beater, whip the egg whites and cream of tartar until the whites hold firm, but not stiff, peaks. Stir one-quarter of the whites into the yolk mixture. Fold in the remaining whites in 3 stages, blending until there are no white streaks.

Place the tart pan on a jelly-roll pan. Pour the filling into the shell, using a rubber spatula to even the top. Bake 20 minutes, until the filling is puffed, set, and light golden. Cool in pan on a rack. Dust the top of the tart with powdered sugar before serving.

The tart will keep up to 4 days at room temperature, tightly wrapped in foil.

Poppy Seed—Citrus Cheesecake

Lemon and orange zest give fresh citrus undertones to this lush cheesecake. This is very rich, so it's best to serve thin slices, which makes it perfect for a crowd.

Makes 1 (9½-inch) cake, 14 to 18 servings.

◆ ◆ ◆

1 tablespoon unsalted butter, softened, for pan

Crust

1½ cups crushed graham cracker crumbs
½ cup walnuts
2 tablespoons sugar
½ teaspoon ground ginger
½ stick (4 tablespoons) unsalted butter, melted

Filling

2 pounds cream cheese, softened
1¼ cups sugar
4 large eggs at room temperature
1 cup sour cream
½ cup heavy whipping cream
Zest of 1 large lemon, finely minced
Zest of 1 medium orange, finely minced
1 tablespoon lemon extract
1 teaspoon orange extract
1 teaspoon pure vanilla extract
⅓ cup poppy seeds

Crust

Position a rack in the center of the oven. Preheat oven to 325F (165C). Using the 1 tablespoon of butter, generously coat the inside and bottom of a 9½-inch springform pan.

In the work bowl of a food processor fitted with a steel blade, combine the graham cracker crumbs, walnuts, sugar, and ginger. Pulse the mixture until it is finely ground, about 2 minutes. With the machine on, pour the melted butter through the feed tube. Continue to process until the mixture holds together. Transfer the crust to the springform pan and press it evenly over the bottom and up the sides. Chill the crust while preparing the cake.

Filling

In the bowl of a stand mixer or a medium bowl, using the flat-beater attachment or a hand-held mixer, beat the cream cheese until fluffy, about 2 minutes. Add the sugar and blend well, stopping and scraping down the sides and bottom of the bowl with a long-handled rubber spatula as necessary. Add the eggs, one at a time, beating well after each addition. Add the sour cream and whipping cream and blend well. Stir in the lemon zest and orange zest, then add the extracts and the poppy seeds. Blend the mixture thoroughly.

Wrap a double layer of heavy-duty foil around the bottom and up the sides of the springform pan, then pour the batter into the chilled crust. Place the springform pan in a larger pan that can easily hold up to 1 inch of water. Place the pans in the oven and carefully pour boiling water into the bottom pan, extending halfway up the sides of the springform pan.

Bake the cake 1 hour and 15 minutes. Turn off oven and hold the door ajar with a wooden spoon. Leave the cake in the oven 1 hour, then remove the cake from the water bath and cool to room temperature on a rack. Cover the cake with foil and chill in the refrigerator at least 4 hours or overnight.

To unmold the cake, run a thin-bladed knife carefully around the inner edge of the pan and gently remove the outside rim of the pan. Store the cake up to 1 week in the refrigerator, loosely tented with foil.

Saffron

...Pale in a saffron mist...

—Conrad Aiken, *Senlin*, morning song

Saffron is the world's most expensive spice because it is harvested and processed entirely by hand. It is also one of the world's oldest spices. Its documented use goes back to the ancient Assyrians. Saffron is mentioned in the Song of Solomon in the Bible, by Homer in the *Iliad*, and in the ancient Egyptian medical book *Ebers Papyrus*. Virgil's poems praise saffron and it is also cited by the first-century gourmet Apicius in his cookbook.

Saffron was used not only in food but also as a perfume and as a dye. The Egyptians scented the oils used to anoint their kings with saffron. It was used by the ancient Greeks and Romans, who took it all over Europe in their travels. During the Dark Ages saffron's use in Europe died out almost completely.

When the Moors conquered Spain in the late eighth century, they brought saffron with them and it has remained a prominent feature of Spanish cuisine. In fact, the name comes from the Arabic word *za'faran*. Saffron is one of the characteristic ingredients in Spain's famous rice dish, *paella*. Saffron traveled from Spain to continental Europe and England, where it became a prominent and lavishly used ingredient in the Middle Ages.

Saffron Walden, a town in Essex, north of London, took its name from the saffron fields that used to flourish nearby. For 400 years these saffron fields produced significant quantities of the spice. Saffron buns, a traditional specialty of the region, are still made to this day. In Cornwall, in southwest England, they also make saffron bread and cakes, a legacy from the ancient Phoenicians, who were said to have brought the spice there in their travels.

Because saffron is so costly, it has often been adulterated by less than scrupulous merchants. In fifteenth-century Germany, the *Safranschau* was a special tribunal set up to discourage and eliminate such practices. So seriously did they take the offense of adulterating saffron that the punishment meted out was being burned or buried alive.

Today saffron is still highly prized. It is the hallmark of many European dishes; without saffron, they would not be the same. It is used mostly in savory dishes, such as rice, soups, and meats, but is also used in making rolls, breads, and in many desserts.

Lore and Myths

◆　◆　◆

Saffron was thought to have reviving qualities, to slow down the aging process, and to be an aphrodisiac. In India, it was used as a digestive aid. Saffron's golden color was deemed to signify wisdom, enlightenment, and illumination.

Characteristics

◆　◆　◆

The spice is the dried threadlike stigma of the fall-blooming crocus flower, *Crocus sativus*, a perennial plant grown from a bulb. Purple flowers top a thin, erect stem that grows to heights of 15 inches. The dried wiry threads are about 1 inch long, very light in weight, and deep red-orange in color, although occasionally some are yellow-orange. The better-quality saffron comes from the threads with deeper color.

Saffron is also available ground, but to be sure of the purity of the spice, it is better to buy the threads and crush them as needed.

Where and How It's Grown

• • •

Saffron is native to Asia Minor and the eastern Mediterranean. It grows well in the sun in sandy, well-drained soil. Today it is grown extensively in Spain, particularly in the La Mancha region, which is reputed to grow the world's best. Turkey, Greece, and Morocco also grow saffron. Iran and India are also big producers of saffron. Some of the world's finest saffron, Mogra Cream, which is often difficult to obtain in the United States, comes from the Kashmir region of India.

When the flower petals open, usually in the fall, they are plucked from their stems. Then the three stigmas in each flower are removed and dried. There is no mechanical way to do this work. It is all done by hand, which is the main reason saffron is so expensive. It takes about 100,000 flowers to make 1 pound of saffron.

How It Tastes and Smells

• • •

Saffron imparts a very distinctive golden color to food. It has a pungent, aromatic, earthy fragrance and a sharp, rich, almost bitter, slightly sweet flavor. The taste of saffron is at first startling, but once acquired, it is unforgettable and enjoyable.

Use and Preparation

• • •

Saffron is either used as threads or crushed. Often the threads are infused in liquid before use. Use saffron sparingly. Only a small amount is needed for both coloring and flavoring. Too much imparts a medicinal, bitter flavor. To obtain a uniform golden color and even flavor, soak the threads in a little warm liquid before using. Add both the liquid and the threads to the dish. Saffron threads can also be crumbled by hand or crushed with a mortar and pestle, then measured by placing loosely in a measuring spoon before they are added directly to a dish. A good way to bring out the flavor of saffron is to toast the threads in a dry pan over low heat until they become brittle, about 5 minutes. Then they are infused with hot liquid and the mixture can be reduced slightly before it is added to food.

Tips for Choosing and Storing

◆ ◆ ◆

Buy saffron threads from a credible source to be sure of the quality. Crushed saffron loses its flavor quickly and it is easily adulterated with other spices or dyes, so it is best to buy threads. It is easy for unscrupulous merchants to substitute turmeric for crushed saffron. Buy only small quantities at a time, because saffron does not keep well.

Store saffron in airtight containers in a cool, dark, dry place. It can be wrapped well and stored in the freezer, where it will keep for up to 1 year.

Saffron Rice Pudding

In the Middle East, saffron has been used to enhance sweets for centuries. Traditionally it is used to lend its delicate flavor and color to rice pudding. Here is my version of this classic dessert. I prefer to use Kashmir Mogra Cream saffron, long known as the world's premiere saffron, because it is sweeter than Mancha. Kashmir Mogra Cream is traditionally used for rice dishes. However, if it's hard to find, Spanish Mancha saffron will work very well.

Makes 12 servings.

◆　◆　◆

1 tablespoon unsalted butter for pan	2 pinches Kashmiri or other saffron
½ cup long-grain white rice	threads
3 cups milk	½ stick (4 tablespoons) unsalted butter,
½ cup sugar	softened
⅓ cup currants	2 large eggs at room temperature
Zest of 1 large orange, finely minced	2 large egg yolks at room temperature
Pinch of salt	1 tablespoon pure vanilla extract

Generously butter the inside of a 9 × 2-inch-round cake pan with the 1 tablespoon of butter. Set aside. Combine the rice and milk in a heavy 1-quart saucepan over medium heat. Cover and bring to a boil. Reduce the heat to low and cook the mixture 45 minutes. Stir in the sugar, currants, orange zest, salt, saffron, and butter and cook the mixture 30 minutes, until the liquid is completely absorbed by the rice. Remove the saucepan from the heat.

Position a rack in the center of the oven. Preheat oven to 325F (165C). In the bowl of a stand mixer or a medium bowl, using the wire-whip attachment or a hand-held mixer, beat the eggs and egg yolks together until they are thick, about 3 minutes. Stir the beaten eggs and vanilla into the rice mixture, blending thoroughly.

Pour the pudding into the prepared pan, place the pan on a baking sheet, and bake 35 minutes, until the pudding is golden brown and the sides have slightly pulled away from the pan. Cool in pan on a rack.

Serve the rice pudding warm, at room temperature, or cover with foil and refrigerate up to 3 days.

Lemon-Saffron Tea Cake

Saffron imparts its golden color and special taste to this delicate tea cake.

Makes 1 (8-inch-square) cake, 16 servings.

◆　　◆　　◆

2 teaspoons unsalted butter, softened,
　for pan

2 teaspoons all-purpose flour for pan

2 cups all-purpose flour, sifted

2 teaspoons baking powder

½ teaspoon salt

1 stick (8 tablespoons) unsalted butter,
　softened

¾ cup granulated sugar

2 large eggs at room temperature,
　lightly beaten

¼ teaspoon baking soda

Pinch of saffron threads, finely crushed
　(approx. ⅛ teaspoon)

Zest of ½ lemon, finely minced

¾ cup water

2 tablespoons fresh lemon juice

Powdered sugar

½ cup heavy whipping cream (optional)

1 cup fresh berries such as strawberries,
　raspberries, blueberries (optional)

Use the 2 teaspoons of butter to generously coat an 8-inch-square baking pan. Dust the pan with the 2 teaspoons of flour and tap out the excess. Position a rack in the center of the oven. Preheat oven to 350F (175C).

Sift together the flour, baking powder, and salt; set aside.

In the bowl of a stand mixer or a medium bowl, using the flat-beater attachment or a hand-held mixer, beat the butter until light and fluffy, about 2 minutes. Add the sugar and beat until thoroughly blended. Add the eggs and beat well, stopping occasionally and scraping down the sides and bottom of the bowl with a rubber spatula. Combine the baking soda with the saffron and lemon zest and add to the mixture, blending well.

Combine the water and lemon juice and add to the batter alternately with the dry ingredients. Beat the batter to blend well after all ingredients are added.

Pour the batter into the prepared pan and bake 45 to 55 minutes, until a wooden pick inserted in the center comes out clean. Cool in pan on a rack.

Remove cake from pan and dust the top lightly with powdered sugar before serving. Cut the cake into 4 strips, then cut each strip into 4 squares.

If using the whipping cream, pour it into the bowl of a stand mixer or a medium bowl. Using the wire-whip attachment or a hand-held mixer, whip the cream on medium speed until it holds soft peaks, 2 to 3 minutes. Serve each square of tea cake with a dollop of whipped cream and a spoonful of fresh berries, if desired.

Store the cake up to 4 days at room temperature, tightly covered with plastic wrap, or freeze up to 4 months. If frozen, defrost in the refrigerator for 24 hours before serving.

Saffron Ice Cream

This seductive ice cream was inspired by a conversation with my good friend and colleague Kitty Morse, who is a native of Morocco and a specialist in the cuisines of North Africa. It's important to use only a small amount of saffron to create just the right flavor balance. I used Kashmir Mogra Cream saffron, which I prefer to Mancha for its sweetness, but if you have trouble finding it, substitute Mancha and use a pinch less.

Makes 1 pint, 4 servings.

◆ ◆ ◆

¼ (scant) teaspoon saffron threads

¾ cup milk

1¼ cups heavy whipping cream

4 large egg yolks at room temperature

⅓ cup plus 1 tablespoon sugar

Crumble the saffron threads into a dry, heavy 2-cup saucepan. Place the saucepan over low heat and toast the saffron until it becomes brittle, 5 to 8 minutes. Use the back of a spoon to lightly crush the saffron threads.

Meanwhile, combine the milk and cream in a heavy 3-quart saucepan. Heat the mixture over medium heat to just below the boiling point, 10 to 12 minutes. Stir the toasted saffron threads into the mixture. Remove the pan from the heat, cover, and let the mixture infuse 30 minutes.

In the bowl of a stand mixer or in a medium bowl, using the wire-whip attachment or a hand-held mixer, whip the egg yolks and sugar together until they are pale yellow and hold a slowly dissolving ribbon when the beater is lifted, about 5 minutes.

Reheat the cream mixture to just below the boiling point. Reduce the mixer speed to low and slowly pour 1 cup of the hot cream mixture into the egg and sugar mixture. Stir to blend well, then return the egg mixture to the mixture in the saucepan. Reduce the heat to low and stir the mixture constantly with a wooden spoon until it registers 185F (85C) on a candy thermometer, 10 to 15 minutes. At this point the mixture will be thickened and when a line is drawn through the custard on the back of the spoon, it will leave a clearly defined path.

Remove the saucepan from the heat and pour the mixture into a 2-quart bowl. Cover the mixture tightly with plastic wrap, cool to room temperature, then chill in the refrigerator for several hours or overnight. Process the mixture in an ice cream maker according to the manufacturer's instructions.

Store the ice cream in a covered container in the freezer for up to 1 month. If it is frozen solid, soften it in the refrigerator for a few hours before serving.

Lemon and Saffron Sabayon

Sabayon is a classic light, creamy dessert that originated in Italy, where it's called *zabaglione* and is traditionally made with Marsala wine. The French adopted the dessert and made it versatile by changing the liquid. Here I've replaced the wine with freshly squeezed lemon juice that balances well with the saffron. This makes a delicious dessert paired with Tuiles (page 144) or Nutmeg Madeleines (page 140). It's also a great accompaniment to Summer Fresh Fruit Salad (page 53), Triple Berry Bundles (page 150), or Mixed Spice Cake (page 152).

Makes 3¹/₂ cups, about 4 servings.

◆   ◆   ◆

¼ (scant) teaspoon saffron threads

4 large egg yolks at room temperature

⅓ cup granulated sugar

½ cup fresh lemon juice

½ stick (4 tablespoons) unsalted butter, cut into small pieces, softened

⅓ cup heavy whipping cream

1 tablespoon superfine sugar (see Note, page 21)

4 to 6 sprigs of fresh mint (optional)

½ cup fresh berries (optional)

Crumble the saffron threads into a dry, heavy 2-cup saucepan. Place the saucepan over low heat and toast the saffron until it becomes brittle, 5 to 8 minutes. Use the back of a spoon to lightly crush the saffron threads.

Combine the egg yolks and granulated sugar in a heatproof 3-quart bowl and whisk to blend. Add the saffron and lemon juice. Place the bowl over a saucepan of simmering water and whisk constantly until the mixture is thick and holds a slowly dissolving ribbon when the whisk is lifted from the mixture, about 5 minutes.

Remove the bowl from the heat and whisk to cool, 1 to 2 minutes. Add the butter in 3 to 4 stages, whisking to blend thoroughly after each addition. Place the bowl over a larger bowl of cold water and whisk until the mixture is cool, about 5 minutes.

Pour the whipping cream into the bowl of a stand mixer or a medium bowl. Using the wire-whip attachment or a hand-held mixer, whip the cream on medium speed until it is frothy. Add the superfine sugar and whip until the cream holds soft peaks.

Gently fold the cream into the sabayon, leaving no white streaks. Leave the sabayon in the large bowl or divide it between individual serving bowls. Cover tightly with plastic wrap and chill about 2 hours or up to 1 day before serving.

Decorate the top of the sabayon with fresh berries and mint leaves, if desired.

Fresh Raspberry & Fig Tart with Saffron Pastry Cream

In the early fall (late August through early October) fresh raspberries and figs are at their peak. It's best to buy the fruits the day they are picked, either from a farmer's market or from a produce stand. They are the perfect topping for this tart, which has unusual pastry cream.

Makes 1 (9½-inch) tart, 8 to 10 servings.

◆ ◆ ◆

Saffron Pastry Cream

4 to 5 saffron threads
1 cup milk
3 large egg yolks at room temperature
⅓ cup sugar
2 tablespoons cornstarch

Pastry (page 102)

Assembly

3 medium to large fresh, ripe figs
½ pint fresh raspberries
⅓ cup apricot preserves
1 tablespoon Grand Marnier or other
   orange liqueur

Saffron Pastry Cream

Crumble the saffron threads into a dry, heavy 2-cup saucepan. Place the saucepan over low heat and toast the saffron until it becomes brittle, about 5 to 8 minutes. Use the back of a spoon to lightly crush the saffron threads. Place the milk in a heavy 2-quart saucepan, stir in the saffron threads, and heat the mixture over medium heat to just below the boiling point.

Combine the egg yolks and sugar in the bowl of a stand mixer or a medium bowl. Using the wire-whip attachment or a hand-held mixer, whip the mixture on medium-high speed, until it is very thick, pale yellow, and holds a slowly dissolving ribbon as the beater is lifted, about 4 minutes. Sift the cornstarch and blend into the mixture, stopping and scraping down the sides of the bowl with a rubber spatula as needed.

Turn the mixer speed to low, add half of the hot milk slowly to the egg mixture and blend well. Then pour the mixture into the remaining hot milk in the saucepan, stir to blend thoroughly, and bring the mixture to a boil over medium-high heat, whisking constantly.

Remove the saucepan from the heat and turn the pastry cream into a 1-quart bowl. Cover the cream immediately with waxed paper or plastic wrap, and cool to room temperature, about 1 hour. Refrigerate the pastry cream at least 3 hours before using. (The pastry cream can be prepared up to 4 days in advance.)

Pastry

Prepare and chill pastry as directed on page 102.

Remove the dough from the refrigerator. If it is very cold, let it stand at room temperature 10 to 15 minutes. Roll out the dough on a lightly floured work surface to a thickness of about ¼ inch. Turn the dough often and dust with flour as needed to keep it from sticking. Gently roll the pastry dough around the rolling pin, then carefully unroll it into a 9½-inch fluted tart pan with a removable bottom. Lift up the edges of the dough and fit them into the bottom and against the sides of the pan. Trim off the excess pastry dough at the top of the pan, leaving a border of ½ inch. Turn this under, reinforcing the sides of the pastry shell. Pierce the bottom of the pastry shell in a few places and chill in the freezer 30 minutes.

Position a rack in the center of the oven. Preheat oven to 375F (190C). Place the tart pan on a baking sheet. Line the pastry shell with a large piece of foil and weight with pie weights or a combination of rice and beans. Bake 10 minutes, remove the foil and weights, and bake another 12 to 15 minutes, until the shell is golden and set. Cool completely on a rack. (The pastry shell can be baked and held up to 2 days at room temperature, covered with foil, before assembling.) When ready to assemble, gently remove the sides of the tart pan and place the pastry shell on a serving plate.

To assemble

Stir the pastry cream vigorously to remove any lumps. Spread it evenly in the pastry shell. Cut the figs lengthwise into quarters and arrange 4 of the quarters in the center of the tart with the wide ends facing the center. Arrange the remaining fig quarters evenly around the outer edge of the tart shell with the wide ends facing in to the center. Use the raspberries to fill the spaces between the figs.

Combine the apricot preserves and liqueur in a small saucepan and bring to a boil over medium heat. Stir to combine and boil for about 2 minutes. Remove from the heat, cool slightly, and strain the glaze, pushing as much of the fruit pulp through the strainer as possible. Lightly brush the top of the fruit with the glaze. Tent the tart with foil and refrigerate until ready to serve or up to 3 hours; otherwise the pastry cream will seep into the pastry shell and make it soft.

Saffron Crème Caramel

Crème caramel is a well-known and much-loved dessert in many countries. It is a classic light egg custard baked in a caramel-coated mold. After baking, the custard is chilled. When turned out of its mold the caramel forms a topping and a sauce for the custard. In Spain this dessert is called *flan*. Here I've used saffron, which also comes from Spain, to add an extra flavor dimension to an already delicious dessert.

Makes 8 servings.

◆　◆　◆

¼ (scant) teaspoon saffron threads	2½ cups milk
1 cup sugar	3 large eggs at room temperature
¼ cup plus 2 tablespoons water, divided	3 large egg yolks at room temperature

Crumble the saffron threads into a dry, heavy 2-cup saucepan. Place the saucepan over low heat and toast the saffron until it becomes brittle, 5 to 8 minutes. Use the back of a spoon to lightly crush the saffron threads.

Place 8 custard cups in a large roasting or baking pan. Position a rack in the center of the oven. Preheat oven to 350F (175C).

Combine ½ cup of the sugar and ¼ cup water in a dry, heavy 2-cup saucepan over high heat. Cook the mixture until it turns a rich golden brown, about 8 minutes. Remove the pan from the heat and carefully stir in the remaining 2 tablespoons water. Return the pan to the heat, and using a long-handled wooden spoon, stir the mixture 1 to 2 minutes to remove any lumps. Carefully pour caramel into the bottom of each custard cup and tilt the cup so the caramel completely covers the bottom.

Combine the milk and toasted saffron in a heavy 2-quart saucepan over medium heat and heat the milk to just below the boiling point. Remove the pan from the heat, cover, and leave the milk to infuse while preparing the rest of the custard.

In the bowl of a stand mixer or a medium bowl, using the wire-whip attachment or a hand-held mixer, whip the eggs and egg yolks together lightly, then slowly blend in the remaining ½ cup of sugar. In a steady stream, pour the hot milk into the eggs, and blend together well.

Pour the custard into a 4-cup liquid measure, then divide it evenly among the caramel-coated custard cups. Set the roasting pan on a rack in the oven and pour hot water into it until the water reaches halfway up the sides of the cups.

Reduce oven temperature to 325F (165C) and bake 40 minutes, until a wooden pick inserted in the center of the custard comes out clean.

Remove the pan from the oven. Remove the custard cups from the roasting pan and cool on a rack. Chill the custard until ready to serve. To unmold, run a thin-bladed sharp knife around the edges of the cups to loosen the custard. Place a small serving place over the top of each cup and invert the custard onto the plate. The custard will keep up to 3 days in the refrigerator, tightly covered with plastic wrap.

Sesame Seeds

• • • • • • • • • • • •

Open sesame!

—Anonymous, *The History of Ali Baba*

Sesame seeds are an old spice, known to have been cultivated as far back as 3000 B.C. in Africa, where they are called *benne* seeds. A 4,000-year-old drawing showing a baker mixing sesame seeds with dough has been found in an Egyptian tomb. Wine and oil were made from sesame seeds by the ancient Babylonians. The *Ebers Papyrus*, an ancient Egyptian medical book, mentions sesame seeds as a medicinal plant. Sesame seeds were eaten for energy by ancient Greek soldiers on the march. "Open sesame" was the secret command that could open the cave in the well-known tales of the legendary Ali Baba. Sesame seeds came to the United States with African slaves.

Today sesame seeds are used in many of the world's cuisines in both savory and sweet dishes, and in many confections. They are a prominent ingredient in many Middle Eastern countries, where they are ground into a paste known as *tahini*. *Halva*, a well-known Turkish confection, is made with sesame seeds. The seeds are also widely used in India. In China, sesame seeds are used to coat foods before cooking to give them a crunchy texture. In Japan, they are sprinkled on many traditional dishes. Oil pressed from the seeds is widely used for cooking and salad oil in the Western world. In China, sesame oil is made from toasted seeds and has a deeper color and nutty, rich flavor.

Lore and Myths
◆ ◆ ◆

African slaves who brought sesame seeds with them when they came to the United States believed them to be good luck symbols. Old herbal books claimed sesame seeds to be an antidote to spotted lizard bite.

Characteristics
◆ ◆ ◆

Sesame seeds are the dried seeds of the annual herb plant *Sesamum indicum*, which grows to a height of 4 feet. It has fuzzy, deeply veined, oval alternating leaves, with flowers that range in color from off-white to pale pink and four-sided pods containing chambers that hold the seeds. The oval, flat seeds are tiny, measuring about 1/8 inch long. The most common color of the seeds is creamy-white, but they also come in tan and black, depending on the variety.

Where and How It's Grown
◆ ◆ ◆

There is some confusion as to the exact origin of sesame, but it is thought to be native to the Sundra Islands in Indonesia and to East Africa. It thrives in warm climates. Today Mexico and Central America are the biggest producers of sesame seeds.

Because the seeds will burst out of their pods when ripe, the plants are harvested just as the lower pods begin to ripen and the upper pods are still green. They are cut and threshed, then dried and hulled.

How It Tastes and Smells

◆ ◆ ◆

Sesame seeds have a pleasant, mildly nutty aroma and a delicate, sweet, almondlike flavor that intensifies when toasted. Sesame oil made from toasted seeds is dark brown with a nutty, rich aroma and flavor. Oil made from white sesame seeds is light and almost flavorless.

Use and Preparation

◆ ◆ ◆

Sesame seeds are used whole, either raw or toasted, depending on the dish. They are also ground to a paste. Raw sesame seeds are sprinkled directly onto the surface of many baked goods. If they are added to doughs or batters, it is best to toast them first to bring out their flavor. Place them in a single layer in a baking dish and toast in a preheated 350F (175C) oven 15 to 20 minutes, shaking the pan every 5 minutes. They can also be toasted in a skillet over low heat 5 to 8 minutes until they turn golden brown. Be sure to stir them frequently so they don't burn.

Tips for Choosing and Storing

◆ ◆ ◆

Buy sesame seeds from a reputable source to be sure of the quality. Check the seeds for even color. Store sesame seeds in a tightly sealed container in a cool, dark, dry place for up to 2 years. They can also be stored in an airtight container in the freezer.

Benne Wafers

Sesame seeds were called *benne* seeds by African slaves who brought them to the American South. These rich, chewy wafers are classics.

Makes about 48 wafers.

◆   ◆   ◆

2 cups raw sesame seeds

½ cup pecans

6 tablespoons (¾ stick) unsalted butter, softened

¾ cup firmly packed golden brown sugar

1 large egg at room temperature, lightly beaten

1 teaspoon pure vanilla extract

½ cup all-purpose flour

¼ teaspoon baking powder

⅛ teaspoon salt

2 tablespoons unsalted butter, melted, for baking sheets

Position a rack in the center of the oven. Preheat oven to 350F (175C). Place the sesame seeds in a single layer on a jelly-roll pan. Toast about 15 minutes, shaking the pan every 5 minutes, until the seeds are lightly browned. Cool in pan on a rack. Place the pecans in a shallow baking pan and toast 8 minutes. Cool in the pan on a rack, then chop them finely.

Place the 6 tablespoons of butter in the bowl of a stand mixer or a medium bowl. Using the flat-beater attachment or a hand-held mixer, beat until light and fluffy, about 2 minutes. Add the sugar and beat until thoroughly blended, then add the egg and vanilla. Beat the mixture 2 minutes, stopping and scraping down the sides of the bowl with a long-handled rubber spatula.

Sift together the flour, baking powder, and salt. Add 1 cup of the toasted sesame seeds, then add the dry ingredients to the butter mixture in 3 stages, blending well after each addition. Stir in the pecans and beat until well mixed, about 30 seconds.

Sprinkle half of the remaining toasted sesame seeds on a large rectangle of waxed paper. Place half of the dough on the waxed paper and form into a roll about 2 inches in diameter. Coat the outside of the roll with the sesame seeds. Roll up the dough tightly in the waxed paper and chill in the refrigerator until firm, about 2 hours. Repeat with the remaining half of the dough. (The rolls can be kept in the refrigerator 1 week, if well wrapped.)

Position racks in the lower and upper thirds of the oven. Preheat oven to 350F (175C). Line 3 baking sheets with foil and brush with the 2 tablespoons butter.

Slice rolls of dough crosswise into ¼-inch-thick rounds and place on the foil 2 inches apart. Bake 5 to 6 minutes. Switch the baking sheets and bake another 5 to 6 minutes, until lightly browned. Cool on baking sheets on racks. Gently peel the foil from the cookies when cooled. The wafers will keep 1 week at room temperature in an airtight container.

Sesame Seed Brittle

This is a captivating candy. Once you start munching on it, it's hard to stop. Because it is prone to becoming soft when exposed to any moisture, be sure to keep the candy in an airtight container at room temperature.

Makes 4½ cups.

♦ ♦ ♦

2 cups raw sesame seeds

2 tablespoons flavorless vegetable oil,
    such as safflower oil

2 cups sugar

½ cup water

½ teaspoon cream of tartar

Position a rack in the center of the oven. Preheat oven to 350F (175C). Place the sesame seeds in a cake pan, pie plate, or on a jelly-roll pan. Toast 15 minutes, shaking the pan every 5 minutes, until light golden brown. Cool in pan on a rack.

Coat the back of a baking sheet with the vegetable oil and set aside. In a heavy-bottomed 3-quart saucepan over high heat, cook the sugar, water, and cream of tartar until mixture is a medium-caramel color, about 8 minutes. With a pastry brush dipped in warm water, brush down the sides of the pan twice to prevent the sugar from crystallizing. Add the toasted sesame seeds and stir quickly with a wooden spoon to coat them completely with the caramel. Remove the pan from the heat, pour the mixture onto the oiled baking sheet, and spread it out with a wooden spoon. It is necessary to work very fast, because the mixture sets up rapidly.

Let the brittle cool completely, about 30 minutes, then break it into pieces with your hands. The brittle will keep 1 week at room temperature stored between layers of waxed paper in an airtight container.

Sesame Biscotti

Sesame seeds are an unusual addition to these Italian twice-baked cookies. Biscotti are welcome at any time of day—after lunch or dinner, as a snack, or with afternoon coffee and tea.

Makes 24 biscotti.

◆　◆　◆

½ cup plus 2 tablespoons raw sesame
　　seeds
2 cups all-purpose flour
1 teaspoon baking powder
¼ teaspoon salt

1 cup sugar
2 large eggs at room temperature
2 large egg yolks at room temperature
1 teaspoon pure vanilla extract

Position a rack in the center of the oven. Preheat oven to 350F (175C). Line a baking sheet with parchment paper. Place the sesame seeds in a cake pan or pie plate and toast in the oven 8 minutes, until light golden. Cool in pan on a rack.

Sift together the flour, baking powder, and salt. Place mixture in the bowl of a stand mixer or a medium bowl. Add the sugar and toasted sesame seeds. Using the flat-beater attachment or a hand-held mixer, blend together at low speed 30 seconds. Combine the eggs and yolks in a small bowl and beat together lightly. Stir the vanilla extract into the eggs, then add to the dry ingredients and mix well.

Turn the dough out onto a lightly floured work surface. Knead lightly 30 to 60 seconds, until the dough holds together. Divide the dough into 2 equal pieces. Shape 1 piece into a log about 8 inches long, 2 to 3 inches wide, and ½ inch thick. Transfer the log to the lined baking sheet. Repeat with remaining dough.

Bake the biscotti 25 minutes, until lightly browned and set. Cool on baking sheet on a rack 8 minutes.

Reduce oven temperature to 325F (165C). Slice each log on the diagonal into ½-inch-thick slices, then place the slices on their sides on the baking sheet. Return the baking sheet to the oven 10 minutes, until the biscotti are firm. Cool on baking sheet on a rack. Store the biscotti up to 3 weeks at room temperature in an airtight container.

Honey and Sesame Seed Ice Cream

This ice cream has a unique texture that is both velvety and crunchy. The rich, intriguing flavor has a way of lingering and making you want more.

Makes 1 quart, about 8 servings.

◆　◆　◆

¾ cup raw sesame seeds

1¼ cups milk

½ vanilla bean

½ cup honey

3 large egg yolks at room temperature

½ cup heavy whipping cream

Position a rack in the center of the oven. Preheat oven to 350F (175C). Place the sesame seeds in a cake pan, pie plate, or on a jelly-roll pan. Toast 15 to 18 minutes, shaking the pan every 5 minutes, until light golden brown. Cool in pan on a rack.

Pour the milk into a heavy 2-quart saucepan over medium heat. Split the vanilla bean lengthwise, scrape out the seeds, and add along with the pod to the milk. Bring the mixture to a boil, add the honey, and stir to blend. Remove pan from heat, cover the mixture, and infuse 10 minutes. Remove vanilla pod.

In the bowl of a stand mixer or a medium bowl, using the wire-whip attachment or a hand-held mixer, whip the egg yolks until they are pale yellow and hold a slowly dissolving ribbon when the beater is lifted, about 8 minutes.

Reheat the milk mixture to just below the boiling point. Reduce the mixer speed to low and slowly pour 1 cup of the hot liquid into the egg and honey mixture. Stir to blend well, then return the mixture to the hot milk in the saucepan. Reduce the heat to low and stir the mixture constantly with a wooden spoon until the mixture reaches 185F (85C) on a candy thermometer, 5 to 8 minutes. At this point the mixture will be thickened and when a line is drawn through the custard on the back of the spoon, it leaves a clearly defined path.

Remove the saucepan from the heat and pour the mixture into a 2-quart bowl. Stir in the sesame seeds. Cover the mixture tightly with plastic wrap, cool to room temperature, then chill in the refrigerator for several hours or overnight.

In the bowl of a stand mixer or a medium bowl, using the wire-whip attachment or a hand-held mixer, whip the cream to soft peaks. Fold the whipped cream into the ice cream custard, blending thoroughly. Immediately process the mixture in an ice cream maker according to the manufacturer's instructions.

Store the ice cream in a covered container in the freezer for up to 1 month. If it is frozen solid, soften it in the refrigerator for a few hours before serving.

Vanilla

• ◆ • ◆ • ◆ • ◆ • ◆ • ◆ • ◆ • ◆ •

Ah, you flavor everything;
you are the vanilla of society.

—Sydney Smith, *Lady Holland's Memoir*

Vanilla is the world's most popular flavor. What would ice cream be without it? Because of the methods used to produce it, vanilla is one of the three most expensive spices in the world, along with saffron and cardamom.

Unknown to Europe until the New World was explored by Columbus and Cortez in the sixteenth century, vanilla has had a major impact on the course of history, certainly culinary history. The exact origin of vanilla is unknown, but it has been in use as far back as 1,000 years ago. Vanilla was used by the Aztec Indians in Mexico, who called it *tlilxochitl*, to flavor their chocolate drinks long before Cortez arrived on the scene in 1520. They considered vanilla to be precious and held it in such high regard that it was used for currency and was given to the Emperor Montezuma as a tribute.

Cortez brought vanilla pods back to Spain, where they were enthusiastically embraced and used to flavor chocolate. The name "vanilla" comes from the Spanish *vainilla*, via Latin, and means "sheath" or "pod," referring to its shape. From Spain, vanilla traveled throughout the continent and to England. In 1602, Hugh Morgan, apothecary to Queen Elizabeth I, suggested using vanilla as a flavoring on its own instead of only with chocolate.

Eventually the Spanish's use of vanilla waned as they took up the use of cinnamon to flavor their chocolate, but its consumption remained at high levels in England and France. It was in France that Thomas Jefferson discovered vanilla. When he returned to the United States in 1789, he missed vanilla so much that he had pods sent over from France for his use. Not long after that vanilla was found in many American kitchens.

Today vanilla is used throughout the world, but the Western European countries, Canada, Japan, Australia, and the United States are the biggest consumers. Vanilla's primary use is in desserts, pastries, and confections, but it also adds its intoxicating aroma and intriguing flavor to many savory dishes.

Lore and Myths
◆　◆　◆

When Cortez first brought vanilla pods to Europe, they were thought to be an aphrodisiac. In seventeenth-century Mexico, vanilla beans were thought to have healing qualities.

Characteristics
◆　◆　◆

Vanilla is the fruit of a climbing perennial orchid, *Vanilla plainfolia*, that climbs to heights of 50 feet. It has flat, broad, oval, smooth leaves with yellowish-green trumpet-shaped flowers that cluster in groups of about twenty. The vanilla pods, also called beans, are green, thin, and cylindrical. The pods measure up to 12 inches long and hang in clusters from the vines before harvesting. They are filled with thousands of tiny seeds. At this point they hardly resemble vanilla beans and have no vanilla aroma.

Vanilla tahitensis is similar to *Vanilla plainfolia*, yet slightly different. Its beans are shorter and broader, with a thicker skin and fewer vanilla seeds. *Vanilla tahitensis* ultimately produces a vanilla with its own special aroma and flavor.

After vanilla pods are cured they are plump, supple, dark brown and covered with a layer of tiny white crystals, *vanillin*, which is the secret of their aroma and flavor.

Pure vanilla extract is a clear, dark brown liquid made from vanilla beans that has an intense aroma.

Where and How It's Grown

◆ ◆ ◆

Vanilla is native to the humid, tropical climate of southern Mexico, where it was first grown exclusively. In 1793, the vine was smuggled out of Mexico to the island of Reunion, a French protectorate called *Ile de Bourbon*, from which a variety of vanilla beans take their name. At first the vines produced only flowers, not beans. In 1836 Charles Morren, a Belgian biologist, discovered that the trumpet shape of the flower made pollination impossible without help. A tiny bee, found only in Mexico, pollinated the flowers grown there. In 1841 a former slave from the Island of Reunion, Edmond Albious, developed a method for fertilizing the flowers by hand that is still in use today. Because of this discovery and his subsequent invention, vanilla is now grown in Madagascar, Reunion, the Comoro Islands, Tahiti, Tonga, the West Indies, Indonesia, and Mexico. The best-quality vanilla beans are reputed to come from Madagascar and Mexico. Madagascar, Reunion, and the Comoro Islands produce about 80 percent of the world's supply of vanilla. Mexico produces barely enough for its own consumption and practically none for export.

Once a vanilla vine is planted, it can take up to 3 years to reach the stage where it will bear fruit and then will continue to produce for about 12 years. The vanilla flowers open for only part of each day and if they are not pollinated that same day, they will not produce a pod. The vines are checked daily for flowers, which are hand-pollinated. It takes about 6 weeks for pods to grow from the fertilized flowers and 6 to 9 months until they are ready to harvest.

There are different methods for beginning the lengthy curing process, depending on where the vanilla pods are grown. The first step begins the critical enzymatic reaction that brings out the flavor and aroma of vanilla. The beans are either wrapped in blankets and straw mats and placed in ovens for 24 to 48 hours or immersed in hot water for a short while. In Java they are smoked. Any of these processes stops the beans' growth. After the first step, they are spread out in the sun to dry, then again wrapped in blankets and placed in wooden boxes to sweat overnight. This process of sweating and drying is repeated many times over a period of 3 to 6 months. The vanilla pods shrink, turn dark brown, and produce an outer covering of crystallized vanillin. It takes 5 pounds of fresh vanilla pods to produce 1 pound of cured beans.

After the curing process, the vanilla beans are graded according to appearance and size, wrapped in bundles, and packed for shipment.

Vanilla extract is made by macerating the beans in a mixture of water and alcohol. Then the residue is extracted from the liquid. The resulting liquid is filtered, sugar is added to it, and it is aged. Vanilla extract is highly concentrated. There are different strengths of pure vanilla extract, called "folds," which are graded according to standards set by the Food and Drug Administration. To be labeled "pure" the extract must contain at least 35 percent alcohol. If it contains less, it is given the label "vanilla flavored."

Imitation vanilla extract is made from either coal tar or the by-products of the paper industry. The liquid chemicals used to clean conifer trees that are to be made into paper are used to produce this synthetic vanilla, also called "vanillin."

How It Tastes and Smells

♦ ♦ ♦

Vanilla has a sweet, deep, mellow flavor with a complex aroma that is characterized as mellow, highly aromatic, and slightly tobaccolike. Tahitian vanilla has more flowery notes, with a sweet, almost licorice flavor.

Imitation vanilla has a strong aroma and a bitter, unpleasant aftertaste.

Use and Preparation

♦ ♦ ♦

Both whole vanilla beans and vanilla extract are used. To use a whole vanilla bean, split it lengthwise with a sharp knife to expose the thousands of edible seeds. Scrape out the seeds and add them with the bean to liquid such as milk or cream. Heat the liquid, then cover, and leave to steep off the heat for several minutes. The vanilla bean is usually removed after steeping, before the liquid is added to the rest of the ingredients in a recipe. The tiny black seeds will remain with the liquid.

Vanilla extract is measured and added to a recipe before baking. When vanilla extract is used in savory dishes, it is added toward the end of cooking so its flavor will not evaporate.

Tips for Choosing and Storing

♦ ♦ ♦

Choose plump, supple, slightly greasy, dark-brown vanilla beans with good aroma. Avoid beans that are dry and brittle. Read the label of the vanilla extract to be sure it is pure and not imitation. The label should state that it contains at least 35 percent alcohol if it is called "pure." Top-quality pure vanilla extract should be dark amber with a rich aroma. Buy vanilla from a reputable source to be sure of the quality.

Store vanilla extract tightly capped in a dark, dry place at room temperature where it will last for up to 5 years. It benefits with aging, but the more it is exposed to heat and light, the quicker it will lose its potency. Store vanilla beans tightly wrapped in airtight plastic bags in a cool, dark, dry place for up to 2 years. Vanilla beans can also be buried in granulated sugar, but they will dry out faster.

Very Vanilla Crème Brûlée

I love the textural contrasts of crème brûlée. A crisp caramel crust is broken through to unlock the velvety, rich custard underneath. Classic crème brûlée is traditionally flavored with vanilla. For this recipe I wanted a very intense vanilla flavor, which I was able to achieve by using Tahitian vanilla beans, with their flowery overtones.

Makes 8 (½-cup) servings.

◆ ◆ ◆

1½ vanilla beans, preferably Tahitian

2 cups heavy whipping cream

6 large egg yolks at room temperature

½ cup granulated sugar

½ cup superfine sugar (see Note, page 21)

Place the cream in a heavy 3-quart saucepan over medium heat. Using a sharp knife, split the vanilla beans lengthwise and scrape the seeds from the pods. Place both the seeds and pods in the cream, then bring the mixture to a boil. Remove the pan from the heat, cover, and let the mixture infuse 30 minutes.

In the bowl of a stand mixer or a medium bowl, using the wire-whip attachment or a hand-held mixer, whip the egg yolks and sugar together until they are pale yellow and hold a slowly dissolving ribbon when the beater is lifted, about 5 minutes.

Reheat the cream mixture to just below the boiling point. Reduce the mixer speed to low and slowly pour 1 cup of the hot cream into the egg and sugar mixture. Stir to blend well, then return the mixture to the hot cream in the saucepan. Reduce the heat to low and stir the mixture constantly with a wooden spoon until the mixture reaches 185F (85C) on a candy thermometer, about 5 minutes. At this point the mixture will be thickened and when a line is drawn through the custard on the back of the spoon, it leaves a clearly defined path.

Remove the saucepan from the heat and strain the mixture into a 2-quart bowl. Discard vanilla pods. Place 8 (½-cup) custard cups on a jelly-roll pan or in a large rectangular baking pan. Pour some of the custard into a liquid measuring cup, then pour the custard into the individual cups. Cover the custard tightly with plastic wrap, and chill in the refrigerator for several hours or overnight.

Sprinkle 1 tablespoon superfine sugar in an even layer over the top of each custard cup, taking care to wipe the edges clean. Using a propane torch held about 8 inches above the surface, caramelize the sugar in each cup. Swirl the torch in concentric circles working from the outside edge toward the center to achieve even caramelization. Let the custards cool, then cover with plastic wrap, and refrigerate until ready to serve. The custard will keep up to 3 days in the refrigerator.

Nutty Vanilla Caramels

These creamy caramels are brimming with the full-bodied flavor of vanilla. They keep well, so they can be made in advance. They would be a welcome addition to an assorted gift box of candies and other treats.

Makes 64 caramels.

◆　◆　◆

1 cup whole unblanched almonds
2 tablespoons flavorless vegetable oil,
　　such as canola
1½ cups superfine sugar (see Note, page 21)

¼ cup honey
½ cup light corn syrup
1½ cups heavy whipping cream
2 vanilla beans, split lengthwise
2 tablespoons unsalted butter, softened

Position a rack in the center of the oven. Preheat oven to 350F (175C). Spread the almonds in a single layer in a cake pan and toast 15 minutes, until light golden, shaking the pan every 5 minutes. Remove from the oven and cool, then chop coarsely.

Line an 8-inch-square baking pan with foil, extending the foil over the sides. Use 1 tablespoon of the vegetable oil to coat the foil.

In a heavy 2-quart saucepan, combine the sugar, honey, and corn syrup. Bring the mixture to a boil over medium heat, stirring constantly with a long-handled wooden spoon. Brush down the sides of the pan with a damp pastry brush twice while the mixture is cooking, to prevent sugar crystallization. Increase the heat to medium-high and cook the mixture until it reaches 305F (150C) on a candy thermometer.

At the same time, in a separate saucepan, heat the cream with the vanilla beans over medium heat to just below the boiling point.

Stir the butter, 1 tablespoon at a time, into the caramel while keeping the mixture boiling. Slowly pour the hot cream into the caramel and continue to cook the mixture, stirring constantly, until the mixture reaches 250F (120C), about 15 minutes.

Remove the pan from the heat. Use a fork to remove the vanilla pods. Stir the toasted almonds into the mixture thoroughly, then transfer the mixture to the prepared pan. Let the caramels stand at room temperature 4 hours to set.

Use the foil to lift the candy from the pan. Turn it out onto a cutting board, peel off the foil, and turn the candy top side up. Use the remaining vegetable oil to coat a large chef's knife. Cut the caramels into 8 (1-inch-wide) strips, then cut each strip into 8 pieces.

Serve the caramels at room temperature. Store them up to 10 days at room temperature between layers of waxed paper in an airtight container.

Fresh Fruit Pizza

This is a fresh fruit tart in a striking and unusual form. Serve this delicious dessert for your next backyard barbecue or garden party and watch your guests' eyes light up with delight.

Makes 1 (12-inch) round, 12 to 14 servings.

◆　◆　◆

Pastry

2¼ cups all-purpose flour
¾ cup powdered sugar, sifted
Pinch of salt
1¾ sticks (14 tablespoons) unsalted
    butter, cut into small pieces, softened
2 large egg yolks at room temperature,
    lightly beaten
1 teaspoon pure vanilla extract

Topping

1 (8-oz.) package regular or low-fat
    cream cheese, softened
⅓ cup powdered sugar, sifted
1 tablespoon pure vanilla extract
3 cups fresh berries (raspberries,
    blackberries, blueberries, or
    strawberries) or other fruit, such as
    peaches, bananas, or kiwi fruit
¼ cup finely shaved top-quality white
    chocolate

Pastry

Combine the flour, powdered sugar, and salt in the work bowl of a food processor fitted with a steel blade. Pulse 5 seconds to mix. Add the butter and pulse until the butter is cut into very tiny pieces, about 1 minute.

In a small bowl, beat the egg yolks with the vanilla. With the machine on, pour egg mixture through the feed tube. Process the dough until it wraps itself around the blade, about 1 minute. Cover the dough in plastic wrap and chill 3 to 4 hours before using.

The dough will keep 4 days in the refrigerator or can be frozen up to 4 months, if very well wrapped. If frozen, defrost at least 24 hours in the refrigerator before using. If the dough is very cold, let it sit at room temperature until it is pliable, but not soft, then knead it briefly before using.

Preheat the oven to 375F (190C). Roll out the dough on a lightly floured work surface to a 14-inch circle about ⅛-inch thickness. Gently drape the pastry over the rolling pin and unroll onto a 12-inch-round pizza pan.

Cut off the excess dough that hangs over the rim of the pan, then use a fork to make a decorative design in the edge of the dough all the way around. Line the dough with foil and weight with pie weights. Bake 10 minutes, then remove the foil and weights and bake another 10 to 15 minutes, until set and lightly golden all over. Cool completely in pan on a rack. (The crust can be baked up to 2 days in advance and held at room temperature tightly covered with foil.)

Topping

Place the cream cheese in the bowl of a stand mixer or a medium bowl. Using the flat-beater attachment or a hand-held mixer, beat until light and fluffy, about 2 minutes. Add the powdered sugar and mix thoroughly. Add the vanilla and beat until thoroughly blended.

Spread the cream cheese mixture evenly over the cooled pastry dough, leaving a 1-inch border all the way around. Cover the cream cheese with the fresh fruit, then sprinkle the top of the fruit with the shaved white chocolate. Cut the pizza into wedges to serve.

Assemble the pizza no more than 3 hours before serving and keep refrigerated. Let the pizza stand at room temperature 20 minutes before serving.

Vanilla Bean Ice Cream

The essence of vanilla is captured in this superb ice cream. It has a velvety texture with a rich, full-bodied vanilla flavor. Once you eat this, I doubt you will ever go back to eating store-bought vanilla ice cream.

Makes about 1 quart, 8 servings.

◆　◆　◆

2 cups milk

2 cups heavy whipping cream

5 vanilla beans

8 large egg yolks at room temperature

¾ cup sugar

Place the milk and cream in a heavy 3-quart saucepan over medium heat. Using a sharp knife, split the vanilla beans lengthwise, scrape out the seeds, and add both the seeds and the pods to the liquid. Heat the mixture to just below the boiling point, 10 to 12 minutes. Remove the pan from the heat, cover, and let the mixture infuse 30 minutes.

In the bowl of a stand mixer or a medium bowl, using the wire-whip attachment or a hand-held mixer, whip the egg yolks and sugar together until they are pale yellow and hold a slowly dissolving ribbon when the beater is lifted, about 5 minutes.

Reheat the cream mixture to just below the boiling point. Reduce the mixer speed to low and slowly pour 1 cup of the hot liquid into the egg and sugar mixture. Stir to blend well, then return the mixture to the saucepan. Reduce the heat to low and stir the mixture constantly with a wooden spoon until the mixture reaches 185F (85C) on a candy thermometer, 10 to 15 minutes. At this point the mixture will be thickened and when a line is drawn through the custard on the back of the spoon, it leaves a clearly defined path.

Remove the saucepan from the heat. Strain the mixture through a fine sieve into a bowl. Discard vanilla pods. Cover the mixture tightly and chill in the refrigerator several hours or overnight. Process the mixture in an ice cream maker according to the manufacturer's instructions.

Store the ice cream in a covered container in the freezer for up to 1 month. If it is frozen solid, soften it in the refrigerator for a few hours before serving.

Vanilla Custard

This rich custard is very versatile. You can vary the firmness of the texture by using only flour, only cornstarch, or a combination, to thicken it. All cornstarch will make it very firm. The custard is delicious on its own, but try it layered in a parfait glass or dish with fresh fruit or as the filling in a tart or cake.

Makes 3 cups.

◆ ◆ ◆

2 cups milk

1 vanilla bean

6 large eggs yolks at room temperature

⅔ cup sugar

4 tablespoons all-purpose flour or
   cornstarch

Place the milk in a heavy 2-quart saucepan over medium heat. Using a sharp knife, split the vanilla bean lengthwise, scrape out the seeds, and add both the vanilla pod and seeds to the milk. Heat the mixture to just below the boiling point, 10 to 12 minutes.

Whip the egg yolks and sugar together in the bowl of a stand mixer or a medium bowl, using the wire-whip attachment or a hand-held mixer on medium-high speed, until the mixture is very thick, pale yellow, and holds a slowly dissolving ribbon as the beater is lifted, about 5 minutes. Sift the flour or cornstarch and add to the mixture, stopping and scraping down the sides of the bowl with a rubber spatula, as necessary.

Add half of the hot milk slowly to the egg mixture, with the mixer on low speed, and blend well. Then pour the mixture into the saucepan, stir to blend thoroughly, and bring the mixture to a boil over medium-high heat, whisking constantly.

Remove the saucepan from the heat and pour the custard into a 1-quart bowl. Discard vanilla pod. Cover the custard immediately with waxed paper or plastic wrap, and cool about 30 minutes. Refrigerate the custard at least 3 hours before using.

Stir the custard vigorously before using to remove any lumps. It will keep up to 4 days, well covered in the refrigerator, but cannot be frozen.

Vanilla Macadamia Nut Tart

Vanilla is used in two forms—beans and extract—to contribute its rich, full-bodied flavor to this yummy tart. The filling is soft and chewy yet crunchy with the texture of the macadamia nuts.

Makes 1 (11-inch) tart, 14 to 16 servings.

◆ ◆ ◆

Pastry (page 102), omitting nutmeg and cloves

Filling

⅓ cup firmly packed golden brown
    sugar
¼ cup granulated sugar
¼ cup light corn syrup
¼ cup dark corn syrup
2 large eggs at room temperature
2 large egg yolks at room temperature

1 tablespoon pure vanilla extract
1 tablespoon unsalted butter, softened
2 vanilla beans, split
1½ cups macadamia nuts, toasted and
    coarsely chopped

To serve

½ cup heavy whipping cream
2 teaspoons superfine sugar (see Note,
    page 21)
1 teaspoon pure vanilla extract

Pastry

Prepare and chill pastry as directed on page 103.

Position a rack in the center of the oven. Preheat oven to 350F (175C). Roll out the pastry on a lightly floured work surface to a 14-inch circle, about ⅛ inch thick. Gently roll the pastry around the rolling pin and unroll carefully into an 11-inch fluted tart pan with a removable bottom. Lift up the sides of the pastry and fit it into the bottom and against the sides of the tart pan. Trim off the excess pastry at the top. Line the pastry with a large piece of foil and weight with pie weights. Place the tart pan on a jelly-roll pan and bake 10 minutes. Remove the foil and weights and bake another 10 to 12 minutes, until light golden and set. Cool in pan on a rack.

Filling

Combine the brown sugar, granulated sugar, light and dark corn syrup, eggs, egg yolks, and vanilla extract in the bowl of a stand mixer or a medium bowl. Using the wire-whip attachment or a hand-held mixer on medium-high speed, whip until light, about 1 minute.

Place the butter in a small saucepan. Using a sharp knife, split the vanilla beans lengthwise, and scrape out the seeds. Add both the vanilla pods and seeds to the butter and brown over medium heat, 3 to 4 minutes. Remove the vanilla pods and add the butter to the sugar mixture. Blend in the macadamia nuts and pour the mixture into the pastry shell.

Bake the tart 30 minutes, until set and golden. Cool in pan on a rack 30 minutes, then remove the sides of the tart pan. The tart is best served within 4 hours, but will last for up to 3 days in the refrigerator, tightly covered.

To serve

Whip the cream in the bowl of a stand mixer or a medium bowl, using the wire-whip attachment or a hand-held mixer on medium speed, until it is frothy. Add the sugar and vanilla and continue to whip the cream until it holds soft peaks. Serve a dollop of whipped cream on top of each slice of tart.

Vanilla Sugar

Vanilla sugar adds an extra depth of vanilla flavor to any dessert. It can be used in place of granulated, superfine, or powdered sugar in any recipe. After I use a vanilla bean I rinse and thoroughly dry it, then add it to my sugar canister. When I use any of the sugar I simply replenish it, so I can always have vanilla sugar on hand.

Makes 4 cups.

♦   ♦   ♦

4 cups granulated, superfine, or
powdered sugar

1 vanilla bean

Score the vanilla bean lengthwise, place it in a tall glass jar or other container, and cover it with the sugar. Tightly cover the container and let the sugar stand at least 24 hours so the vanilla can permeate the sugar.

Orange Flower Water

• • • • • • • • •

If I were yonder orange-tree
And thou the blossom blooming there,
I would not yield a breath of thee
To scent the most imploring air!

—Thomas Moore, "If I Were Yonder Wave"

Orange flower water, also called orange blossom water, is a unique and exotic flavoring that has been in use for hundreds of years in the Middle East, where it originated. The Arabs invented the process of distillation, which they used to extract the essence from the flowers of the orange tree to make orange flower water. It is assumed that this occurred in the third century, although the exact time is not known. This unusual flavoring was introduced to many cultures by the Arab traders, who traveled widely.

During the Middle Ages, orange flower water was a very popular flavoring used extensively by Europeans for sweets and drinks. In the seventeenth century, orange flower water was widely used in England. Although it is still popular in Eastern Europe, its use in Western Europe has declined in modern times.

Orange flower water is used in sweet and savory dishes and is a classic flavoring in the cuisines of North Africa and the Middle East. It is widely used in Africa, Eastern Europe, Morocco, Greece, Turkey, Lebanon, Syria, India, and other Middle Eastern countries.

Characteristics

◆　◆　◆

Orange flower water is a clear, straw-colored liquid.

Where and How It's Manufactured

◆　◆　◆

Orange flower water is distilled from the blossoms of bergamot and Seville (bitter) orange trees. It was probably first distilled at the medical school founded by the Persian king Shapur I in Jundishapur, in Mesopotamia, about the third century A.D. Today orange flower water is produced throughout the Middle East and in Europe.

The ancient method of distillation involved simmering orange blossoms in boiling water in a large copper pan covered with a dome-shaped lid with a tube attached to it. This tube was placed into a glass bottle. As the steam rose into the dome, it passed out through the tube, which was cooled by cold water. This caused the steam to condense into drops, which completed traveling through the tube and dropped into the bottle. After distillation, orange flower water was warmed again to bring the oil to the surface, which was then skimmed off.

Today steam distillation is used to extract the fragrance from the orange blossom petals after they have been macerated. This method allows for the best-quality orange flower water because the oil evaporates easily and no fragrance is lost.

The orange blossoms are put into a container through which steam is forced under pressure. As the steam exits, it carries suspended with it, the delicate oil that holds the orange flower fragrance. This oil, neroli oil, stays on the surface as a thin film as the steam condenses and is skimmed off to be used by the perfume industry. It is also used as essential oil to flavor food. The remaining liquid is orange flower water. It takes approximately 7 pounds of orange blossoms to produce 1 gallon of orange flower water.

How It Tastes and Smells
• • •

Orange flower water has a slightly sweet, mild orange flavor and a delicate, flowery fragrance, reminiscent of gardenias.

Use and Preparation
• • •

Orange flower water is always used in liquid form. It is sprinkled on finished dishes just before serving so its delicate flavor doesn't evaporate during cooking. Use orange flower water with a light touch since it is very strong. It is used to make orange sugar by sprinkling it onto sugar cubes that are then dried and finely ground for use in making pastries, desserts, and confections.

Tips for Choosing and Storing
• • •

Buy orange flower water that is labeled for culinary, not cosmetic, use. It is available in stores that specialize in Middle Eastern foods, some gourmet and cookware shops, some natural food stores, and some supermarkets. Store orange flower water tightly sealed in its bottle in a cool, dark place, where it will last for years.

Orange Blossom Disks

These delicate, rich cookies, perfumed with fragrant orange flower water, are perfect for afternoon tea. They make a splendid addition to an assortment of cookies or small pastries.

Makes about 36 cookies.

◆　◆　◆

2 cups all-purpose flour
¾ cup powdered sugar, sifted
1¾ sticks (14 tablespoons) unsalted
  butter, chilled, cut into small pieces

Zest of ½ large orange, finely minced
2 tablespoons plus 1½ teaspoons orange
  flower water
2 tablespoons granulated sugar

Place the flour and powdered sugar in the work bowl of a food processor and pulse briefly to blend. Add the butter and pulse until it is cut into very tiny pieces, about 1 minute. Add the orange zest and orange flower water and process the mixture until it forms a ball and wraps itself around the blade, about 30 seconds.

Place a large piece of waxed paper on a work surface. Sprinkle the granulated sugar over the waxed paper. Turn the dough out onto the waxed paper and, using your fingertips, roll it in the sugar to form a cylinder about 14 inches long, 1½ inches wide, and 1¼ inches thick. Tightly wrap the cylinder in the waxed paper and chill in the refrigerator at least 1 hour.

Position the racks in the upper and lower thirds of the oven. Preheat to 350F (175C). Line 2 baking sheets with parchment paper.

Remove the dough cylinder from the refrigerator, remove the waxed paper, and place the cylinder on a cutting board or other cutting surface. Using a sharp knife, cut the cylinder crosswise into ½-inch-thick slices. Transfer the cookies to the baking sheets, leaving 1 inch of space between them.

Bake the cookies 4 minutes. Switch the baking sheets and bake another 4 to 6 minutes, until the edges are golden. Cool cookies on the baking sheets on racks. The cookies will keep up to 1 week at room temperature in an airtight container.

Orange and Honey—Baked Figs

This dessert was inspired by one I ate when I traveled through Greece many years ago. Orange flower water adds its fragrant flavor to the sauce for the figs and again when they are served. The figs can be served either hot from the oven or at room temperature.

Makes 4 servings.

◆　　◆　　◆

8 large ripe, fresh figs

⅓ cup honey

½ cup fresh orange juice

2 tablespoons orange flower water

Position a rack in the center of the oven. Preheat oven to 325F (165C). Rinse the figs, pat them dry on paper towels, and cut off their stems. Place them with the stem end up in a 2-quart baking dish.

Combine the honey, orange juice, and 1 tablespoon of the orange flower water in a 1-quart saucepan over low heat. Heat to dissolve the honey, about 5 minutes. Pour the mixture over the figs.

Bake the figs 1 hour, until they are soft when pierced with a knife, basting the figs occasionally as they bake. Remove from the oven and use a slotted spoon to transfer the figs to a serving plate.

Transfer the orange syrup to a 1-quart saucepan over medium heat and bring to a boil. Cook until syrup is reduced to two-thirds the original amount, about 3 minutes. Pour the syrup over the figs and sprinkle them with the remaining tablespoon of orange flower water. Serve immediately.

Baklava

Baklava is a classic pastry with a rich nut filling enclosed between layers of flaky, crisp phyllo dough. It is found throughout the Middle East in many variations. Some use only almonds or walnuts or pistachio nuts; others use assorted mixtures of these nuts. I have chosen to use all three types in this recipe. Different flavorings are also emphasized in baklava, depending on the country or region. In my version, I use orange blossom water in both the filling and the sugar syrup to lend its subtle floral flavor. Phyllo pastry dough is available frozen in packages in many supermarkets and gourmet shops.

Makes about 21 (2-inch) pieces.

◆　◆　◆

1¼ cups whole unblanched almonds
1½ cups pistachio nuts, toasted
1½ cups walnuts
¼ cup sugar
1 teaspoon ground cassia cinnamon
Pinch of freshly ground cloves
1 tablespoon orange blossom water
½ pound (½ box) frozen phyllo pastry
 dough, thawed
1 stick (8 tablespoons) unsalted butter,
 melted

Sugar Syrup

1½ cups sugar
¾ cup water
2 teaspoons fresh lemon juice
2 tablespoons orange blossom water

Combine the nuts in the work bowl of a food processor fitted with a steel blade. Pulse until they are coarsely chopped, about 1 minute. Transfer the nuts to a 2-quart bowl. Add the sugar, cassia, cloves, and orange blossom water and toss to blend thoroughly.

Position a rack in the center of the oven. Preheat oven to 375F (190C).

Unroll the phyllo dough. Remove 8 sheets. Cut these in half lengthwise, making 16 sheets approximately 12 × 8 inches. Re-roll the remaining dough, wrap tightly with plastic wrap, and freeze for another use.

Brush a 12 × 8-inch baking pan with butter. Place 1 layer of phyllo dough in the pan and brush with butter. Repeat with 7 more layers of phyllo dough. Spread the nut filling evenly over the phyllo dough and cover with 8 more sheets of phyllo, buttering each. Use a sharp knife to cut the pastry into crisscrossing diagonal lines to create diamond shapes.

Bake pastry 20 minutes. Reduce oven temperature to 325F (165C) and bake the pastry another 20 minutes, until light golden brown and crisp.

Sugar Syrup

While the pastry is baking, combine the sugar and water in a heavy 1½-quart saucepan over medium-high heat and bring to a boil. Boil 10 minutes, until the syrup begins to thicken. Add the lemon juice and boil another 2 to 3 minutes. Remove from the heat, stir in 1 tablespoon of the orange blossom water, and cool slightly.

When the pastry is baked, remove from the oven and place on a rack. Use a sharp knife to cut through the previously cut lines. Pour the warm syrup over the pastry, then sprinkle on the remaining 1 tablespoon orange blossom water. Serve immediately or cool completely, cover tightly with plastic wrap, and refrigerate up to 1 week.

Rosewater

And the rose herself has got
Perfume which on earth is not.

—Keats, "Bards of Passion and of Mirth"

Rosewater is one of the most exotic and unusual flavorings. It has been in use for hundreds of years in the Middle East, where it originated. Roses and their water have long been valued for their medicinal qualities. Roses were grown in the gardens of Babylon for use in medicines as far back as the eighth century B.C. The Persians exported rosewater to China long before Christ was born. Ancient Greeks, Romans, and Egyptians extracted the fragrance from rose petals by steeping them in oil, alcohol, or water.

It is believed that the Arabs invented the process of distillation that was used to extract the essence from rose petals to make rosewater. Exactly when this occurred is not known, but it is speculated to have taken place in about the third century. The Arabs traveled far and wide as traders and brought this unique flavoring to many peoples. In several of the countries where rosewater is used, it is the only form of roses known because the flowers are not grown. There, the Arabic word for rosewater, *ma ward*, is also the word used for roses.

Rosewater was brought to Europe with the returning Crusaders. The particular rose that is most favored for making rosewater is the Damask rose, which takes its name from Damascus. Rosewater was a very popular flavoring used heavily by Europeans during the Middle Ages, the Renaissance, and in sixteenth-century Elizabethan England in sweet and savory dishes and in drinks. In the last 200 years its use has declined.

Rosewater is used primarily in sweet dishes and is a classic feature of cuisines of North Africa and the Middle East. It is also used in Eastern Europe, India, Afghanistan, Indonesia, and Africa. Rosewater is always found in Turkish delight, a classic sweet; in *kheer*, an Indian rice dish made for festival celebrations; in Iranian and Afghani sorbet; and often in baklava.

Lore and Myths

◆ ◆ ◆

Rosewater was thought to have medicinal qualities. Afghani and Persian *faqirs*, poor holy men, sprinkled rosewater on people as a blessing in exchange for the food given them. Rosewater has long been used as a perfume and in cosmetics.

Characteristics

◆ ◆ ◆

Rosewater is a clear, colorless liquid.

Where and How It's Manufactured

◆ ◆ ◆

It is speculated that rosewater was first distilled at the medical school founded by the Persian king Shapur I in Jundishapur, in Mesopotamia, about the third century A.D. Today rosewater is produced throughout the Middle East and in Europe.

Rosewater is distilled from rose petals that are grown for this particular purpose. The ancient method of distillation is still in use in Afghanistan today. Rose petals are simmered in boiling water in a large copper pan covered with a dome-shaped lid that has a tube attached to it. This tube is placed into a glass bottle. As the steam rises into the dome it passes out through the tube, which is cooled by cold water. This causes the steam to condense into drops, which complete their travel through the tube and drop into the bottle. Often after it is distilled, rosewater is warmed again to bring the *attar*, or oil, to the surface, which is then skimmed off.

Modern technology uses steam distillation to extract the delicate fragrance from the petals. This method allows for the best-quality rosewater because the oil evaporates easily and no fragrance is lost.

The rose petals are put into a container through which steam is forced under pressure. As the steam exits, it carries suspended with it the delicate oil that holds the rose fragrance. This oil is called *attar* of roses, from Persian, meaning "perfume" or "essence." It stays on the surface as a thin film as the steam condenses and is skimmed off to be used by the perfume industry. The remaining liquid is rosewater. Another way to make rosewater is to add rose oil to distilled water in the proportion of one drop to a gallon of water.

How It Tastes and Smells

◆ ◆ ◆

Rosewater has a slightly sweet, flowery taste and a soft, delicate, flowery fragrance. It is definitely a unique flavor.

Use and Preparation

◆ ◆ ◆

Rosewater is always used in its liquid form. It is sprinkled on finished dishes just before serving so its delicate flavor doesn't evaporate during cooking. Use rosewater with a light touch, too much will taste medicinal.

Tips for Choosing and Storing

◆ ◆ ◆

Buy rosewater that is labeled for culinary, not cosmetic, use. It is available in stores that specialize in Middle Eastern foods, some gourmet and cookware shops, some supermarkets, and some natural food stores. Store rosewater tightly sealed in its bottle in a cool, dark place, where it will last for years.

Greek Butter Cookies

These classic rich, buttery cookies are found in Greece as part of practically any celebration. Traditionally, whole cloves are pressed into the cookies after they are formed, but I found that including ground cloves in the dough gives them a rounder, fuller clove taste. Rosewater is sprinkled on the cookies while they are warm, adding its special flavor.

Makes about 72 cookies.

◆　◆　◆

2 sticks (16 tablespoons) unsalted
　butter, softened
5 cups powdered sugar, sifted
1 large egg yolk at room temperature
2 tablespoons brandy or Cognac
1 teaspoon pure vanilla extract

2 cups all-purpose flour
1 teaspoon baking powder
1¼ teaspoons ground cloves
¾ cup walnuts, finely ground
1 to 2 tablespoons rosewater

Position the racks in the upper and lower thirds of the oven. Preheat oven to 350F (175C).

In the bowl of a stand mixer or a medium bowl, using the flat-beater attachment or a hand-held mixer, beat the butter until it is fluffy, about 5 minutes. Gradually add ½ cup of the powdered sugar, then blend in the egg yolk, brandy, and vanilla, stopping and scraping down the sides of the bowl with a rubber spatula a few times during the mixing.

Sift together the flour, baking powder, and cloves into a medium bowl. Add to the first mixture in 4 or 5 stages, making sure each batch is well blended before adding the next and stopping and scraping down the sides of the bowl with a rubber spatula as necessary. Stir in the walnuts and blend thoroughly.

Line 3 baking sheets with parchment paper. Break off walnut-size pieces of the cookie dough and roll into balls with your hands. Place the cookies on the baking sheets, leaving 1 inch of space between them.

Bake the cookies 6 minutes. Switch the baking sheets and bake the cookies another 5 to 6 minutes, until light golden. Place the baking sheets on racks. Lightly sprinkle the warm cookies with the rosewater. Cool cookies until warm.

Place half of the remaining powdered sugar on a baking sheet. Place the warm cookies on the sugar and sift more powdered sugar on top of them. Leave them to cool completely, then roll the cookies in the powdered sugar.

The cookies will keep 1 week at room temperature, stored in the powdered sugar in an airtight container.

Fresh Berry Gratin

This dessert is a real treat when summer berries are at their peak! Use any combination of sweet, fresh berries that you choose.

Makes 4 servings.

◆　◆　◆

4 cups ripe, fresh berries (raspberries, blackberries, blueberries, or strawberries)

½ cup low-fat sour cream

4 tablespoons buttermilk

6 tablespoons superfine sugar (see Note, page 21)

1 tablespoon plus 1 teaspoon rosewater

Rinse the berries and pat dry with paper towels. If using strawberries, hull them, then slice them lengthwise into quarters. Divide the berries evenly among 4 (4½-inch-round) shallow heatproof dishes.

Blend together the sour cream and buttermilk until smooth. Divide the mixture equally and spread over the tops of the berries. Sprinkle 1 tablespoon superfine sugar on top of each dish. Use a propane torch to lightly caramelize the sugar. Sprinkle another half tablespoon of sugar over each dish and caramelize again. Sprinkle 1 teaspoon of rosewater over each dessert and serve immediately.

Persian Ice Cream

The inspiration for this unusual ice cream came from a dinner my husband and I ate in a Persian restaurant in La Jolla, California. Our meal was delicious, so of course we wanted to know what was available for dessert. The proprietress recommended we try their specialty, Persian ice cream. This recipe re-creates our delightful discovery. The ice cream highlights rosewater and saffron, flavorings classically used in Persian cuisine, as well as pistachio nuts. Be sure to use a light hand with the saffron, so it doesn't overpower the other flavors.

Makes 3 cups, 6 servings.

◆   ◆   ◆

¼ (scant) teaspoon saffron threads

¾ cup milk

1¼ cups heavy whipping cream

¼ teaspoon ground cardamom

4 large egg yolks at room temperature

⅓ cup plus 1 tablespoon sugar

3½ tablespoons rosewater

½ cup plus 1 tablespoon unsalted, shelled pistachio nuts, toasted

1 teaspoon sugar

Crumble the saffron threads into a dry 2-cup saucepan. Place the saucepan over low heat and toast the saffron until it becomes brittle, 5 to 8 minutes. Use the back of a spoon to lightly crush the saffron threads.

Combine the milk and cream in a heavy 3-quart saucepan over medium heat. Heat the mixture almost to the boiling point, 10 to 12 minutes. Stir the toasted saffron threads and cardamom into the mixture. Remove the pan from the heat, cover, and let the mixture infuse 30 minutes.

In the bowl of a stand mixer or a medium bowl, using the wire-whip attachment or a hand-held mixer, whip the egg yolks and sugar together until they are pale yellow and hold a slowly dissolving ribbon when the beater is lifted, about 5 minutes.

Reheat the cream mixture to just below the boiling point. Reduce the mixer speed to low and slowly pour 1 cup of the hot liquid into the egg and sugar mixture. Stir to blend well, then return the mixture to the hot mixture in the saucepan. Reduce the heat to low and stir the mixture constantly with a wooden spoon until the mixture reaches 185F (85C) on a candy thermometer, 10 to 15 minutes. At this point the mixture will be thickened and when a line is drawn through the custard on the back of the spoon, it leaves a clearly defined path.

Remove the saucepan from the heat and pour the mixture into a 2-quart bowl. Cover the mixture tightly with plastic wrap, cool to room temperature, then chill in the refrigerator several hours or overnight.

Stir in the rosewater and ½ cup of the pistachio nuts and blend well. Process the mixture in an ice cream maker according to the manufacturer's instructions.

Place the remaining 1 tablespoon of pistachio nuts and the 1 teaspoon sugar in a spice or coffee grinder, or in a blender. Pulse until finely ground. Sprinkle each serving of ice cream with some of the ground pistachio nuts.

Store the ice cream in a covered container in the freezer up to 1 month. If it is frozen solid, soften it in the refrigerator for a few hours before serving.

Roseberry Sorbet

I named this sorbet after its main ingredients, rosewater and fresh, ripe raspberries. The combination of ingredients is a natural match in which each highlights and enhances the other.

Makes 1 pint, 4 servings.

◆　◆　◆

3½ cups fresh raspberries (3 boxes)　　⅔ cup sugar
1 tablespoon rosewater　　　　　　　　½ cup water

Puree the raspberries in the work bowl of a food processor fitted with a steel blade, in a blender, or in a food mill. Strain the puree to remove the seeds. Mix the berry puree with the rosewater, cover with plastic wrap, and chill thoroughly in the refrigerator.

Combine the sugar and water in a small heavy saucepan over medium heat and bring to a boil. Transfer to a bowl, cover tightly with plastic wrap, and chill thoroughly in the refrigerator.

Combine the raspberry puree and the sugar syrup, blending thoroughly, then process in an ice cream maker according to the manufacturer's instructions.

Store the sorbet in a covered container in the freezer up to 1 month. If it is frozen solid, soften it in the refrigerator for a few hours before serving.

Mail-Order Sources for Spices

• • •

Aphrodesia Products
264 Bleeker Street
New York, NY 10014
212/989-6440

Frontier Herbs
3021 78th Street
P.O. Box 299
Norway, IA 52318
800/786-1388
FAX: 800/717-4372

La Cuisine
323 Cameron Street
Alexandria, VA 22314
800/521-1176; 703/836-4435
FAX: 703/836-8925

Paprikas Weiss Importer
1572 Second Avenue
New York, NY 10026
212/288-6117

Pendry's
1221 Manufacturing
Dallas, TX 75207
800/533-1870
FAX: 214/761-1966

Penzeys, Ltd.
P.O. Box 1448
Waukesha, WI 53187
414/574-0277
FAX: 414/574-0278

The Spice Corner
904 South 9th Street
Philadelphia, PA 19147
800/774-2371; 215/925-1660
FAX: 215/592-7430

San Francisco Herb Company
250 14th Street
San Francisco, CA 94103
800/227-4530; 415/861-7174
FAX: 415/851-4440

The Ultimate Herb & Spice Shoppe
111 Azalea, Box 395
Duenweg, MO 64841
417/782-0457

Weight and Measurement Equivalents

♦ ♦ ♦

CAPACITY	APPROXIMATE CAPACITY	
⅕ teaspoon	1	milliliter
1 teaspoon	5	milliliters
1 tablespoon	15	milliliters
¼ cup	60	milliliters
1 cup (8 fluid ounces)	240	milliliters
2 cups (1 pint, 16 fluid ounces)	470	milliliters
4 cups (1 quart, 32 fluid ounces)	0.95	liter
4 quarts (1 gallon, 64 fluid ounces)	3.8	liters

WEIGHT	APPROXIMATE WEIGHT
1 fluid ounce	28 grams
1 dry ounce	15 grams
2 ounces	30 grams
4 ounces (¼ pound)	110 grams
8 ounces (½ pound)	230 grams
16 ounces (1 pound)	454 grams

Liquid Measurement

MEASUREMENT	FLUID OUNCES	OUNCES BY WEIGHT	GRAMS
2 tablespoons	1 fluid ounces	1¼ ounces	28 grams
¼ cup	2 fluid ounces	3½ ounces	100 grams
⅓ cup	3 fluid ounces	4½ ounces	130 grams
½ cup	4 fluid ounces	6½ ounces	170 grams
⅔ cup	5 fluid ounces	8 ounces	230 grams
¾ cup	6 fluid ounces	9½ ounces	250 grams
1 cup	8 fluid ounces	12 ounces	340 grams

MEASUREMENT	EQUIVALENT
¼ cup (2 fluid ounces)	4 tablespoons
⅓ cup (3 fluid ounces)	5 tablespoons
½ cup (4 fluid ounces)	8 tablespoons
⅔ cup (5 fluid ounces)	10 tablespoons
¾ cup (6 fluid ounces)	12 tablespoons
1 cup (8 fluid ounces)	16 tablespoons

Dry Measurement

MEASUREMENT	EQUIVALENT
3 teaspoons	1 tablespoon
2 tablespoons	⅛ cup
4 tablespoons	¼ cup
5 tablespoons	⅓ cup
8 tablespoons	½ cup
16 tablespoons	1 cup

Granulated Sugar

MEASUREMENT	OUNCES	GRAMS
1 teaspoon	1/6 ounce	5 grams
1 tablespoon	1/2 ounce	15 grams
1/4 cup	1 3/4 ounces	50 grams
1/3 cup	2 1/4 ounces	65 grams
1/2 cup	3 1/2 ounces	100 grams
2/3 cup	4 1/2 ounces	130 grams
3/4 cup	5 ounces	145 grams
1 cup	7 ounces	200 grams

Brown Sugar

MEASUREMENT	OUNCES	GRAMS
1 tablespoon	1/4 ounce	7 grams
1/4 cup	1 1/4 ounces	35 grams
1/3 cup	1 3/4 ounces	50 grams
1/2 cup	2 3/4 ounces	75 grams
2/3 cup	3 ounces	85 grams
3/4 cup	3 1/2 ounces	100 grams
1 cup	5 ounces	145 grams

Flour (Unsifted)

MEASUREMENT	OUNCES	GRAMS
1 tablespoon	1/4 ounce	7 grams
1/4 cup	1 1/4 ounces	35 grams

⅓ cup	1½ ounces	45 grams
½ cup	2½ ounces	70 grams
⅔ cup	3¼ ounces	90 grams
¾ cup	3½ ounces	100 grams
1 cup	5 ounces	145 grams

Nuts

WEIGHT OF 1 CUP, SHELLED	OUNCES	GRAMS
Almonds, sliced	3 ounces	85 grams
Cashews	4½ ounces	130 grams
Hazelnuts	4½ ounces	130 grams
Macadamia nuts	4 ounces	110 grams
Peanuts	4 ounces	110 grams
Pecans	4 ounces	110 grams
Pistachio nuts	5 ounces	145 grams
Walnuts	3½ ounces	110 grams

Butter

MEASUREMENT	OUNCES	GRAMS
1 tablespoon	½ ounce	15 grams
2 tablespoons	1 ounce	30 grams
4 tablespoons (½ stick, ¼ cup)	2 ounces	60 grams
8 tablespoons (1 stick, ½ cup)	4 ounces (¼ pound)	115 grams
2 sticks	8 ounces (½ pound)	230 grams
4 sticks	1 pound	454 grams

Converting
to and from Metric

• • •

WHEN THIS FACTOR IS KNOWN	MULTIPLY BY	TO FIND

Weight

Ounces	28.35	Grams
Pounds	0.454	Kilograms
Grams	0.035	Ounces
Kilograms	2.2	Pounds

Measurement

Inches	2.5	Centimeters
Millimeters	0.04	Inches
Centimeters	0.4	Inches

Volume

	MULTIPLY BY	
Teaspoons	4.93	Milliliters
Tablespoons	14.79	Milliliters
Fluid ounces	29.57	Milliliters
Cups	0.237	Liters
Pints	0.47	Liters
Quarts	0.95	Liters
Gallons	3.785	Liters
Milliliters	0.034	Fluid Ounces
Liters	2.1	Pints
Liters	1.06	Quarts
Liters	0.26	Gallons

	DIVIDE BY	
Milliliters	4.93	Teaspoons
Milliliters	14.79	Tablespoons
Milliliters	236.59	Cups
Milliliters	473.18	Pints
Milliliters	946.36	Quarts
Liters	.236	Cups
Liters	.473	Pints
Liters	.946	Quarts
Liters	3.785	Gallons

Sugar Temperatures and Stages

◆ ◆ ◆

A reliable candy thermometer is the best way to determine when sugar has cooked to the correct temperature. The following table shows the temperature ranges and characteristics of each stage of cooked sugar. To determine the stages without a candy thermometer, drop a teaspoon of the sugar syrup into a glass of cold water, then gather it into a ball and press it gently between your thumb and forefinger.

TEMPERATURE RANGE	STAGE	CHARACTERISTICS AND USES
223–234F (106–112C)	Thread	Forms a loose, thin thread.
234–240F (112–115C)	Soft ball	Forms a soft, sticky ball that deflates when removed from the water.
242–248F (116–120C)	Firm ball	Forms a firm but malleable, sticky ball that holds its shape briefly, but deflates when left at room temperature for a few minutes.
250–266F (121–130C)	Hard ball	Forms a stiff, sticky ball that holds its shape against pressure.
270–290F (132–143C)	Soft crack	Divides into threads that are firm but pliable.

| 300–310F (148–153C) | Hard crack | Separates into brittle threads that splinter easily. The sugar is no longer sticky. |
| 320–360F (160–182C) | Caramel | Becomes transparent and undergoes color changes ranging from light golden to dark amber. |

Comparative Volume of Standard Baking Pan Sizes

◆ ◆ ◆

PAN SIZE	VOLUME

Round cake pans

5" × 2"	2⅔ cups
6" × 2"	3¾ cups
7" × 2"	5¼ cups
8" × 1½"	4 cups
8" × 2"	7 cups
9" × 1½"	6 cups
9" × 2"	8⅔ cups
10" × 2"	10¾ cups
12" × 2"	15½ cups
14" × 2"	21 cups
9" × 3" bundt	9 cups
10" × 3½" bundt	12 cups
9" × 4" kugelhopf	12 cups
9" × 3" tube	10 cups
10" × 4" tube	16 cups

9" × 2¾" springform	10 cups
10" × 2¾" springform	12 cups
9" × 3" cheesecake	14 cups
2¾" × 1½" muffin cup	½ cup

Pie plates

8" × 1¼"	3 cups
9" × 1¼"	3½ cups
9" × 1½"	4 cups
9" × 2"	6 cups

Square pans

8" × 8" × 1½"	6 cups
8" × 8" × 2"	8 cups
9" × 9" × 1½"	8 cups
9" × 9" × 2"	10 cups
10" × 10" × 2"	12 cups
12" × 12" × 2"	16 cups

Rectangular and loaf pans

10½" × 15½" × 1" (jelly-roll pan)	10 cups
12½" × 17½" × 1" (jelly-roll pan)	12 cups
11 " × 7" × 2" rectangle	8 cups
13" × 9" × 2" rectangle	15 cups

8" × 4" × 1½" loaf	4 cups
8½" × 4½" × 2½" loaf	6 cups
9" × 5" × 3" loaf	8 cups

To determine the volume of any other size pan, use a liquid measure to pour water into the pan until it reaches the top.

Bibliography

Bloom, Carole. *The International Dictionary of Desserts, Pastries, and Confections*. New York: Hearst Books, 1995.

Claiborne, Craig. *An Herb and Spice Cookbook*. New York: Bantam Books, Inc., 1963.

David, Elizabeth. *Spices, Salt and Aromatics in the English Kitchen*. New York: Penguin Books, 1975.

Farrell, Kenneth T. *Spices, Condiments, and Seasonings, Second Edition*. New York: An AVI book, published by Van Nostrand Reinhold, 1990.

Hazen, Janet. *Vanilla*. San Francisco: Chronicle Books, 1995.

Labensky, Sarah, and Alan M. Hause. *On Cooking: A Textbook of Culinary Fundamentals*. Englewood Cliffs, NJ: Prentice-Hall, 1995.

Lang, Jenifer Harvey, ed. *Larousse Gastronomique: The New American Edition*. New York: Crown Publishers, Inc. 1988.

McGee, Harold. *On Food and Cooking: The Science and Lore of the Kitchen*. New York: Collier Books, 1984.

Miloradovich, Milo. *Cooking with Herbs and Spices*. New York: Dover Publications, Inc., 1977.

Mulherin, Jennifer. *The Macmillan Treasury of Spices & Natural Flavorings*. New York: Macmillan Publishing Company, 1988.

Norman, Jill. *The Complete Book of Spices*. New York: Viking Studio Books, 1991.

Ortiz, Elisabeth Lambert. *The Encyclopedia of Herbs, Spices & Flavorings*. New York: Dorling Kindersley, Inc., 1992.

Rain, Patricia. *The Vanilla Cookbook*. Berkeley, CA: Celestial Arts, 1986.

Rosengarten, Frederic, Jr. *The Book of Spices*. Wynnewood, PA: Livingston Publishing Company, 1969.

Schivelbusch, Wolfgang. *Tastes of Paradise: A Social History of Spices, Stimulants, and Intoxicants*. New York: Vintage Books, 1993.

Spicing Up the Palate: Studies of Flavourings—Ancient and Modern. Proceedings of the Oxford Symposium on Food and Cookery 1992. Devon, England: Prospect Books, 1992.

Stobart, Tom. *Herbs, Spices and Flavorings*. New York: McGraw-Hill Book Company, 1970.

Tannahill, Reay. *Food in History*. New York: Stein and Day, 1973.

Toussaint-Samat, Maguelonne. *A History of Food* (English translation). Cambridge, MA: Blackwell Publishers, 1992.

Trewby, Mary. *A Gourmet's Guide to Herbs & Spices*. Los Angeles: HPBooks, 1989.

Walker, Jane. *Creative Cooking with Spices*. Seacaucus, NJ: A Quintet Book, published by Chartwell Books, 1985.

Index

• • •

JAN 2 97
JAN 21 97
FEB 8 97
FEB 25 97
MAR 1 97

MAR 5 97
MAR 22 97
JUN 18 97

14 DAY!

2

Keep this card in the book pocket
Book is due on the latest date stamped

APR 0 2 1997

DO NOT TOUCH THE DATE CARD

BAKER & TAYLOR